Night Wind

Night Wind

STEPHEN MERTZ

Five Star • Waterville, Maine

Five Star First Edition Romance Series.

Published in 2002 in conjunction with Stephen Mertz.

Set in 11 pt. Plantin by Myrna S. Raven.

Printed in the United States on permanent paper.

Library of Congress Cataloging-in-Publication Data

Mertz, Stephen, 1947–
    Night wind / Stephen Mertz.
    p. cm.—(Five Star first edition romance series)
    ISBN 0-7862-4353-8 (hc : alk. paper)
    1. Mothers and sons—Fiction. 2. Divorced mothers—Fiction. 3. Missing children—Fiction. 4. New Mexico—Fiction. I. Title. II. Series.
    PS3613.E788 N54 2002
    813'.6—dc21
                                   2002067752

"The unexamined life is not worth living."
- Plato

"Fear of life in one form or another is the great thing
to exorcise."
- William James

"Break on through to the other side!"
- Jim Morrison, *THE DOORS*

Chapter 1

They left Albuquerque about noon that day, later than she'd planned, taking the Interstate south across a seemingly endless expanse of high desert that was emerald green with scrub brush. Towering, lunar rock formations in the distance shimmered in the heat. It was a clear, sunny day, not too hot. A perfect day for travel. Eighty miles south of the city, they exited I-25, taking a secondary state highway that angled west toward the mountains. Before long the two-lane blacktop began a winding ascent that was as gradual as the change of vegetation along the road that cut through the sparsely populated countryside of ranches and homesites. Scant, low, scraggly trees gave way to more numerous, darker, greener, bushier ones. Then came high, full-foliaged trees, pinions, and junipers and, towering beyond them, thickening, deepening forests of pine that carpeted the sides of the mountains.

It was minutes after sunset, with the western sky turning from gold to crimson, when the front right tire of the Subaru blew with a *bang!* that sounded like a rifle shot. The car began wobbling, wildly out of control.

Robin Curtis had been about to slip a Celine Dion cassette into the tape deck. The tape flew to the floor. Instinctively lifting her foot from the accelerator, she began pumping the brake pedal, the Subaru already veering across the centerline.

Beside her, Paul forgot about the paperback he'd been reading, his young face pale, knuckles white as he gripped the dashboard, bracing for a possible impact.

7

Robin was able to apply the strength necessary to steer the car back into her lane, then concentrated on not over-compensating and going off her side of the road, aware that the ground dropped off sharply only a few feet beyond the gravel shoulder. She worked the brake more gently now, steering the car into a gravel-spewing skid, the moment seeming to extend itself, unfolding in slow motion. The grinding sounds of the skid intensified, enveloping her senses.

The Subaru slowed, the wobbling decreased, and the skid subsided as she finally regained full control, remaining well clear of the precarious drop. They coasted to a stop on the shoulder.

Robin switched off the ignition key, and the abrupt silence was excruciating. She switched on the hazard lights and touched her forehead to the cool steering wheel, closing her eyes. Now it was the thumping of her heart that filled her senses.

"Oh, hell," she sighed quietly.

"Mom, I hate to say it," Paul spoke matter-of-factly, pure deadpan, "but I don't think teachers are supposed to cuss in front of kids. At least, that's how it was in Illinois. Maybe it's different in New Mexico."

She looked up to see that the color was returning to his cheeks. He was falling back on that wiseguy sense of humor that could be oh-so-precocious at times, but more often than not had helped buoy and sustain her spirits during the tough times they'd shared. Paul was only twelve years old but he didn't miss much.

"I believe it's acceptable to say hell when you get a flat tire no matter what state you're in," she said. The adrenaline rush was beginning to subside, her heartbeat returning to normal. "Let's take a look."

They stepped from the car and once again, the sheer vastness and beauty of the land swept over her. Behind them the highway curved, winding into and out of sight along the base of the mountains.

She had been unprepared, six weeks earlier, for her first impressions of the wide open spaces of the American West when she'd flown out to interview for her new job. To gaze in every direction and see breathtaking vistas of mountains and sky and prairie, to taste the dry, crisp cleanness of the air, to hear the breeze whispering through trees and cactus and mesquite; these were sensations and perceptions unlike any she had known in the suburbs of Chicago. Western landscapes were something in western movies or on the cover of the Louis L'Amour novels Paul used to read before he began devouring science fiction.

"We almost made it," Paul said.

She followed the direction of his gaze and saw the green highway sign:

DEVIL CREEK

1 MILE

"We'll make it," she said. "The town is just around that bend up the road."

The low rumble of thunder sounded from not very far away.

She'd made a point of keeping a wary eye on the sky beyond the jutting, craggy mountain peaks, where the golden red afterglow of sunset was merging with a bank of dark, threatening clouds, purple with gray in between. That was another thing about these wide-open spaces, the weather changes could be seen moving in long before they arrived. A cool breeze played with strands of her chestnut hair and the hem of her blue print summer dress. The breeze carried with it the scent of pine, but she did not smell rain.

Walking around to the front of the car, she and Paul appraised the damage to the tire, which was considerable. The tire had been chewed up, twisted around the metal rim. The pungent stench of burnt rubber hung heavy in the air.

"I'll get the jack," Paul said, starting toward the back of the car.

Her son's quick wit was mercifully leavened with a more serious, introspective nature than most twelve-year-olds she knew. A solid "A" student, he was at that awkward age where he was still shy around girls, but in many ways Paul was mature for his age. He was inclined to be a loner, and Robin liked to think that this independence was her positive influence showing through. Paul had her brown eyes, but he also had his father's sandy hair, and when he was serious about something, as he was now, he reminded her of Jeff.

She blinked away that thought. *Stop thinking about Jeff,* she told herself for the thousandth time since leaving Chicago. *That life is behind you. This is a new start. The pain is behind you and so are the hard times. This is the beginning of a new life. Everything is going to be all right.*

Another peal of thunder rumbled from those ominous clouds behind the mountains and, for some reason, a momentary chill coursed down her spine.

Chapter 2

Paul insisted on single-handedly changing the tire.

Robin did assist him in removing their bicycles from the carrying rack attached to the rear bumper, then the boy opened the trunk and wrestled out the jack, jack handle, and spare tire. Boxes filled the trunk, crammed with their belongings. The back seat was also jammed to capacity. They were carrying with them everything they owned.

They'd been living in a furnished apartment in Chicago. She'd held a garage sale to get rid of whatever they couldn't take, donating what didn't sell to a St. Vincent de Paul store. They were only bringing the essentials to start this new life. Except for his bicycle, Paul hadn't seemed attached to any more material possessions than would fit into a few cardboard boxes, which was something else that endeared him to her on this trip.

She returned with him to the front of the car, where he knelt at the front bumper and placed the jack in position. He went about removing the lug nuts that had been tightened with a power tool when she'd outfitted the Subaru with new tires before leaving Illinois. At first the lug nuts did not want to loosen, but Paul leaned into his work with his full strength and eventually they gave. Physically, he was of average build, hardly skinny but not muscle-bound, either. He went about the task with a quiet strength and purpose that made her proud.

She loved him because he was her son, of course, but she also enjoyed his company as a friend. He had proven to be a first-rate traveling companion during their four

11

long days on the road together.

Paul stood after having pumped up the jack. He looked down the highway, behind her.

"Someone's coming."

She turned at Paul's observation. A shabby old pickup truck that had been heading in the opposite direction had crossed over to their side of the highway. It came gliding to a halt on the gravel shoulder, stirring up a small cloud of dust. The setting sun reflected off the truck's cracked windshield, making it impossible to see the occupants. The engine was switched off, creating a cacophony of wheezing, rattling noises that seemed to match the pickup's grubby appearance. Both doors swung open. The occupants tumbled, more than stepped, from the cab. She didn't like them at first glance. A strange, momentary sensation of dread coursed through her, similar to the inexplicable chill that had traced its way down her spine minutes earlier when she'd heard thunder. She estimated their age at eighteen or nineteen. Their hair was long, unkempt. They favored denim, and not very clean denim at that. The driver was large-boned and hefty with a well-developed beer belly. The one from the passenger side was smaller of build, but they shared a facial similarity of widely-spaced, squinting eyes and weakly-defined jawlines that could only be family resemblance. The pair both swaggered as they approached.

Beside her, Paul stepped away from the Subaru, removing the tire iron from the jack. He let it hang loosely at his side.

The one who had been driving wore a natural sneer. His eyes were mean and hostile, reminding Robin of small, black marbles. He spat a brownish stream of tobacco juice that arced onto the ground close to her feet. He used the back of a soiled shirtsleeve to clean away some of the juice that glistened from his stubbled chin.

"Well, well." The eyes traveled up and down her figure. At a well-proportioned 110 pounds, Robin worked to keep in shape. His eyes lingered here and there, making her cringe inwardly, although she tried not to let it show. He grinned, showing broken teeth that were the same color as the tobacco juice. "All broke down out here in the middle of nowhere, all helpless like. Now ain't that something?"

When she spoke she tried to sound natural, even friendly; tried to keep the escalating sense of alarm she felt out of her voice. "Thank you, but we don't need any help. Thanks for stopping, though."

The smaller of the two cackled. "Thanks for stopping," he mimicked. "Sure is polite, ain't she, Bobby?"

Bobby spat another stream of tobacco juice, closer to her than the one before. He made a production of studying the Subaru's license plate. "Can't be a local gal. Way too god-damn polite to be one of them hogs from around here. Look at that, little brother. All the way from Illinois." He pronounced the *s* in Illinois. "Ain't that something?"

Little brother said, "We ain't here to change no tire, lady. We pulled over so's we could get a better look at you, that's all. And darlin', you're worth a second look. Mighty fine, yes sir. Guess you could say we're the Devil Creek welcome wagon." He thought that was funny, and cackled.

"Tobe's right," Bobby snickered. The tobacco Bobby chewed formed a bulbous protrusion from one cheek. "Welcome to Devil Creek."

Paul advanced to stand in front of his mother, placing himself between her and them. She started to step around him. She would let her son change a tire, but *this* mom would defend her twelve-year-old son, not the other way around! She tried to recall the martial arts defensive posture she'd learned at that night class two years ago. A bird cawed somewhere overhead, an aching, plaintive cry carried away on the wind, and the sound stabbed into her senses an acute awareness of the uninhabited desolation of this lonely stretch of highway.

Paul raised the tire iron, holding it like a club. "Leave us alone." The boyish voice held a sharp edge she'd never heard him use before. "Get away from us."

Bobby and Tobe had been ignoring Paul. Now Bobby laughed at him. "Whoa, little dude. Don't make me take that thing away from you or I'll break your head with it."

Robin forced herself to maintain steady eye contact with Bobby as she said in what she hoped was a calm, self-assured tone, "These are just foolish boys, Paul. They're only trying to scare us. They're going to get back into their truck and leave us alone. Aren't you, Bobby?"

Before Bobby could respond, a vehicle approached from the direction of town, from behind her. A surge of hope coursed through her. She was about to run into the highway, to wave the driver down, when she realized that this vehicle was already coasting to their side of the highway. She looked around to see a Ford Bronco stop behind the shabby pickup.

She felt the situation instantly defuse.

Bobby and Tobe seemed to forget about her and Paul. They lost some of their swagger.

A man emerged from the Bronco. A burly, red-haired man in his fifties with a weathered, intelligent face. A bright red, trimmed beard was streaked with gray, like his close-cropped hair. The backs of his hands were splattered with freckles. A brown denim jacket matched his slacks and polished boots. He stood beside the Bronco, not stepping forward, taking in the scene. His eyes settled on

14

Bobby, but he spoke to Robin.

"These boys causing you trouble, ma'am?"

Paul lowered the tire iron, but still held it like a club.

Robin rested both hands on her son's shoulders and didn't take her eyes from Tobe and Bobby. "As a matter of fact, they are. Thank you for stopping."

"Maybe you boys had better pile into that bucket of bolts you're driving and skedaddle out of here," the man suggested to Tobe and Bobby in a quiet voice.

A car whooshed by on the highway without slowing. Robin barely noticed its passing.

Tobe was watching his big brother to see how Bobby would react. Bobby faced the man.

"You old bag of wind. You've let that rag you call a newspaper go to your head. This is a free country. We can talk to anyone we've a mind to. We were just having some fun. Guess this here gal didn't know we was joking."

Without changing his stance, the man extended an arm into the Bronco. "I've got a .357 on my front seat, Bobby Caldwell, and I've got a cell phone I can use to get Chief Saunders out here right quick if I need backup. Not that I'd need backup with a runny-nosed little twerp like you. Now are you and your brother going to climb back in that bucket of bolts and get the hell out of here, or are we going to have us a serious tussle?"

"Aw, hell," Bobby grumbled. "People just flat out don't like other people having fun. Don't have a heart attack, old-timer. We're out of here."

"I know," the man said.

Bobby and Tobe got into their pickup without a backward glance. The engine turned over noisily, then the truck sped away in a squeal of tires, leaving a brownish cloud of dust drifting across the highway and derisive howling and hooting from the truck's open windows until it disappeared around a bend in the road.

The man next to the Bronco removed his arm from the vehicle. There was no gun in his hand.

Paul stopped holding the tire iron like a club. "Jeez, mister, that was like in a western, the way you faced them down. That was cool."

The man chuckled. Crisp blue eyes crinkled in the weather-seasoned, leathery face. "Heck, son, those weren't any big bad outlaws, just a couple of juvenile delinquents acting too big for their britches. And I'm no gunslinger. Matter of fact, Bobby was right. I am an old bag of hot air. I don't have any gun on my car seat."

"The important thing is that you convinced them that you did," Robin said. She extended a hand. "Thank you for stopping. I'm Robin Curtis. This is my son, Paul."

The red-haired man's hand may have been huge, but his handshake, while firm, was not rough. "Pleased to meet you, ma'am. I'm Charlie Flagg. Matter of fact, I kind of guessed who you were when I saw those Illinois license plates of yours. Devil Creek's too out of the way for tourists. You'd be the new fourth grade teacher they hired over to the school."

"Guilty as charged. So you run the town newspaper?"

"Yes, ma'am. We're just a small town weekly. Not much of a newspaper but then, Devil Creek's not much of a town. Size-wise, that is. It's a good town, though, with good folks. Don't let those two no-accounts give you the wrong impression."

"You're the first impression I'll remember, Mr. Flagg, and it's a good one, believe me."

"Do you own a gun?" Paul blurted with genuine, undisguised fascination.

16

Robin gave him a look. "Paul, I think we'd better get into town before it gets dark." She added, for the man's benefit, "Paul's read a lot of westerns. It was no trouble talking him into moving out here."

"Billy the Kid rode this country," Paul said. "A lot of the books I've read took place around here."

Thunder rumbled again in the distance. Shadows were lengthening across the land from the foot of the mountains. The sultry air of the day was dissipating on a cool breeze.

"Does it rain often in this country, Mr. Flagg?" Robin asked.

"Rare as hen's teeth except for the monsoon and that was finished last month. It won't rain tonight, except maybe in the mountains. Those clouds build around the peaks like that every evening, make a few rude noises like they're doing now and they're gone by the morning."

"I'm looking forward to getting to know this land. It's all so new to me. I hope we won't have trouble finding a place to rent."

"Matter of fact, you're talking to the right man on that score. I know a lady with a place to rent. Took in her classified ad down at the paper just this afternoon. Mrs. Lufkin. She's good people, the best, and it's a real nice place if it's the one I'm thinking of. She owns a few houses around town. You'll find her in the book under Florence Lufkin. You call her and tell her Charlie Flagg told you to get in touch."

"Thank you. I'll call her when we get into town."

"Here, son, let me help you change that tire."

It was as if Paul suddenly remembered what he'd been doing. "No, thanks, Mr. Flagg, I'll take care of it."

As Paul went back to work, the man nodded to Robin, a look that only she could see, and it conveyed that he was impressed with the boy. "Would you like me to wait around? I can follow you back into town."

She gave the idea consideration. Paul was already replacing the flat with the spare. The job would be done in minutes. There was at least a half-hour of daylight remaining.

"We'll be all right from here on. You've been very helpful, Mr. Flagg. Thank you again."

"Just being neighborly. You need anything, you come by the newspaper office or give me a call, hear?" He waved to the youngster. "Paul, see you around."

Paul paused in his labor. "See you, Mr. Flagg."

The Bronco made a wide U-turn and drove off in the direction of town.

They stood for a moment watching its taillights recede into the gathering dusk before disappearing around the bend in the road.

"It really was like in a movie, Mom, the way he backed down those guys."

"I was proud of you, Paul, the way you were ready to fight for us. You're quite a young man, do you know that?"

She accompanied the words with a warm hug. She tried not to think about how close she and Paul had been to becoming victims.

"Aw, Mom."

"Come on, tough guy. Let's finish loading up. We've come this far and our new home is just around that bend in the road."

Chapter 3

Devil Creek formed a rectangle on a small flat among rolling hills at the foot of the mountains, straddling the highway that lead south to Las Cruces. Robin had noted during the drive out from Illinois that western communities, on their city limits signs, often took more pride in their elevation than their population. Paul quipped that this was probably because the smaller towns were embarrassed because they were so small. But she did not need to be told the population of this community, having researched the town before making her decision to relocate here.

Devil Creek, including outlying ranches, farms and homesites, had a population of 3700. Except for a convenience store with gas pumps at either end of town, the approach from either direction was mercifully free of the strip shopping malls, the garish fast food chain neon and the drive-up motels that marred the landscape of most American small towns. The streets leading into the central district were shaded, lined with homes of varying vintage, mostly one-story structures, adobe with wooden frame, and some mobile homes on small, well-maintained lots. Devil Creek was the kind of close-knit community where neighbors took pride in their homes and yards. There was a church for most of the Christian denominations. The center of town was pleasant and clean. A handful of modernized brick and plate glass structures—a small branch bank office, a gas station, a hardware store and a locally owned supermarket—lined one of the two blocks that constituted downtown.

In the next block, to one side were *Ritchie's Tavern,* *Donna's Café,* a lawyer's office and a medical building where a dentist and a pair of family physicians shared space with a pharmacy. The opposite side of the street was evenly divided between a park and the Town Hall. The park, complete with a fountain and half-a-dozen picnic tables, was lined with ash trees and dogwoods whose tops were tinted with leaves just beginning to turn yellow, the first hint of approaching autumn. Town Hall, where the city government offices and the police department and jail were located, was a one-level structure of red brick.

Robin and Paul stopped at the gas station to replace the flat tire when they reached town. The attendant, a cheery teenager, had shaken his head while removing the ruined rubber from the rim.

"Never seen one tore up this bad, even for a blow out. You were real lucky, ma'am. Something must have sure tore into it."

Robin had called Mrs. Lufkin and introduced herself from the pay phone at the gas station, and made an appointment at nine o'clock the following morning for a look at the house for rent. With a new tire purchased and mounted on the Subaru, she and Paul had then proceeded to spend the night in the town's only motel. They'd gone to Devil Creek's only restaurant for breakfast the next morning.

Mrs. Lufkin was waiting in a Datsun pickup when they arrived for their appointment. Florence Lufkin couldn't have been more than five-one, and weighed no more than one hundred pounds. Yet her diminutive frame seemed to embody a spunky, downright feisty energy and spirit that belied her years. Her features were creased with the lines of a life of honest work. It was a wise face, with sparkling, kindly eyes and a smile that was warm and genuine. Snowy white hair, tied back, retained streaked traces of blonde. She had been a stunningly beautiful young woman and, though the mahogany skin was deeply-lined, the natural beauty remained. She wore a faded red bandanna knotted around her neck, a western-style shirt, well-worn jeans, and scuffed tennis shoes.

"Well, my dear, what do you say?" she asked when they'd completed their tour of the house. "Five hundred dollars a month and utilities, and you and young Paul can call it home." Her tone implied that, personally, she liked the idea.

It was a small adobe home of windows that splashed golden sunlight across the hardwood floors and white walls, filling the furnished house with a warm, soothing ambiance that appealed to Robin as soon as she set foot inside. The comfortable furnishings were Southwestern in motif. There were two bedrooms, a bath with a shower, a small kitchen-dining room combination and an airy living room. Best of all, behind the carport was a room attached to the house with a washer and dryer. The laundry room was adjacent to a patio that overlooked the mountains.

"We'll take it, Mrs. Lufkin." Robin felt fresh in a pressed blue blouse and white skirt. Despite Charlie Flagg's tip, she'd been prepared to spend the entire day house hunting if necessary. However, she had taken an instant liking to her new landlady. "Would you like me to sign a lease?"

"Heavens, no." The older woman waved a hand, dismissing the thought. "I like you, Robin, and I always trust people I like. I think you'll be happy here and I know you'll take good care of the place."

"We will, I promise you that."

"The gas, cable, and electricity are already on. I know how hard it can be to make ends meet when a person moves halfway across the country and doesn't know a soul. I came west from Pennsylvania when I was twenty-one." Florence Lufkin chuckled. "In some ways that seems so long ago, like I was another person. In other ways, it seems like yesterday." She cleared her throat. "Anyway, you can have the billing for the utilities changed to your name and that way you won't have to pay a deposit for a new account."

"That's very kind of you. I don't mind telling you that Paul and I are on a pretty tight budget until my first paycheck."

"The whole country's having troubles like that, it seems. Times like these, we little people have to stick together."

They stood on the patio after a tour of the house that could have been completed in five minutes, but which had in fact become a pleasant, rambling conversation that consumed almost an hour. The *Welcome to Devil Creek* sign had stated that the elevation was 4900 feet, and last night had brought on chilly temperatures with a bite. This morning, though, the thermometer was already climbing nicely.

The house was situated on an acre and a half of land, the last residence on a graveled country road on the edge of town, surrounded on three sides by open field. Rolling hills began practically at the back property line, the land sweeping upward into ravines and tree-covered slopes beneath a sky that was crisp and blue.

"The mountains look completely different now from when Paul and I drove in last night," Robin commented.

Mrs. Lufkin nodded. "The beauty of this land is in its shifting shadows and changing colors. You notice a lot for someone from the city."

"I love nature. Always have. But I feel that I'm really getting acquainted with it for the first time in my life by moving out here."

"Well, there's plenty of nature to love in these parts." A trace of pride sparkled in the woman's voice. "Those mountains we're looking at will be changing colors all day. Do you see how those peaks over yonder are a light tan? They'll be a deeper brown by this afternoon and before sunset, why, you won't believe it. They'll be a warm, rosy red. Then they start turning purple. They're black silhouettes after the sun goes down. I watch those mountains from my house when there's a moon, sometimes for hours."

"They're lovely. The whole town is lovely. I'm so glad Mr. Flagg suggested that I call you. With this house on the same end of town as the school, it couldn't be more perfect. I especially like the large lot."

Mrs. Lufkin sniffed with mock disdain. "Heck, an acre and a half isn't large. There's hundred-acre spreads and better all over this county."

"Still, where we come from the houses are practically right on top of each other. It will be good to have some breathing space."

"Glad you feel that way. You're at the end of the road so it's all open country to three sides, and I don't think that new tenant next door will bother you any. Mr. Landware, his name is. I rented to him yesterday. I liked him, too. He brought boxes of books with him and that's about all he had except for a typewriter and one suitcase. But, like I said, I trust my instincts. That doesn't mean I'm a pushover, but I'm usually right."

"What does he do?"

"He's a writer, so he said."

Robin recalled the feeling of isolation last evening outside town when the teenage toughs had accosted her and Paul. "I suppose it's good to have a neighbor in case of an emergency."

23

"It's always good to have a man around," said Mrs. Lufkin. "Oh, they can be a nuisance, right enough. Reckon I'm as liberated as an old gal my age can be. I run my own business. I've done men's work all my life. But doggone it, there's something reassuring about having them around." A trace of moisture glistened in her eyes. "I lost my Billy in Vietnam when he was nineteen and my Joe died of cancer a couple years later and I've been alone ever since. I think of those two men every day. I visit their graves every Sunday. You see, I know what it's like to have menfolk around and not want to lose them . . . and lose them."

Robin didn't know what to say. "Mrs. Lufkin, I'm sorry."

The woman brushed at her eyes, as if wiping away specks of dust, and shook her head once, banishing the mood. "Forgive me, child. At my age a body tends to ramble." The brightness returned. "Anyway, except for Mr. Landware, your next neighbor is a half-mile down the road. It's not a bad thing for a single woman to know her neighbors out here, just in case. I think you and Mr. Landware will get along fine."

"I'm sure we will. With school starting on Monday, I expect to be very busy."

"That's important work you're doing, educating young minds. If there's anything I can do to help you get settled in, you be sure to let me know."

"I certainly will. Mr. Flagg offered to help last night. People are so friendly out here."

"Comes from living so far off the beaten path, I expect. We don't get many newcomers. Some people make it their summer home, but most of them are gone by now. I think you and Mr. Landware are the first new arrivals in, oh, it's been a year since Charlie Flagg moved here." Mrs. Lufkin

24

cleared her throat. "Now don't think I'm being a nosey old so-and-so, because your business is your business. I just want to say that I respect you for coming all this distance like you have."

Robin felt embarrassed. And a little perplexed. "What do you mean?"

"I mean you being a single mother and all, picking up and moving all the way here from where you're from. It does my heart good to see a young woman like you striking out on her own. That's what the West is for. It's always been that way. It's a place of new beginnings. That's the pioneer spirit."

Robin smiled. "I'm not that young, Mrs. Lufkin. I'm thirty-four."

"Honey, when you're seventy-eight, everyone is young. You're a knockout. You'll find there's not much nightlife out here. Las Cruces is an hour away. That's where most of the single folks hereabouts go to meet other single folks."

"I like Devil Creek just the way it is."

"I hope that young one of yours likes it. A child that's used to the big city could get mighty restless out here."

"Paul will meet kids his age, and he's good at entertaining himself. Oh, he likes his TV and video games, but I started reading to him when he was still a baby, and he's grown up loving to read. You'll never know how thankful I am that he knows how to amuse himself quietly."

"Paul is a good, solid old-fashioned name."

"He was named after his grandfather, Paul Samuel."

It was then that the realization struck home that she had become so enchanted with this new acquaintance and so engrossed in their conversation that she'd lost track of Paul's whereabouts. She had enough faith in Paul's intelligence and resourcefulness to generally allow him a reasonable degree of personal freedom, to the extent that he was a twelve-year-old. But for one moment, that inexplicable sense of alarm she'd experienced last night on the highway tremored through her despite the sunshine and the pleasant company. She found herself compelled to hurriedly cross the patio to where she could glance in either direction across the backyard.

Something in her manner prompted Mrs. Lufkin to ask, "What is it? Is something wrong?"

"I was just wondering where Paul is." She was startled at the concern she heard in her own voice. "He must be out in the car waiting for me, reading a book."

"He can't have gone far. Let's go find him."

The older woman led the way back through the house toward the front door. Robin followed, feeling mildly embarrassed. And yet her stomach muscles were cramped. As she followed Mrs. Lufkin through the house, she found herself at one level rationally trying to analyze these strange flashes of alarm and urgency she'd begun experiencing. It was weird. *This isn't like me,* she thought. *This isn't like me at all.*

Chapter 4

She could not hold back a sigh of relief when she and Mrs. Lufkin stepped onto the front porch and she saw Paul in the driveway. Her son was engaged in earnest conversation with a man who was busily adjusting the front wheel of Paul's bicycle, which was still attached to the bike rack at the rear of the car.

Paul was positively beaming. "Hi, Mom. This is Mike. He lives next door."

The man gave the wrench a final twist. "There you go," he said to Paul. "Must have worked itself loose on the trip down."

"Thanks!" Paul bubbled with enthusiasm. "Mom, Mike's a writer."

The man slipped the wrench into his back pocket and strode forward, smiling. "Part time journalist, actually. Ex-full time."

He was in his late forties. About five-ten, he moved with an easy grace that suggested a strongly-centered self-confidence. Muscular enough, though not in an overly-developed, body-building sort of way. He wore an open-necked shirt, brown corduroy slacks and athletic shoes. Ebony hair was touched with gray at the temples. Not movie star handsome. There was the shiny sliver of an old, slight scar over his left eye. The eyes were dark blue and steady, cordial, yet somehow cool and distant.

Mrs. Lufkin made the introductions.

"Michael Landware, Robin Curtis. You two are not only neighbors, you're the first new arrivals we've had in

Devil Creek in some time."

They shook hands. A brief handshake.

"It's nice to meet you, Mr. Landware." His handshake was firm, the touch warm. "I appreciate you helping Paul with his bike."

"My pleasure. Please, call me Mike. And how are you today, Mrs. Lufkin?"

Mrs. Lufkin glanced at her wristwatch. "As a matter of fact, I'm late! Reverend Kroeger asked me to stop by the church to help with preparations for the bake sale. I hope you kids don't mind, but I've got to run."

"Of course not," Robin said.

Mike Landware cracked a smile and for an instant the coolness, that aloofness she'd sensed, gave way to what sounded like sincere fondness for the landlady. "Mrs. L., I haven't known you for long, but I'd be willing to bet you've always got somewhere to go and something to do."

Mrs. Lufkin enjoyed hearing this. It was obviously how she saw herself, just as it was obviously true. "I reckon a writer has to be an observant fella," she acknowledged with a lowering of the eyes, which Robin could only think of as coquettish. "Well, I'll see you both later."

"Stop by anytime," Mike called after her.

The woman waved goodbye from inside her Datsun, then backed out of the driveway and drove off down the road.

"She certainly is a nice person," Robin said, to make conversation. She felt slightly uncomfortable, standing there speaking with a man who was a complete stranger to her.

"Mrs. L. is one of the good ones," he agreed. "Say, I was planning to barbecue up a burger for myself later this afternoon. Since we're neighbors, maybe you and Paul would like to join me for a get acquainted dinner. What do you say?"

"Hey, that would be great!" Paul enthused.

Robin felt put on the spot. "Uh, I don't think so, Paul. That's very nice of you, Mike, but—"

"Please don't think I'm coming on," he added. "I'm not. I just thought it would be a nice way to get acquainted, since we are neighbors."

"No, it isn't that. Really." She could feel Paul staring daggers at her. "It's just that . . .it's been a long couple of weeks, the move, the drive out here and all. We still have to unpack and clean the house and . . . it's a very nice offer. Could we take a rain check?"

"Of course. Maybe after you're settled in."

"That would be nice."

"So I guess I'll let you guys get to work. See you later."

"See you, Mike," Paul said.

Paul waited until Mike had reached the house next door; an adobe practically identical to theirs, across twenty yards of open scrub brush already brown and brittle from the lowering night temperatures. When Mike Landware entered his house, disappearing from their sight, Paul faced his mother with a pained expression.

"Mom—"

"Paul, he seems like a very nice man. But I was telling him the truth. We do have a lot to do and we'd better get started."

Paul wasn't too happy about that but, thankfully, he didn't argue about it, either, choosing instead to throw himself into the task of unloading the car.

How did you explain to a boy of Paul's years that, in her mind and heart, she still felt too—well, too roughed up and confused by wounds not yet healed. She wasn't sure if she was ready to let a man into her life at this point even if it was just as a friendly neighbor who also happened to be a good-looking, buff, intelligent, *eligible* man. She did not want her mind even starting down that direction! She didn't like the needs she felt when her mind drifted towards those kind of thoughts. No, she could not explain these feelings to Paul. She could hardly explain them to herself.

At one point, she noticed her neighbor glancing out his side door in their general direction. Or maybe he was looking at the mountains. When she returned his gaze, directing her attention in his direction, he turned away, retreating into his house, again disappearing from sight.

Chapter 5

Sunday night after Paul went to bed, Robin sat at the kitchen table, intending to review her notes and lesson plans for the first day of school. But her mind kept wandering.

They'd spent Saturday and Sunday unpacking, moving in. The former tenants had left the house clean enough, yet she could never really feel comfortable in a new place until she had personally given every room a good cleaning. Then there had been grocery shopping and doing the laundry that had accrued during the trip.

There had been no recurrence of those brief, peculiar flashes of panic and dread she'd experienced that first night on the highway or the morning when Mrs. Lufkin was showing her the house. She decided that those sensations were due to a combination of travel exhaustion, the sensory overload of the whole relocation process and that initial uncertainty and trepidation anyone experiences when adapting to new surroundings. She was not an experienced traveler. She was thousands of miles away from everything and everyone she knew, in a place foreign to any previous experience she'd had, surrounded by strangers.

Throughout the weekend, Paul had been his usual helpful self, doing his fair share without being asked. She didn't work him too hard, though. He hadn't said much yet about what he thought of Devil Creek, as if still in the process of forming an opinion. She hoped it would be a favorable opinion as he got out, made friends, and in general became acclimated to the place. She wasn't concerned, as she would have been back in Chicago, about Paul being on his own, riding his bike or walking around Devil Creek. There were always terrible crimes being committed against children back in Chicago, it seemed. The TV and newspapers were full of such stories. But this was a world away from Chicago.

During the weekend when she had looked out a window for Paul, he'd usually been sitting under a tree, reading. Twice she saw him standing at the property line, conversing with their next door neighbor, the conversation appearing animated and good natured. When she asked Paul later what they'd been discussing, he said science fiction writers, that Mike also liked science fiction and had been suggesting authors Paul hadn't heard of. When her son had first started reading westerns, Robin read one to monitor his tastes and had approved of the clear-cut, black and white parables of good versus evil. She'd read enough science fiction on her own to know that novels in that genre were thematically far more complex, that their moral statements could be ambiguous, but she accepted Paul's reading of them as a healthy sign of an inquisitive nature. She decided it was good he had someone like Mike to discuss these books with.

She too had some contact with their neighbor. Mike seemed like a nice guy. He'd been working under the raised hood of his Jeep late Saturday afternoon while they were unloading the car and they'd exchanged friendly waves. Then, as they were returning from the supermarket the next day, he'd been leaving his house for a walk down the road that fronted their properties. They'd exchanged pleasantries, talked about the weather, and spoke again of their mutual fondness for Mrs. Lufkin. Friendly, neighborly chitchat, which she appreciated.

So now the unpacking was completed, the house still had the vaguely aseptic scent of a hospital room after all the cleaning they'd done, and the refrigerator and cupboards were well-stocked. There still remained a tentative feel to the house, which she knew only living here would erase. And here it was, Sunday night, and Robin finally had some quiet quality time alone, all set to prepare for her first day as a teacher . . . when she realized how totally exhausted she was.

Not too exhausted, though, to prevent her mind from wandering, and she found herself considering, more than she wanted to, the man who lived next door. This was somewhat irritating. What she needed in her life at this point was a new place to live, a new job, and a new start. What she definitely did not need was romance.

She couldn't deny that there was a throaty timbre to the man's voice that was pleasant to her ear. Mike's manner suggested intelligence, sensitivity, and a quiet strength. He was not unattractive to her. She sensed something tragic about him. He smiled easily enough, yet there was a sadness not far beneath the surface. She wondered about that.

He was nothing like Jeff.

Robin had met her ex-husband in college. They'd married a month after graduation and she was soon pregnant with Paul. She became a housewife. At first she'd experienced some guilt and frustration at becoming so domesticated, but she convinced herself, and Jeff had agreed, that it would be in their child's best interest for her to stay home and be a full-time mom. Jeff had gone on to amass considerable real estate holdings, masking his cold, shrewd, calculating intelligence beneath a breezy, flippant outer facade. The facade also masked a manipulative personality driven by blind greed and ambition. As their marriage and their son grew older, she had witnessed this side of him gradually blot out the good qualities she once saw and loved about him. Or perhaps those qualities too had only been part of the facade. As they climbed the social ladder in their suburban community, as Christmas after Christmas found a perfect family pictured on the cards she sent out, she eventually, inexorably found herself falling out of love with the man she had vowed to love and cherish forever.

Then, when Paul was seven, she found out that Jeff was regularly and routinely cheating on her. At first, after the shock, the hurt, the rejection, and the determination to do something about it, she'd told herself that it had to have been some lack on her part, that she was not fulfilling her duties as a good wife. But the more she thought about it, the more hurt and angry she became. She had always been faithful to him. The perfect little wife. Initially, she thought it was just his secretary. She confronted the woman. Woman? Girl was more like it. A dumb, busty little twenty-three-year-old with a big butt. During their ugly, catty confrontation, Robin was stunned when the girl brazenly told her that Jeff had had affairs with other women in his office, too.

Jeff conned her when she initially confronted him with his infidelity. He sobbed confessions and remorse and begged her forgiveness, pledging his love for her alone. He lavished her with presents. They went to a marriage counselor until Robin discovered that Jeff had never stopped carrying on his affair with Little Miss Big Butt. Theirs became a marriage in name only. Jeff didn't want a divorce because of his standing in the community. He was entertaining the notion of entering local politics and a failed marriage would not have helped. He never did get into politics, for which Robin thought the local electorate should have been profoundly grateful, apparently deciding that there was more money to be made in shady real estate deals than by lying to voters and taking graft. Ultimately, she realized that she was only holding the marriage together for Paul's sake. She came to understand that the real reason she could not let go was her fear of losing the comfort and false security of the materialistic life she had become used to.

Then one day she and Paul came home unexpectedly, when they had planned to be gone for the day, and she found Jeff in bed with another woman. It wasn't even Little Miss Big Butt. It was some bimbo she'd known nothing about. She packed one suitcase for her, one for Paul and they moved out that day. She took a sales clerk job at a mall, filed for divorce, and began applying by mail for teaching jobs around the country, accepting the furthest offer from Chicago that she could find.

Devil Creek would be her first teaching job. She'd always had a great rapport with kids. She considered herself a perceptive, caring person and she assumed that these qualities and her degree were what sold her during the job interview despite her lack of experience.

She'd been a bit surprised at how easily she'd adapted to being a single working mom. There were pressures and day-to-day problems, of course, but she found it a giant step up from being emotionally victimized in a bad marriage. She'd recognized long ago that while her mother had ingrained into her a compassion and sensitivity for others, her father, a career military man, had taught her to be self-reliant in most things. In fact, she'd become a loner years ago, even while still living with Jeff.

But sitting at her kitchen table this Sunday evening with her mind drifting from the notes and lesson plans spread out before her, she had to admit that at moments like this, late at night, when the world was a quiet place and she was alone with her thoughts, she was plagued with an elusive insecurity, a pestering self-doubt that sprung mostly from the fact that this really was the first time she'd ever truly set out on her own to make a go of it without the help or support of anyone else. Even as a college student, her parents had generously paid for her education.

Of course, she was not totally alone. She had Paul. Jeff had not offered to discuss alimony or child support, and she would have refused it anyway, though she understood that she was legally entitled. She wanted it this way, as long as she could provide for Paul on her own. She'd effectively cut loose from her cushy life and struck out on her own. She welcomed the challenge. This was a turning point in her life and she *would* make it. This was no time for romance. Or was she being presumptuous and foolish, self-delusional even, to think that her next door neighbor could be attracted to her? Either way, this was no time to complicate things by allowing herself to become attracted to him.

So why did her thoughts tonight keep drifting over to that single light visible from the house next door, that pale silver square shining in the nighttime gloom? He was an interesting man, and there could be the beginnings of some sort of attraction between them, unless she was completely off base. Intuitively, she didn't think she was. She sensed that it was a mutual attraction, or at least a mutual interest in a man-woman kind of way. She hoped her curiosity about him was not reciprocated because he was just a nice guy, friendly to her as he would be to anyone else. She hadn't dated in Chicago in the year since her divorce. At the age of thirty-four, the whole concept of dating, not to mention going to bed with someone, terrified her. Talk about insecurities. Jeff was the only man she'd ever slept with.

She rose from the kitchen table, drew the curtain so she could not see the light from the house next door, and returned to her notes and lesson plans, mentally reprimanding herself for succumbing to such dopey, late night thoughts. Tired or not, she had to be fully prepared tomorrow when she showed up for work. A small corner of her mind continued to consider Michael Landware, the man with the cordial, aloof smile and the sad aura. She wondered what he was doing right now. What was he thinking, next door in that house?

Stop it, she told herself. *Stop it.* It was just that Mike Landware was so different from Jeff.

The ringing of the wall phone struck her nerve ends like the detonation of a bomb. She found herself grasping the receiver with both hands before the end of the first ring.

"Hello?"

"Hello, sweetheart."

Jeff . . .

Her blood ran cold. She hadn't heard that voice—that oh-so-pleasant salesman baritone—since she'd moved with Paul out of their house. Her ex-husband hadn't made contact once throughout her and Paul's apartment life together in Chicago. Lawyers had handled all communication between them, and that in itself had seemed a clear enough message to her and Paul from Jeff: good riddance, and stay away. And now, after all this time, after all those miles traveled, to be sitting here in her home hearing his voice as if he were here across from her at the kitchen table.

"Jeff. Jeff, where are you calling from?"

He laughed; more of a snicker. "I'd think you'd be wondering why I was calling, sweetie pie."

"Don't call me that."

"Well, don't you wonder why I'm calling?"

37

She glanced through the archway, into the living room. Paul and the television were beyond her line of vision, but the sounds of the science fiction movie continued unabated.

She struggled to suppress her rising emotions, which included panic.

"Very well, Jeffrey," she said with exaggerated patience. "Why are you calling? *And* where the hell are you calling from?" Nothing else came across the connection, and she thought they may have been disconnected. "Jeff?"

"I just want you to know, you bitch." His words hissed like the rattle of a snake, dangerous and cruel; not quite sane. "I don't care if you and that brat of yours move to the other side of the goddamn earth. I just want you to know that I can find you. Understand? I can mess with this 'start a new life' pipe dream of yours anytime and any way I feel like it."

"Jeff, please—"

"You think you can run out on me, you *bitch?* I know exactly where you are at this very minute."

The cold blood in her veins froze to ice.

"Jeff, where are you calling from?"

"Think about it, darling." His sneer slithered across the connection like a slurred obscenity. "You never understood how powerful I am, Robin, or how many people I know who can see to it that things happen."

"Jeff, please. Don't threaten me. Let us go. It shouldn't come to this. Please."

"Quit your whining." He snickered. "I'm just wanted you to know that I can turn that paradise you think you've found into a living hell whenever I feel like it. And you know what, you bitch? I think I feel like it."

The line went dead in her ear.

She sat at her kitchen table, holding the telephone receiver until the *beep-beep-beeping* of the unused line startled her, and she hung up the phone.

She left the table, left her kitchen, the schoolwork forgotten. She would not tell Paul about the call. But she did need to be in front of that television with him, giving her son a hug with all her strength whether he liked it or not.

Chapter 6

He sat, trying to write at the battered old IBM Selectric he'd set up on the kitchen table. Its soft, quiet purr hummed contentedly, a relaxing sound that usually drew him into that space where the ideas came from. Tonight, though, the ideas would not come. He was blocked. The well, at least for tonight, was dry. He could not write.

He kept thinking about his neighbors. The woman, Robin, and her son. He found himself thinking about Robin's eyes. He blocked these thoughts, blocked those eyes, from his mind. He tried to concentrate on the blank piece of paper in the typewriter.

Nothing would come.

Damn, he thought. *Damn.*

He thought about the bottle on the top shelf of the kitchen cabinet. The sealed bottle. It would be so easy to unseal. Then the memories would stop, and so would the pain, and so would his thinking about the eyes of the woman next door. No, he told himself. No. That would be too easy. That bottle was not the answer. He'd bought the bottle the same day he'd had his last drink. The same day he'd told himself that he would never take another drink. The bottle had traveled with him ever since, a sealed bottle allowing him to prove to himself that he was strong enough to resist. So far, he had been strong enough. So far.

He stared at the blank sheet of white paper.

He'd used computers at the newspaper in Denver and at the university, but for writing fiction he found that nothing would do but the pounding of typewriter keys, hearing the snappy punch of the element on paper, watching those sheets of paper fill up with scenes and characters.

"Yeah, right," he told himself.

He'd completed forty pages, all of them in the three days since he'd come to this town, moved into this house, begun this new life. Yet tonight the words would not come. Memories triggered by the eyes of the woman next door gnawed at his mind. The blank sheet of paper in the typewriter was like a movie screen upon which he viewed the past.

His past.

The dark past.

And he thought about the recent past.

He thought about his job interview with the owner of the town's weekly newspaper. He'd been leaving the town's little supermarket on his first day in Devil Creek, the afternoon of the day he'd rented his house from Mrs. Lufkin. On his way to his car in the parking lot, he happened to glance across the street and had noticed the sign, *County Clarion*, on the front lawn of a private residence, a brown brick single story structure with a two car garage. An ancient dogwood tree provided a wide swath of shade, a precious commodity in the southwest. A Ford Bronco was parked in the shade. He strolled across the street, went in and within a few minutes heard himself asking the editor, a good old boy named Charlie Flagg, for a job.

The "office" of the *County Clarion* was actually the front half of the remodeled residence. A few file cabinets, a pair of computers, some tables for layouts, and a wide oak desk comprised the furnishings. Charlie introduced himself as "chief cook and bottle washer of this one horse operation." Naturally, he had some questions.

Mike was general, bordering on vague.

"Gave up teaching at the university in Albuquerque because I couldn't put off writing this book that's in my gut anymore," was what he told Charlie. "Hunted around for some place, some small town where I could find some peace and quiet and get the work done."

"You'll find plenty of that in Devil Creek," Charlie had chuckled. Charlie smiled a lot from behind his obviously well-tended red beard. "Going to write the Great American Novel, eh?"

"Maybe a couple of 'em," Mike said with a grin that was meant to be self-deprecating.

"So what's the book about?"

"Uh, actually, I've decided not to talk about it until I get the first draft finished." *And there goes the job,* Mike added mentally.

Charlie surprised him. He didn't skip a beat. "Don't want to diffuse the energy before you get it down on paper, is that it?"

So Charlie Flagg was sharp and his interest appeared real. But how did you break down into a few sentences a novel you'd been thinking about and planning for close to twenty years and not have it come out sounding trite and hackneyed? Another book about a guy coming of age in Vietnam and what happened after he came home and took a cross-country road trip . . . hell, maybe it *was* hackneyed. But it *was* his life and he was going to put it down on paper, and maybe he would create art.

"You're right," he told Charlie. "I'd rather not talk about it. Thanks for asking, and thanks for not taking offense. A buddy from the old days asked to see an outline when he heard what I was working on. He liked it enough to send it on to an agent he knows in New York."

"New York, huh?" Charlie's red eyebrows lifted. "Sounds like you are serious."

"The agent likes what I've done. He landed me a contract and a small advance. A real small advance. Enough to make ends meet. But a supplemental income wouldn't hurt."

"Never does," Charlie agreed amiably. "But I'd best warn you. I'll only be needing an article or two a week and it won't pay much."

"Pay me what you can. It's something I want to do. It's occurred to me that for all the solitude I need, I'll need some interaction with people too, or I could go stir crazy."

Charlie had crossed his ankles and placed his polished boots on the corner of his desk. He stroked his beard. "Tell you what, Mike. You caught me at a good time. Frankly, I don't have any positions here to have openings for, as such. This paper is only four pages and I write most of the copy myself. A few folks contribute columns. Matter of fact, Mrs. Lufkin has a recipe column and another fellow, a retired professor from the university down in Cruces, he contributes a column every other week about the history of the area. And of course there's a letter column and the obituaries. Reverend Kroeger does a weekly inspirational column. Most of the rest of it is club meetings, accident reports, and stuff like that. But as a matter of fact, I have been considering expanding coverage a little bit. I want to cover more local and regional goings-on besides highway accidents and high school sports. 'Course, there's not a whole lot that happens that's newsworthy around these parts. I'm thinking human-interest stuff. Feature articles, like the city papers run. That'd be something new for us. Might pick up sales some. That'll sell more advertising."

Though on the surface it was an idle conversation, Charlie had continued to adroitly probe into Mike's background.

Mike had seen no reason to avoid or alter the basic facts. Born and raised in Denver. Drafted following high school graduation and sent to Vietnam for the final days of that increasingly forgotten war. The war had already been mostly forgotten when he was there. At least that's the way it had seemed to most of the troops in country, taking heavy casualties while self-serving politicians in the "real world" talked peace, telling that world that an American withdrawal from Vietnam was imminent, only a matter of time before our boys would be coming home after a done deal that only had to be negotiated. The problem, if you were an American foot soldier in the world of Vietnam, was in maintaining your morale; to continue being a good soldier, to stay alive, to keep from coming home in a body bag until that "done deal" was actually negotiated.

Mike had been a platoon sergeant. While politicians talked peace, he'd seen too many of his buddies sent home in those body bags. He had come close. He still carried a chunk of shrapnel near the base of his spine where the doctors had said it was too risky to tamper with; too close to too many nerve endings. It still throbbed to let him know it was there whenever the weather changed.

He'd moved on psychologically from his combat experiences long ago. He appreciated that posttraumatic stress was a real thing. In previous wars they'd called it battle fatigue or shell shock. In fact, he didn't go a day without his thoughts at least once grazing on those distant, horrific images, of seeing friends die and of killing men and, yes, some women in combat. The Viet Cong had been an equal opportunity employer. A man never outlived the memories like that, no matter how many years intervened. But neither was his permanent self-image that of a "Vietnam vet." His philosophy was that life was to be lived, and bad crap was to be dealt with. Enough time had passed; nearly a quarter of a century. Enough had happened between then and now for him to be living in the present, having a life. Things he'd seen and done in Vietnam had compelled him to make the vow, over the graves of his parents, to never again take another human life.

He did not reveal these things to Charlie Flagg. He stayed with autobiographical fact.

After being wounded and shipped stateside, he'd received his medical discharge. Having healed physically, he had then proceeded to heal his psyche with travel around the States before enrollment in college on the GI bill, graduating with a journalism degree. Those were the facts. He mentioned that he'd worked at one of the Denver dailies for five years, but did not mention his reason for leaving. He did not mention the alcoholism. Did it matter which came first? The booze, or the burnout from having to record for the afternoon edition and posterity the sewer depths of human depravity that his newspaper job had daily brought him into contact with, year after endless year. When the gangs started gaining turf and guns started flooding the streets, Denver became too violent. He didn't elaborate and Charlie didn't push. He also glossed over the relocation to Albuquerque; taking the job as instructor in the journalism department. He did tell Charlie about Carol. But of course, he didn't tell everything . . .

He met her at a faculty dinner. She was in the English Department. There had been some sort of instant magic thing that happened between them right from the start, and she later told him that she'd felt it too. He'd read once somewhere that we know our friends as soon as we meet them and that had certainly been the case with Carol. She was intellectual. She was earthy. She was tender. She was strong. She was beautiful, and she was good for him. When he asked her to marry him after a year long courtship, she said yes. Yes . . . if he would dry out. He'd already cut way back on the booze ever since they'd started dating. Somehow, putting the booze behind him was easy. He did it for her. He did it because of her. He did it. And the bottle still sat in the cupboard, unopened. Much as Carol loved teaching, they'd both wanted a family. She became pregnant soon after they were married. He found teaching a hell of a lot less compelling than soldiering or big city journalism, but a whole lot less stressful too, so he stayed with it. They enjoyed weekly trips out of town, into the desert or into the mountains, always enjoying each other's company, talking about their future. He had as many pictures of her as he had of the scenery. He had never been happier . . .

Another thing he hadn't told Charlie Flagg was the real reason why he left the University; why he left Albuquerque.

And one other fact he omitted was that he had not altogether severed contact with his "former" military life. While he had not *technically* been in government service since his army discharge, he had—in a manner of speaking—been part of American covert operations on three separate occasions when an old friend from Vietnam had tempted him back into "temporary civilian duty." Some friends cannot be turned down, and the fact of the matter was that Mike hadn't even wanted to say no those times when Gil called. Gil Gilman was still in government service, as far as Mike could tell. The three separate calls had each come several years apart, but had been practically identical, word-for-word.

"I need someone to cover me, buddy," Gil had said. "I need a civilian with military training, from outside this little corner of the world I'm boxed into."

Each time Mike had caught the next flight out; once to

46

Honduras, once to Peru and, the last time—a half dozen years earlier—Gil had sent for him from off the coast of Cuba and they had infiltrated that country to meet with an informant Gil needed to contact. On each time, Mike had refused his friend's recommendation to carry a sidearm, honoring that vow over his parents' gravesite. The covert operations had involved Mike following Gil, staying in radio contact with him to report if Mike spotted anyone following Gil in these hostile environments. Each time, Mike's presence had proven unnecessary. And each time he had flown back to the States with expenses paid and at least the satisfaction of knowing that he still had those old instincts even if they hadn't been called up; even if he had forsaken the ways of violence. But he still had the edge. Gil Gilman must have also felt that way, or he wouldn't have requested his services on those occasions.

No, there was no reason to tell Charlie Flagg, or anyone else, about any of this.

Mike and Charlie parted with a handshake, arranging for Mike to report for work at the office at one o'clock "or thereabouts," Monday afternoon.

Tomorrow.

Now, Sunday evening, Mike told himself, *that's* what I should be thinking about if I'm going to think about anything other than what's supposed to be going onto this blank sheet of paper in this typewriter. Instead, his thoughts turned to two people: a kid named Paul, and Paul's mom. He tore the paper from the typewriter, crumpled the paper into a ball and threw it into a corner.

What he'd seen on that blank sheet, like an image on a movie screen, would also not leave his mind. That image would never go away, indelibly seared into his mind's eye. Into his psyche. Into his sleeping and waking nightmares.

And like the pain of loss, or memories of a long ago war, it would forever be a part of him. The last time he looked into Carol's eyes . . .

They'd taken a furnished apartment close to campus. She was in the bedroom. The police officer had brusquely torn away the sheet from her face without giving him any warning and he'd looked down at her, into her eyes.

He'd barely seen the ugly bruises around her throat. Barely saw the purple tongue protruding from her mouth. God. God. He only saw her eyes, then and now. Eyes, wide open.

Staring.

Dead.

Chapter 7

Paul rode with his mom on the first day of school, and during the drive they discussed how things would be.

"Just because I'll be teaching at your school," Robin said, "don't think that anything is going to be different for you than for any of the other kids. You're a student and I'm a teacher."

"I know, Mom."

"If you have any problems, we'll discuss them after school. Okay with you?"

"Okay with me. I don't want to be treated different from the other kids."

The Devil Creek school accommodated all twelve grades; a sprawling, modern two-story structure of glass and tan brick situated on the outskirts of town, adjacent to the highway, abutting a steep, piney slope of the foothills.

By halfway through his first school day, Paul had pretty much determined that, even though he wasn't treated differently, his classmates sure were different from those at his school in Chicago. These were country kids. He hadn't realized that there would be such a difference between them and a suburban kid like himself.

The homeroom class was smaller than he was used to. Everyone seemed to know each other. He was the only new kid. His homeroom teacher, Mrs. Cass, made him stand at his desk and introduce himself, but none of the other kids bothered to introduce themselves to him as the morning progressed. That was okay. Paul liked having friends, but he enjoyed his own company, too. Conversations he overheard between classes were about things he knew nothing about like crops and cattle, or schoolyard gossip about kids he didn't know. Most of the kids appeared intelligent enough when they spoke in class but when many of them spoke among themselves, their grammar was awful. The boys liked roughhousing in the hallways and in the bathroom. The girls mostly stayed off to themselves, separate from the boys, and Paul couldn't blame them for that. It was also okay with him. Younger girls who were impressed by boys his age seemed silly to him. Girls his own age always seemed more mature than he was, and could act snooty and stuck up. When lunch hour recess came, he ate alone in the cafeteria, then he searched for and found a spot where he could sit on the blacktop playground, against a wall of the building. He resumed reading a science fiction book he was halfway through.

After reading only a couple of sentences, he realized that someone was standing directly in front of him, towering over him. He looked up. A small group of boys his own age were clustered around him. He couldn't see their faces because the sun shone in his eyes.

"Hey, new kid," one of them said. "What's so interesting about that book anyway?" Then, over his shoulder to the others, "The new kid would rather read a book than talk to us."

"I'll talk with you," Paul said.

He rose to his feet and slipped the paperback into his back pocket. With the sun out of his eyes, he recognized some of the boys from his homeroom class. He recognized others from seeing them in the hallways. He'd seen this bunch sitting together in the cafeteria. He noticed them because they were loud and pushy in the lunch line and while they ate.

"You look like a faggot sitting there reading your book,"

sneered the boy who acted like he was their leader. He was several inches taller than Paul; a hefty kid who outweighed Paul by about thirty pounds. He had bad breath and pimples and a bad attitude to spare. Long, unwashed hair fell across his face, concealing one eye.

Paul felt his stomach muscles tighten. "You guys leave me alone. I don't want trouble."

"Only queers read books," the boy pressed. He stepped in, started to reach around toward Paul's back pocket. "What're you reading, queer?"

Paul put the palms of both hands against the boy's chest and gave a strong shove. "Stay away from me, I said."

The kid tottered backwards. Then he regained his balance. He laughed. Not a nice laugh. "Yo, the queer likes to fight. Okay, queer, take this."

The boy sailed in, bringing his right fist around in a wide arc. Paul was ready. He raised his left arm, blocking the swing, then he balled his right fist and struck, delivering a punch to the boy's jaw. The boy stumbled back again, his eyes rolling back in his head. His knees buckled. He would have fallen if some of his friends hadn't caught and steadied him. The bully shook his head to clear it and when he looked at Paul now, his eyes were bleary, a trickle of blood at the corner of his mouth. He wiped the blood away with the back of his hand.

"Hey! You didn't have to do that."

"I told you to stay away."

Then one of the teachers on playground duty came over. "You boys. Stop that fighting. What's going on here?"

Paul spoke before the others could. "We were just fooling around."

The teacher's eyes alternated between them, skeptical. "It looked like a fight to me. I'm going to keep my eyes on you two. Watch your step."

He wandered away, soon busy elsewhere on the busy playground.

The one who had started the fight studied Paul for a moment, obviously trying to make up his mind about how to react. He hadn't expected Paul to fight back. Paul hoped that standing up to him would prove something, that they could now be friends. But it didn't happen that way.

"That was real smart, new kid. From now on, let's you and me stay away from each other."

Paul said nothing.

The boy turned and strutted away. His friends trailed after him.

Paul watched them go, the knuckles of his right hand bruised and stinging. He was breathing hard. He became aware of someone else standing beside him. He whirled in that direction and brought up his fists again.

A boy stood there, not one who'd been with the bully's bunch. Paul had noticed this boy earlier, seated on the other side of the class in homeroom. He'd noticed the boy because this kid hadn't interacted with the others. He was on the chubby side with incredibly bright red hair, freckles, and thick glasses.

He lurched back a step. "Hey, don't hit *me*. I'm not one of them. I just want to talk!" He held a book, a paperback with a garish cover portraying a hooded figure holding a bloody axe over a partially decomposed skull.

Paul lowered his fists. "Sorry." He nodded to the book. "So you like to read, too. Do those guys give you a hard time?"

"I not only like to read," the boy said, "I'm going to be a writer someday and write books." He indicated the ones across the schoolyard who had pestered Paul. "They're stupid. Yeah, they used to pick fights with me. Mr. Tutwiler told them to stop or they'd get suspended. They were getting bored messing with me, anyway. They harassed you because you're new. They wanted to see what you'd do. You'll do okay."

"I guess. So what's your name?"

"Jared. Jared Philbin. I know your name. You're Paul. I heard Mrs. Cass introduce you in class. What are you reading?"

Paul displayed the cover of the book he was reading. "I used to like westerns. Now I'm into science fiction."

Jared showed scant interest once he saw that the book was science fiction. "I read horror. Stephen King is my favorite."

Paul returned his attention to the boys who had confronted him. They stood grouped on the far side of the playground, joking among themselves.

"Do you think I'll have any more trouble with them?"

"Naw, they'll let you alone now that they know you can take care of yourself. You might even get to be friends with some of them, it just takes awhile with a new kid. Where'd you learn to fight anyway?"

"I can't really fight. I was just lucky with that punch. Have you lived around here long?"

"All my life. If you want to borrow some of my horror books, you can."

"You can read my sci-fi books when I'm done with them, too."

"No, thanks. I don't like reading about rocket ships and stuff. They're always on other planets, and all those machines bore me."

"Hey, that's okay. I don't believe what happens in those scary books you read, either. Ghosts and monsters and stuff." Paul shook his head.

"They're not all about ghosts and monsters," said Jared. "Sometimes they're about strange things that just sort of happen." A funny look came into Jared's eyes. A guarded look. He glanced around to make sure that no one could overhear them. "I know about a lot of things that go on around here that nobody else knows about," he confided.

"Like what?" Paul had decided that he liked Jared. Even if they didn't read the same kind of books, at least Jared did read. In Chicago, all of Paul's friends liked to read.

"Maybe I'll show you," Jared said. "You'll have to promise not to tell anyone."

"What kind of stuff are we talking about? Not what happens in those horror books, I'll bet."

"No, not like that. But you have to promise not to tell, anyway."

"I won't tell."

"Then I'll show you something tonight, if you want. Something real interesting."

"Tonight? You mean tonight, after dark?"

"Uh huh. Not afraid, are you?"

"Not if you know where we're going. But I don't think my mom—"

"You'll have to sneak out. I always do. What time does your mom make you go to bed?"

"Ten."

"Can you? Can you get away?"

Paul thought about the sliding window over his bed. It would be easy. "I guess I could. Why does it have to be so late?"

"You'll know that when I show you, if they're still there."

"If who's still there?" Paul was already beginning to have second thoughts. "Will it be dangerous?"

"Not if we're careful. You are afraid, aren't you?"

"I'm not afraid if you aren't."

"Well, I'm not afraid. But we do have to be careful. If we're not, then there could be a reason to be afraid."

"Jared, are you pulling my leg?"

Jared's expression was solemn. "No."

"At least tell me what it is you're talking about. I won't tell anyone, I promise."

"I'll show you tonight. After school, let's decide where to meet."

"Okay. But why won't you tell me?"

Jared hesitated. Then he smiled. "I will tell you something else."

"What?"

"It's about that house you and your mother live in."

Chapter 8

Mike showed up for work at the *County Clarion* at precisely one o'clock that afternoon.

Charlie Flagg was seated at his computer, his stubby fingers moving briskly across the keyboard. The bearded man in jeans and western shirt looked like he would have been more at home astride a horse or as a foreman on an oil rig. He paused in his typing, leaned back in his old-fashioned wooden swivel chair and stretched, popping at least a dozen joints in his shoulders and spine. He sighed contentedly, took a swig from a can of Diet Pepsi, and smiled.

"So you've had the weekend to size up our little town. What do you think of it? Quiet enough for you?"

Mike perched on the corner of the other desk in the office. "Devil Creek will suit me fine. Nice and quiet. I just hope there's enough going on for me to write articles about. Where'd the town get its name, by the way?"

Charlie frowned. "I've talked to some of the real old timers about that. Folks don't talk much about it anymore. Matter of fact, I'd hazard to say most folks don't even know about it."

"Know about what?"

"Four hundred years ago there was a massacre along a creek, south of here. At least it was a creek in them days. Now it's just an old dry wash except when the rains come. An old Indian legend has it that a devil spirit settled over where the massacre occurred and has been there ever since. The legend, as I understand it, says the creek ran red with blood. The next day the creek dried up and it's stayed dry ever since. Been a dry creek bed for as long as anyone around here can remember. The name stuck. Most of the Indians are gone now, of course."

"Four hundred years ago is too early for white settlers. It must have been Spaniards and Indians."

"The story goes that the Spaniards discovered a vein of silver near here and forced the inhabitants of an Indian village to mine it for years until the vein ran out."

"So, who massacred who?"

"The Spaniards slaughtered the Indians—every person in the village: man, woman, and child. 'Course, four hundred years is a long time, so no one knows the real facts anymore. Shoot, maybe it never even happened. But old Gray Wolf thinks it did."

"Who's that?"

"Crazy old Indian. Make that Native American. The Stone River tribe. Old boy claims to be a hundred years old. Far as I know, maybe he is. He's no spring chicken, that's for damn sure. Got himself a shack back off the highway south of town that overlooks the old creek bed."

"Ever speak with him?"

"Never have. Hardly anyone has. Caught sight of him once. Some folks around town know his grandson, a fella named Joe Youngfeather. Joe comes in for provisions every now and then. They keep pretty much to themselves. You know, those two could make a good subject for one of those human-interest stories. If they felt like talking, that is. I've heard those two don't take kindly to visitors. That's one of the reasons I've stayed clear. On the other hand, I never had a reason to go calling."

"You've got me curious."

Charlie nodded. "Tell you what. You drive out and see if they'll talk with you. They just might. You come up with anything interesting, we'll run it." He reached for a pencil and a scrap of paper. "Here, I'll draw you a map of how to get there."

South of town, the highway curved away from the mountains and the land flattened out into scrub-covered prairie. After he crossed the bridge spanning the dry creek bed, Mike started watching for the dirt road Charlie had sketched on the crude map. He found it easily enough. It was more of a two-wheel, rutted path than a road, rising away from the highway before dropping out of sight beyond a fold in the terrain. Mike slipped the Jeep into four-wheel drive and followed the rutted path that had long ago been worn into the hard clay, running roughly parallel to the creek bed.

He'd removed the Jeep's canvas covering. A Stetson and sunglasses shielded his face from the afternoon sun. Cobalt blue sky stretched from horizon to horizon without a cloud in sight, the temperature somewhere in the mid-eighties. The wind on his face felt warm and dry.

As Charlie said he would, he found an adobe hut one-and-three-quarter miles from the highway. The hut sat on a cleared piece of land overlooking the wash. An ancient pickup truck and a Harley Davidson motorcycle were parked alongside the shack. Sunlight glinted off the motorcycle's chrome.

He braked the Jeep, shut off the engine and stepped to the ground. The feeling here was one of stark seclusion. His ears required a moment to adjust after the Jeep's engine noise. Then, after he'd taken several steps toward the hut, he became aware of a muted, strangely cadenced murmuring from a short distance away. Turning, he tried to discern the source of the sound that was interwoven with other sounds, with the chirping of small birds in a nearby juniper tree and the breeze that whispered through the mesquite. He pinpointed it coming from the direction of the wash, below where the ground sloped to block his line of vision. He headed in that direction. Beyond the dry wash, a mesquite ball driven by the wind skipped over the ground. Mike's footsteps seemed to him to crunch unusually loud, treading this ground. He knew he was trespassing. Then, he stood gazing down at the old man who sat cross-legged in the center of the wash, no more than one hundred feet from him.

The old Native American was unaware of his presence. Old was hardly an adequate description. In the glare of the sunlight, the Indian looked like a mummy, his flesh wrinkled and dry as parchment; a thin, stick figure, frail yet somehow radiating the impression of a power that was tangible. Eyes remaining closed as he chanted, his arms, like his thin, wizened face, lifted skyward, his long flowing white hair contrasting starkly against a black headband. His lips barely moved. The chanting was rhythmic, authoritative, and impassioned, yet tinged with resignation. A mournful sound.

Mike was captivated. Time hung suspended.

He was unaware of another presence until a stern voice demanded, "What the hell are you doing here?"

He turned, startled, feeling a surge of guilt and embarrassment at having been caught intruding like this. Then he froze at sight of the rifle muzzle aimed at his midsection from less than ten feet away.

"I'm sorry. I should have let you know I was here."

The rifle muzzle did not waver.

"What do you want?"

The man holding the rifle was in his forties. Lean-muscled, he wore black: black shirt, black jeans, black boots. A wide-bladed knife was sheathed in buckskin at mid-chest. His hair was black, worn in braids. His was a warrior's visage; harsh, highlighted by dark, impassive eyes.

"Are you Joe Youngfeather?" Mike asked, knowing the answer.

"I'm holding the rifle. You answer the questions. What the hell are you doing here?"

"My name is Landware. Mike Landware. I came out from town to talk with you and your grandfather."

"Talk about what?"

"I work for the newspaper."

"Get lost."

The old man's chanting continued unabated. A shrike cawed overhead. A dust devil danced along the ground in the distance.

"I'm sorry," Mike said. "I should have called first."

"We don't have a phone. Phones are for talking and we don't talk. Not to newspapers."

"I don't want trouble."

"You've got trouble if you don't get your ass off this property." The man gestured with the rifle. "Like, right now."

"All right, whatever you say. Just stop pointing that thing at me."

"Then get out."

Mike returned to his Jeep. He climbed behind the steering wheel and started the engine. When he looked up, the man had lowered the rifle. Mike felt compelled to say, "I won't write about what I saw."

"You don't know what you saw," said Youngfeather. "It wouldn't matter if you did. My grandfather thinks he can stop what's going to happen. I don't think he can, not even with his powers."

"For someone who doesn't want to talk, why tell me this much? Do you *want* to get me interested?"

"My grandfather is doing what he's doing for the people of your town. If they knew about it, they'd only laugh. They'd scorn him more than they already do. The crazy old Indian."

"I'm not laughing."

Something changed behind the man's impassive features. A decision was made. "My grandfather was a tribal medicine man. There are only a few dozen descendants remaining of our tribe, scattered like grains of sand in the wind. Grandfather is a legend keeper. A healer. A shaman."

"A magic man?" *Go for the opening,* Mike told himself. *He won't tell you any more than he wants to.* "What's the significance of the ritual he's performing?"

"He chants to drive away the evil that is coming."

"Evil spirits?"

"You see what I mean. You do not believe. I hear it in your voice."

"It's difficult for me to believe in spirits," Mike admitted.

"That's what the others would say. You're no different. How could you be? Your race . . . your souls are dead."

"I believe evil exists," said Mike. "Believe me, I've seen my share up close. And I know about the massacre that happened at this site four hundred years ago. Does the evil have something to do with that?"

"Evil has visited this land before. Evil kicked ass here. It will happen again."

"Tell me. Tell me what your grandfather sees."

Youngfeather snorted, an unexpected, rude sound. "I can't tell you because I don't know. I don't think Gray Wolf knows. He *feels,* and he chants to drive it back."

"Can I speak with your grandfather?"

"He's been as you see him for three days. He sleeps four hours out of twenty-four. He fights forces you would never understand, and it saps what energy he has. His heart is weak but he fights like a young brave."

"This evil. Has your grandfather said when he foresees it coming?"

"Soon. Very soon. Now get. I'm tired of talking to you. Go back where you belong. I've said enough."

"That's funny, Joe. Why do I get the feeling you're telling me exactly what you want to tell me?"

Youngfeather pretended not to hear this. "Don't come back. If Gray Wolf is right, nothing will stop what's going to happen. Nothing."

"I'll go. But I will be back. I want to talk with your grandfather."

Youngfeather said nothing. The warrior eyes glittered; brooding, opaque, and unreadable.

Mike backed the Jeep around and drove away.

The sunshine somehow didn't feel quite as warm as it had on the drive in. What had possessed him, he wondered, to act more like some small-town investigative reporter instead of what he was, a guy sent out to do a human interest story if there was one?

He thought he still heard Gray Wolf's rhythmic, endless chanting, although he knew this was impossible. The chanting would hardly have carried across the distance and cut through the Jeep's engine noise.

Mike had never tried to be anything but the born skeptic he was. The other side of skepticism is gullibility. He'd made his share of errors in judgement over the years, but experience had shown that he was shrewd in worldly dealings and a good judge of character. He was not gullible. He found himself respecting and even liking the man who had pointed a rifle at him moments earlier. But what to make of the man's whole acceptance of chanting to keep away spirits? And what about the grandfather? Mike was born and would die a skeptic. He believed what his senses could analyze, and what could be proven to him. Parapsychology and a spiritual world impacting on this reality were not subjects he had ever deemed worthy of contemplation.

And yet he *did* hear Gray Wolf's chanting inside his head all the way back to the highway, and it stayed with him all the way back into town.

Chapter 9

Robin wondered how it was possible to feel frazzled and rejuvenated at the same time. After a night of fitful sleep following the phone call from Jeff, she had gone in early to check her classroom, to insure that there were enough desks, enough paper, pencils, and chalk. But nothing could have prepared her for Monday's hectic pace. So much to keep track of, so many names to remember among faculty and students, so much to keep organized and try to absorb. It would have been totally overwhelming by day's end if she'd afforded herself the luxury of slowing down enough to think about it. One side effect was that by the end of the day, she had pretty much forgotten about Jeff's call. More precisely, she had relegated it to a drunken, late night, and hopefully isolated incident.

Following the final class of the first day, there was a faculty meeting. The other faculty members had seemed friendly enough as she'd met most of them during the day. She, though, was usually the one to initiate introductions rather than receive any particular displays of welcome on the part of the majority of the instructors. She told herself that this reserve toward a new arrival was natural enough in a small town. They were sizing her up, personally and professionally. Fair enough. Or was it wrong to even blame it on Devil Creek being a small town? Maybe that was human nature. It could well be the same on the first day of classes for any new teacher transplanted to Chicago from New Mexico. The faculty was about evenly divided between males and females. Some of the women were approximately her age, but most of the staff was considerably older, reflected in their attire and general attitudes.

One of the women her age was named Connie Silva. Plump and vivacious, with a winning smile and sparkling brown eyes, Connie was open and friendly when they first met. They sat together at the faculty meeting. She hadn't been standoffish at all. Robin liked her immediately. Connie was one of those people whose genuine decency shone through as a first impression; the same feeling Robin had experienced when she'd met Mrs. Lufkin. Different as Connie was on the surface from the spunky landlady, Robin felt blessed to have made the acquaintance of two women of such obvious quality in such short order. She'd been afraid that it would take awhile to make friends in this new place.

After the faculty meeting, Mr. Tutwiler, the principal, made a point of engaging her in conversation while the others filed out, some of them chatting socially among themselves. Tutwiler was a pleasant, heavyset man in his early sixties, possessing a well-coifed silver head of hair and the porous, heavily-veined nose and throaty voice of a seasoned bourbon drinker. He was sober and cordial at the end of this workday, however. Robin had learned that she was the only new instructor this semester. Mr. Tutwiler naturally wanted his own opportunity to size up this newest addition to their ranks. They passed several minutes discussing absolutely nothing, things like how Mr. Tutwiler had been to Chicago once for a convention ten years ago and how much dryer the climate was out west compared to back east. She appeared to pass his inspection, as she believed she probably had in the eyes of the others. Human nature. She was the new kid on the block. She could live with that.

Trading a pleasant goodbye with Mr. Tutwiler, she happened to pass Connie Silva's homeroom on her way out of the building. She glanced in. Connie was working late at her desk.

When Connie looked up with a friendly smile, her eyes sparkled, good-natured and conspiratorial. "Well, did you pass Mr. T's inspection?"

"I think so," Robin said from the doorway. "At least he didn't fire me."

"You'll do fine."

"I hope so. Have you lived in Devil Creek for long?"

"All my life. I'll show you around one of these days, if you'd like."

"That would be nice. Thanks."

Connie leaned back. She emitted a sigh and tossed her pencil onto the stack of papers she'd been poring over, the first indication that she might be as exhausted as Robin felt. "The trick will be finding the time. I have two three-year-olds and between them and my job, that doesn't leave much time for socializing."

"Why not bring your kids along?"

"You wouldn't mind?"

"I wouldn't mind. I love kids."

"Same here. Guess that helps when you're teaching fourth graders."

"I, uh, don't imagine every day is as hectic as the first."

Connie laughed; happy, pleasant. "Hardly. Don't sweat it, teach. You'll do fine."

"Thanks, Connie. I guess I needed that. See you to-morrow."

"See you."

The school parking lot was located behind the gymnasium and adjacent to the playing field. After a day spent indoors, the warmth of the late afternoon sunshine felt good, rejuvenating Robin.

There was no sign of Paul. Paul had already made a new friend, a boy his own age—chubby, red-haired, with glasses—who he'd introduced as Jared. Before the meeting, she'd left the two boys chattering away enthusiastically about the state of the art of special effects in the movies, with Paul promising to meet her by the car in the parking lot an hour later. Which was right now.

"Come on, Paul," she said with mild exasperation to the nearly empty parking lot.

Crossing to the Subaru, she reached into her purse for her keys. She wasn't about to take off in search of her son. He'd show up soon enough. Paul was a good kid but that hardly meant he was an angel by any stretch of the imagination. He was a twelve-year-old boy, after all. Anyway, she could use a few minutes of quality time alone, a little peace and quiet for herself.

Settling behind the steering wheel, she placed her briefcase on her lap and withdrew her lesson plans for the following day. Before she could begin reading, she sensed someone approaching her side of the car. In the brief moment it took for her to look up, she assumed it would be Paul. She was startled to see Bobby Caldwell standing there, leaning down toward her half-lowered window. She almost dropped the papers from her lap. Tobe was barely visible where he stood behind his brother, largely obscured by Bobby's bulk.

Bobby smirked. "Lookee here, little brother. If it ain't our girly friend from the highway, sitting all alone without even her brat to protect her."

"I haven't been a girl in quite a few years," Robin said. "I'm not your friend and I don't need anyone to protect me." It was a bravado she didn't feel. She told herself that these were kids, after all. Bad kids, sure, but this was not some deserted highway. This was a public school parking lot.

Tobe hooted. "Oowee! City gal's got spunk, don't she?"

Bobby rested a hand on the door handle. "I'll give her some spunk." He spoke in a leering whisper for her ears alone. "I'll give her plenty."

She pushed down the lock button. "Get away from this car."

Tobe hooted again. "Don't sound like she's too impressed, Bobby-o."

Bobby said, "Maybe me and her, we just need to get better acquainted." He was about to reach through and unlock the door. She grasped the handle and started to roll up the window.

She heard Tobe say, with feeling, "Aw hell."

Bobby stepped back from the car.

A police car came to a stop beside her vehicle. She'd been too concerned with Tobe to notice its approach. Sunlight reflected off the badge of the officer who stepped from the car. Despite the spare tire that filled out his uniform around the middle, the man looked more than competent. His uniform was sharply pressed. His hand rested on his holstered sidearm.

He said, "Step away from the vehicle, Bobby. Slow and easy."

Bobby obeyed. "Why, sure, Chief. We was just getting acquainted with the new teach, is all."

The officer glanced at Robin. "I'm Chief Saunders, ma'am. I was patrolling and I saw these troublemakers giving you a hard time."

Tobe had not moved from where he stood behind Bobby. "We wasn't giving her no hard time, Chief," he whined. "We was just talking to her."

Bobby added, "Hell, Chief. I wasn't doing nothing but leaning on the lady's car, visiting."

"Ma'am?" the officer asked. "Do you want to press charges?"

Robin considered her options. What could she prove against Bobby and his whining little brother? There was no one to corroborate what they'd said to her, and just because she thought Bobby was about to reach in and unlock the door didn't mean he actually was. She experienced anger, immediately followed by a surge of defeat. She was exhausted. She did not need this.

"I don't want to press charges," she said. "But these boys were harassing me. I'd like them to stay away from me in the future."

Saunders glared at Bobby and Tobe. "You heard her. She's doing you a favor. Now haul your useless selves off these school grounds or I'll run you both in for trespassing. And if I ever find out you've been harassing her again, I'll just have to decide whether I want to throw you both in jail or take my badge off and drive out to your place and kick both your butts. Now scat."

Little Tobe started to withdraw, then hesitated when he realized his brother wasn't with him. Bobby stood his ground, his fists clenched. He and Saunders stared each other down for what Robin guessed had to be at least a half-minute—under the circumstances, a very long time. Then, with a crude snorting noise, Bobby wheeled around, joined his brother and they strutted off toward their beat-up pickup truck, which she now saw parked on the public road fronting the school.

When the two were gone, the bravado she'd mustered disappeared like air from a deflated balloon.

"Thank you, Chief. They were hassling me. I just didn't

want to make it worse for my son and me."

They watched the pickup truck drive away.

"Ma'am, at the next sign of any problem whatsoever from either one of those punks you call 911. I don't reckon Tobe would ever do anything on his own, but that brother of his is one bad apple."

"I should introduce myself. My name is Robin Curtis."

He smiled a kindly smile and tipped his hat brim in a courtly western gesture that she'd seen a million times in the cowboy movies but never in real life. "I know who you are, ma'am. Pleasure to meet you."

Paul chose that moment to appear from the main classroom building, walking toward them, oblivious to what had just occurred.

Before her son was within hearing range, Robin said, "Thanks again, Chief Saunders."

"Just doing my job, ma'am."

Another tip of the hat brim and he was gone. The police car was driving off as Paul got into the Subaru.

"Hi, Mom. What was that all about?"

She shuffled her study plans back into her briefcase, and started the car. "I was meeting the Chief of Police," she said conversationally, as if it really didn't matter.

Paul seemed to have already dismissed the subject.

As they drove home, she watched in her rearview mirror for the brothers' ancient pickup truck, but it was nowhere in sight.

Chapter 10

"Guess what, Mom."

"What, honey?"

"Yo, Mom. You said you weren't going to call me honey anymore."

"All right, *Paul.*" She affectionately emphasized his name. "What?"

"There was a murder in this house. A murder and a suicide, a long time ago."

This was midway through their after-dinner ritual of Paul doing the dishes while she put away the leftovers.

She paused in wrapping meatloaf in a food storage bag. "What are you talking about?"

"Jared told me," Paul did not interrupt or slow his efficient, practiced rinsing of the dishes. "It happened fifty years ago. It was a soldier from that war a long time ago, the Korean one. Jared said that the soldier and his wife built this house. Then he went off to fight in Korea. It happened when he came back. Did we win that war?"

"I'm sure you can find a book all about it in the school library." She heard the sharpness of her tone, and told herself to relax. "Paul, what is supposed to have happened here when that soldier came back from Korea?"

"Jared said the soldier killed his wife, then himself, with a shotgun. It happened right here in the kitchen."

The glass cooking dish with the meatloaf slipped from her fingers, shattering loudly into a million pieces upon the floor.

After that, they concerned themselves with cleaning it up. Paul was contrite. He broomed the mess into a dustpan while Robin used a sponge mop after him, assuring him that dropping the leftovers and breaking the dish was no one's fault but her own. She had pressed him to tell her, right? With that settled, she next had to know if there was anything else that Jared had told him about the tragedy. Paul said no, which was some relief to her at least. But he'd told her more than enough already, and what he'd told her stayed with her throughout the evening like an infection buried deep in the back of her mind.

What could be the emotional truth, she wondered, behind a tragedy like that? Had something snapped psychologically with that soldier while he was off fighting in Korea? Had his wife been unfaithful, falling in love—or lust—with another man during his absence? Robin imagined the man walking into the kitchen where the wife could have been busy at the same spot where she had prepared tonight's dinner. Or had he chased her into the kitchen, the both of them screaming? Had she pleaded for mercy? Begged for her life? Or had he walked up quietly behind her and fired the shotgun? A shotgun. Dear God. He had killed her and in the same fit of insane passion—or despair, or both—had taken his own life. What could twist love into *that?*

Wait a minute, she thought. Looking back on her own life thus far, what she'd thought was love for Jeff was only lust; the hot sex they shared when their relationship was new: his touch, his scent, the way he made her feel between the sheets. But what a stupid thing to base a supposedly life-long commitment on. The passion had left their intimate life even before Paul was born, and they'd had little intimacy whatsoever from the time of their son's birth on.

What a fool I was, she thought.

She consciously set her mind to blocking these thoughts of Jeff as she gathered her work notes together before her on the kitchen table in their new kitchen.

In the living room, beyond the kitchen archway, Paul was indulging in his allotted evening television time. He found a science fiction movie on cable that held him trans-fixed.

She wished Paul hadn't told her about the half-century old tragedy that had happened here. Sadness engulfed her, and she wondered if she would ever again step into her clean, cozy kitchen, in their nice cozy house, without thinking about a long deceased man and woman she'd never known, and their blood and brains splattered across walls and ceiling, their bodies lying for who knew how long before being found . . .

She tried to banish the bleak thoughts, the gruesome image. Every house had a history, and this history Paul spoke of was fifty years ago. Throughout the intervening years, dozens of people had resided here, hundreds more passing through the doorways. Thousands of meals had been prepared and eaten in this kitchen since that event. The intervening years had been kind to the house, as if in compensation for the horrors that had once visited here. The present and the living prevailed over the past and the deceased. Today, tonight, and as long as they lived here, this would be her and Paul's kitchen. This was *their* home. Fifty years ago was long, *long* gone. *Forget it,* she told her-self. *Lighten up.*

Robin sent Paul to bed at his regular time, then forced herself to stop working for the day. She found herself wishing she'd thought to knock off work earlier, so she and Paul could have had some one-on-one time together. She actually enjoyed some of the hokey science fiction and horror films they watched together. She must not allow herself to become so preoccupied with everything that she forgot the important things, like spending time with her son. She decided to reward herself, after such a grueling day, with some strictly pleasure reading. Before long she was drowsing off over Edward Abbey's *Desert Solitaire.*

While preparing for bed, after turning off the lights, she happened to glance out a window and noticed that a single light again shone from the house next door. She hadn't seen her neighbor since yesterday. She did feel a sense of security, knowing that she wasn't alone out here at the end of a country road. At the same time, this mildly irked her. Becoming a single working mom had ingrained in her a determination to be self-reliant. But Mrs. Lufkin was right. It *was* good to know that there was a capable man in the vicinity. Yes, she took pride in her independence. Yet it was Charlie Flagg who had intimidated the Caldwell boys into leaving her alone that day on the highway, and Chief Saunders had done the same in the school parking lot today. What would have happened either time if she'd been alone, without those men being around? Could she have defended herself if those men had not come to her assistance? She had to admit . . . she wasn't sure. And that irked her most of all. She found herself wishing that she had pressed charges against those Caldwell creeps for harassing her.

Lying in bed, trying to banish these thoughts from her mind, she drifted off to sleep.

And that's when the dream began.

Chapter 11

Paul waited for awhile after his Mom went to her room, after she turned off the lights in the house. When his bedside clock told him it was time, he dressed quietly in the moonlight filtering in through his bedroom window. He arranged the sheets around his pillow and a bunched-up clump of clothing to make it appear that he was still curled up and sleeping soundly in the bed, buried beneath the covers, just in case Mom looked in on him while he was gone.

He felt no pride in this. He knew it was wrong, sneaking out like this to meet Jared. His mother worried about him like any good mom would. That didn't necessarily mean there was reason for her to worry. Moms always worried too much. This way his mother wouldn't worry needlessly because she wouldn't even know he was gone. He'd be back within the hour. He'd made Jared promise him that much.

He eased open the window over his bed, the rising sash sounding incredibly loud. He told himself it wasn't really that loud, it only seemed that way. He hoped so, anyway. He pried the screen loose and climbed out, dropping to the ground.

This was something he wanted to do. He wanted to learn more about Devil Creek. This little western town was so different from any place he'd ever known. Back home there was more to do—malls, video arcades, school activities. Kids seemed more into movies and books and different types of music. Night in Devil Creek, especially living on the outskirts of town, meant the *totally* dark quiet of the country, except for moonlight and the chattering of insects and an owl or two. It was so foreign after a lifetime in the 'burbs, he was curious about the things that made everything out here so different from the world he'd known in Chicago.

He took off running across the front yard. The moonlight rendered his surroundings as vague, silvery images like some old, dimly projected black-and-white movie.

Jared was waiting for him under a big cottonwood tree beyond Mike's house, where they'd agreed to meet. The chubby, red-haired boy's thick eyeglasses caught and weirdly reflected the moonlight. He held a flashlight, which was not turned on.

"Ready?" Jared asked.

"Ready."

They started walking. The shadows here were deep and murky. An owl hooted nearby. There was a permeating chill to the air that made Paul glad he'd decided to wear his denim jacket.

He asked, "Now can you tell me where we're going?"

Without hesitation, Jared left the road with the authority of a jungle guide leading the way. "Just over this hill."

A trail cut deeper into the trees, taking them to a ravine.

"Come on, Jared. Tell me *something*."

Jared's breathing was becoming labored from the exertion of walking uphill. "Okay, okay," he said. "From my bedroom I can see a road that leads up here. One night I saw lights coming up here, and I went up to investigate like we're doing now. There are these guys, and almost every week, on the same night—tonight, they . . . well, you'll see."

"You're not going to tell me?"

"You'll see."

76

"You know your way around up here pretty good."

"Sure do. I explore further on up the mountain, too. Most of the time it's during the day. I like to look for a quiet spot where I can be by myself and read."

"Don't your folks mind you coming up here alone?"

"Naw. My folks are divorced. Mom acts like she's glad to get rid of me. Says I never do any housework, but she's the one who never does anything. I do all the housework. I don't know where my dad is. He left when I was a baby, so I don't care. I never knew him anyway. Mom, she's a drunk. Likes to bring guys home on the weekend, or go off to Cruces or Albuquerque. But she never takes me along."

"That's too bad."

Jared shrugged. "I don't care." He spoke between gulps of air. "The old lady's always yelling at me anyway. Only time she doesn't yell is when she's watching her soaps."

"So where does mommy dearest work?"

"She's a waitress at the truck stop. That's where she meets a lot of her boyfriends. She kicks me out when she has company."

"Next time that happens, you come over to my house," Paul said. "My mom won't mind. Back home she let my friends come over and hang out, and some of them came over because they had troubles at home. You'll like my mom. She's way cool."

"Thanks, Paul."

The trail became steeper and more winding. Trees to either side became thicker, more dense; towering giant pillars forming solid walls that disappeared to meet overhead, blocking out most of the moonlight. The path grew narrow. Jared used his flashlight until the trail widened again, then he switched the beam off. Paul could hardly see the end of his arm. He followed Jared more by the sounds of his la-

77

bored breathing, their footsteps muted by the carpet of accumulated dead leaves. Paul's breathing remained normal. He was obviously in much better shape than Jared, though he did clench his teeth to stop them from chattering—it was cold even with the jacket.

He started thinking that maybe he shouldn't have left his warm bed to go out into the night like this. But he would not turn back now. He did wish that he hadn't told his mother what Jared had told him about the murder and suicide in their house all those years ago. It had upset her. He wished he'd kept it to himself. At least he hadn't told her everything. He hadn't told her what Jared had said about the soldier placing the double-barreled shotgun into his mouth after killing his wife. Jared said that after trying to scrub the bloodstains away many times, the ceiling had finally been painted over. The stains were probably still up there, soaked deep into the wood even after who knew how many coats of paint had been applied over the years. Paul hadn't told his mother about how they'd had to use a needle-nosed pliers to pick out the chips of the man's skull that were imbedded in the ceiling from the force of the shotgun blast.

A few feet before the crest of a hill, Paul detected the faint mumble of voices. Jared heard it too. He crouched down, motioning for Paul to do the same.

"They're here again, right on schedule," Jared whispered in Paul's ear. "This is where we have to be real quiet." They advanced the final distance to the crest of the hill. "Take a look," Jared said. "But be *real* careful. And be ready to run."

Pressing themselves to the cold ground, they peered together, side by side, over the crest at the scene below.

Three people sat on a single fallen log around a campfire

in a clearing. Paul saw them clearly in the golden, flickering firelight, and a jolt of fear unnerved him when he recognized the two men, or boys: slobby Bobby Caldwell and his "little bro," Tobe. The Caldwell brothers sat on a log, with a woman perched between them. The woman was skinny to the point of being emaciated, her oily blonde hair long and unkempt. She wore blue jean short-shorts and a halter-top, and a tattoo of barbed wire coiled around one wrist.

"See," Jared whispered. There was a strange undercurrent of anticipation in his voice. "Watch."

Paul didn't reply.

The people sitting on the log were passing what looked like a bottle of whiskey back and forth between them. The ground around the campfire was littered with aluminum beer cans. Paul heard the gravelly voices of the men, but he could not distinguish their words. The woman's drunken giggling laughter rose over the male voices. They all sounded drunk.

Jared whispered conspiratorially into Paul's ear, "Last night I watched them like this for almost an hour. Want to know what happened?"

"What?"

"The two guys . . . they, uh, they did it to the girl. Uh, you know what I mean?"

"I . . ." Paul's words faltered in his throat. "I guess so . . ."

"They were all doing it at the same time, and she didn't even mind. She liked it! It was way cool."

Now that he knew what Jared had brought him here to see, now that he knew what might happen down there in the clearing below, now that he was again in this close proximity to Bobby and Tobe, Paul found himself definitely wishing that he wasn't here. This was nothing he wanted to see. He was as fascinated by and curious about sex as any boy his age. He'd seen some dirty videos and seen—and, yes, *used*—magazines like *Penthouse* and *Playboy*. But this . . . this was different. He felt embarrassed and repulsed, and frightened. He started to say this, started to tell Jared that he wanted to leave, that he *was* going to leave. He was going home. But before he could, things began happening in the clearing by the campfire.

Bobby and Tobe started shouting angrily at each other. The woman had fallen off the log. She was laying on her back upon the ground, whiskey from the bottle splashing across her, glistening on her bared, pale flesh. The Caldwells had temporarily forgotten about her.

"Uh-oh," Jared said under his breath.

Tobe must have said something that made Bobby angry. It happened so fast, Paul could barely believe what he was seeing. Without warning, snarling with rage, each brother threw himself at the other and the struggling Caldwells toppled to the ground, kneeing and slugging each other. Paul clearly heard the impact of fists slamming into flesh, sounds punctuated by grunts of rage and pain.

The woman barely stirred. She stared up at the night sky and began laughing hysterically, a brittle, manic cackling that continued as the Caldwell brothers went on pummeling each other.

Chapter 12

Robin knew she was dreaming but somehow this did nothing to make the dream less real, did nothing to stop the dream from unfolding with color and sound and the sensations of waking reality . . .

She awoke to sounds of whispering. That is, she thought it was whispering. She sat up in bed. Moonlight made the window shade across her bedroom a luminescent rectangle. The whispering was not a voice but the shuffle of slippered feet from upstairs.

Upstairs?

There was no upstairs . . .

The shuffling stopped. Then came a faint clatter and a sharp cry.

She swung her feet to the floor. She listened.

Thunder rumbled. Rain beat a tattoo upon the roof and the window. The wind whistled and moaned around the house. A branch scraped against glass.

She sat there on the edge of her bed for a minute or so, breathing shallowly. Silence enveloped the house except for the raging elements outside. She rose and belted her house robe. She stepped into the hallway outside her bedroom door.

And there was the stairway.

She hadn't noticed it before. It was a lovely piece of work, wide and curving, the stairs and banister of polished mahogany, leading up into impenetrable shadows. *The sounds had come from up there.* She told herself not to go up those stairs. Something terrible, something evil, waited for her up there. But her mind had no control over her body. She glided forward. The shuffling of her feet across the cold floor was like the whispering noise that had awakened her. She ascended the stairs slowly, one hand following the banister, the other drawing the collar of the robe to her throat. Walking up those stairs seemed to take forever. The darkness at the top of the stairs was a magnetic black void drawing her onward, deeper into the dark. She reached the top stair.

There was no landing or hallway. She was standing in a stark, high-ceilinged room of murky wood-paneled walls, barren of any furnishings. The hammering rain was extremely loud up here.

Then she saw it, and the back of her hand flew to her opened mouth to stifle a gasp of shock.

Against a single window was silhouetted a slowly rotating human body hanging at the end of a length of heavy rope suspended from above, one end of the rope secured to a rafter, the other looped around the dead woman's throat. A chair lay overturned beneath her bare, dangling feet. The rafter protested, creaking against the weight.

Robin stood there, rooted to the spot. She could not make out the face of the hanging corpse. Run, her mind screamed. *Run!* But she could not move.

A blinding bolt of lightning.

A deafening thunderclap shook the house, rattling the windows, piercing her eardrums. And in the flare of lightning that filled the room like a strobe light, she saw the face at the end of the rope. *She saw her own face:* the face of a corpse with dead eyes that were distended orbs, the flesh rendered ghostly pale in the lightning. The dead flesh was beaded with moisture like raindrops on marble. The corpse's mouth was frozen open in an eternal silent scream.

Robin screamed, and it was not silent. Her scream was louder than the thunderclap in her dream and it woke her for real.

She sat up in her bed. Moonlight filled the room. She was drenched in sweat. Her flesh looked pale in the moonlight, the beads of perspiration like moisture pearled on cold marble. *Then she saw a human figure, silhouetted by the moonlight, glide past outside the window shade across from her bed!*

She wanted to scream then but she managed to stifle it. She remained motionless, listening intently. She held her breath. She heard nothing. No movement inside or outside the house. Maybe there was no figure, she told herself. Maybe it was a part of her nightmare lingering as she'd awoke; tentacles of the subconscious that had clung from deep sleep into her first waking awareness? Or if there had been someone outside, a prowler, then the prowler must have heard her scream that had ended the nightmare.

She switched on the bedside lamp. She was alone in her bedroom. She thought of Paul. She told herself not to panic.

Throwing on her robe—just like in the dream, she realized—Robin stepped into the moon-splashed hallway outside her bedroom. This time it was the same house she had rented from Mrs. Lufkin, with no exquisitely constructed stairway leading up to a second level that did not exist. She crossed to Paul's door and cracked it open enough to peer in, hopefully without disturbing him. She clearly discerned a shape concealed beneath the covers. With a sigh of relief, she closed the door and returned to her bedroom where she turned off the bedside lamp and stood still for the time necessary to allow her eyes to readjust to the faint illumination of the moonlight.

Moving as lightly as possible, she crossed to the window where she thought she'd glimpsed someone's silhouette outside beyond the drawn shade. Standing with her back to the wall, she used an index finger to part the shade only enough for her to place an eye against the window and look out.

There was no sign of anyone outside. It was not raining. There was no thunder and lightning.

Robin remained like that for some time, her free hand clutching the robe around her throat to ward off the chill within her. *What was nightmare,* she wondered, *and what was real?*

Sometime during the time she had been asleep, the light she'd noticed earlier in Mike Landware's house had been turned off. Was he asleep? Or was her neighbor outside her house, stalking in the moonlight?

The ringing of her telephone, this one on her bedside table, again scared her half out of her skin. She again grabbed it with both hands on the first ring, knowing who it would be.

Before she could say hello, Jeff's snigger slithered across the connection. "Hello, sweetheart. Enjoying your new life?"

She had managed to talk herself into thinking that he would not call again. That his previous behavior had been too stupid even for him to stomach. Now she was just angry.

"Jeff, you bastard, leave us alone."

"And why should I? What favors have you done me? A man in my position is supposed to be an upstanding family man. You lived comfy enough on that notion for a long time. Do you have any idea how my income has been affected by what you put us through?"

"What *I* put us though?" She could barely believe what

she was hearing. "Why you arrogant, self-centered son of a—" A sudden, new notion made her stop as she tried to put a figure, a build, to the shadow that had glided across her window shade. "Wait a minute. There are laws against stalking, Jeffrey." She shivered as if a cold draft had run through the house. "Where are you? Where are you calling from? Are you in Chicago or—" Her throat muscles constricted as if crushed by icy fingers.

Jeff sniggered. "Have you been thinking about it like I told you to, Robin? About how I can reach out to wherever you are and mess up your life anytime I feel like it? I hope you've been thinking about that, sweetheart. Because it's going to happen."

"You bastard."

But she was talking to the droning hum of a dial tone.

Chapter 13

Paul climbed back in through his bedroom window, the raising and lowering of the sash again sounding incredibly loud as he entered and replaced the screen. The interior of the house felt toasty after the cool night air but the sweat coating his face and body was icy and clammy. He wanted to go into the bathroom to wash up, but that would wake Mom. He'd wait until morning.

He'd run all the way home from that ridge overlooking the clearing where Bobby and Tobe Caldwell had fought. He hadn't waited to see what happened next. He'd heard Jared's grunt of disgust at his reaction, but the other boy had left with him, following Paul on the trail that led down the side of the hill, through the ravine and to the road.

Paul couldn't help himself. He didn't care what Jared thought. He wasn't sure himself why he ran away. It wasn't just that the sudden eruption of violence between the two men had surprised him. It was something more. He knew only that he had to get away from there, had to escape. It was one thing when violence occurred in books and movies. That was different. It wasn't real, only pretending to be. But what he'd seen tonight was something different altogether. That was real. Too real. He had to get away and that's what he did.

Pudgy, hard-breathing Jared managed to keep pace with him. After fleeing down the trail, when they finally did reach the road and Paul's house was in sight, they were both out of breath.

Jared said, in between gulps for air, "I sure didn't think

you'd turn chicken." Even in the moonlight, his flushed face was almost the same color as his bright red hair. "I know it's not nice to spy on people like that, but those weren't nice people, dude. Everyone knows what creeps the Caldwell brothers are. Jesus! You didn't have to go crazy and run away like that. What if they'd heard us?"

"I didn't go crazy. I just didn't want to be there." Paul had started to turn away, toward his house.

"You're not going to tell anyone, are you?" Jared asked. His breathing had almost returned to normal.

"I won't tell anyone," Paul promised. "I'll see you at school tomorrow."

He'd left Jared then, crossing the road, and returning to his property. He heard Jared call after him, as if he'd thought of something else to say. Paul pretended he didn't hear the whispered entreaties for him to wait and come back. Then Jared's voice faded behind him altogether, swallowed up by the chirping of insects and the songs of the night birds. Paul had not slowed or looked back.

In his bedroom, he removed the pillow and the bunched-up clothes that he'd placed beneath his bedcovers. He climbed back into bed and lay there, staring at the ceiling. It felt good to be back in the safety of his own home.

Chapter 14

Chief of Police Ben Saunders hadn't heard an M-1 rifle in years but he instantly recognized the angry chatter of its semi-automatic fire shredding the tranquility of this weekday morning.

The source of the gunfire was very close, coming without warning, startling him, making him spill his first cup of morning coffee across the reports on his desk.

Ben was on the far side of fifty. He had something of a spare tire around his middle and a receding hairline. Widowed the previous month after thirty years of marriage, he had one child, grown now and married, living in El Paso. He and Val were close, but not that close. She had her own family, and since the funeral he'd been pretty much left to deal with his grief on his own. Which was how he preferred it. Devil Creek had a small police force; six officers, two cars and only one of them fit to be on the highway. There wasn't much crime to speak of except for the occasional domestic spat, speeders, or break-ins at summer cabins up on Missionary Ridge, or maybe some rowdy farm kids raising a little sand after a Saturday night of drinking down in Cruces. It was, however, enough of a job to keep him busy and occupied. It didn't ease the ache of missing Helen, but it was how he dealt with the gaping hole in his life that he knew could never be filled. He generally put in sixty hours per week, sometimes more if one of his men was out sick or wanted vacation time.

In a lot of ways, this little town of his was a microcosm of American society, much as any small town was no matter the region. Ben thought of Devil Creek as "his" town not because he was the law here, but because he'd been born and raised and would probably die here. He *knew* this town and the people who resided here as only a lawman that had been a lifelong resident could know them.

Ben sprinted from his chair and unlocked the rack of pump shotguns, grabbing one as a second burst of fire sounded from the street. Methodically feeding ammunition into the shotgun, he charged into the corridor outside his office. He reached the outside glass door through which two of his deputies, Perks and Chavez, had exited moments earlier to begin their morning patrol. He moved quickly through the doorway, staying low, chambering a round, holding the shotgun up and ready.

The rifle fire had ceased. The sickening, overly-sweet stench of violent death and the sharp smell of gunsmoke reached him an instant before he rounded the shrubbery that grew alongside the building, bordering the parking lot.

"Oh, no," he heard himself say when he saw their bodies. "Oh God, no."

Perks and Chavez had fallen near each other, sprawled on the blacktop in the morning sunshine, each dead officer with a gaping wound in his back. Someone had come up behind them, or been driven by, and opened fire without either of them suspecting a thing until it was too late and they were cut down in those first bursts of gunfire.

Ben's eyes and the muzzle of his shotgun scanned the street in every direction. Less than twenty seconds had elapsed since the second burst of gunfire. The doorways and windows along the street were overflowing with curious, frightened faces. He saw no sign of anyone with a rifle. Then gunfire resumed from somewhere not far away, from inside a building. He heard screams. Shouts. He pinpointed the source. *Merle's Hardware,* this side of the street, halfway up the block. He stormed in that direction.

Bobby Caldwell emerged from the front door of Merle's, onto the street. He wore polished combat boots and jungle camouflage fatigues. Bandoleers of ammo magazines criss-crossed his chest. He held an M-1 assault rifle. Moans and screams and shouts followed him from inside the hardware store. Without pausing, Bobby opened fire on an old man in coveralls who stood watching from the doorway of *Donna's* across the street. The old man was thrown backwards into the restaurant.

Saunders commanded sharply, "Bobby, goddammit, hold it right there!"

Bobby spun around to face him. He yelped gleefully. "Well there he is! The Chief of Police. Howdy, Mister Chief. How do you like what I done so far?"

Saunders barely recognized Bobby. The kid's face was twisted out of shape and flushed. His glittering eyes were fiery, insane.

"Put that rifle down, Bob." Saunders' voice was cool and even. "You're all finished for today."

"You got that right. See you in hell, Chief."

Bobby bent down and placed the rifle muzzle inside his mouth, sucking the barrel.

Seeing this, Ben lowered his shotgun. "So long, you little shit," he said.

Somewhere across the street a woman screamed.

Bobby Caldwell fired, blowing off the top of his own head.

Chapter 15

News of the massacre reached Robin at school during her second class of the day. She was speaking at the head of the classroom when she heard the earnest, hushed whisperings of adults from outside her open door.

She assigned a class project and stepped into the hallway to join the teachers gathered there from neighboring classrooms. Like the others, she could hardly believe it at first. Random acts of murderous violence on the television news were always numbing reminders of one's mortality and the random nature of fate. But this bloody horror was far worse, infinitely more immediate, because this psycho had gone berserk with a rifle not in some faraway post office or fast food restaurant, but right here in the remote, small town of Devil Creek. Talk about close to home! And because Robin had chosen to make this her home, the news of the atrocity did bite with the same immediacy that shone on the faces of her co-workers as they repeated for her the first vague reports about what had happened minutes earlier. The details were unclear, only that one of the Caldwell boys, Bobby, had gone berserk downtown and started shooting people. Several were dead, others had sustained wounds when the gunman stormed into the hardware store firing his weapon. Miraculously, no one in Merle's was seriously wounded. Not so lucky were two police officers. Bobby Caldwell had then killed himself.

It was, quite naturally, all anyone could talk about for the rest of the day. The education of children and the bureaucratic details that are the daily life of a teacher went on, but Connie Silva and everyone else Robin worked with was affected. You could see it in their eyes. Robin felt no different. During a break Connie told her that one of the policemen slain was the brother of a faculty member who had left hurriedly to attend to the family emergency. The most difficult part of the day was explaining to children what had happened. The kids quickly sensed that something was wrong. None of Robin's students had family members involved in the shooting, but she did hear from a student in her class, after the noon recess, that a ninth grader in another homeroom did have a parent who had been wounded at the hardware store.

When she met Paul after school that afternoon, he acted withdrawn; not nearly as animated and lively as usual. She assumed at first that this was because of the troubling things that had happened that day. The more she reflected on his introspective mood as they drove home, though, the less certain she became that it was directly related to the shootings. It could be something else. He had seemed strangely remote that very morning, *before* the shootings, when she'd gotten him up for school. Some of his introverted mood this afternoon would be his reaction to the bloodbath. But there was something else. She couldn't put her finger on it, but it was there.

As she drove them home, the car radio was tuned to a Las Cruces music mix station. The Eagles were playing, one of her favorite groups. But today their music did nothing to either relax her or pep her up, which was usually the case depending on how she felt when she heard them. The Eagles were that kind of group, good for whatever ailed you. But this afternoon, she barely heard "Take It Easy."

Robin stole a sideways glance at Paul. He wasn't reading. He wasn't commenting on the music, as he often did no matter what was being played. He wasn't commenting on or doing anything, which is why she noticed. He was preoccupied by something he did not wish to communicate with her about. She could tell this even with just a sideways glance.

As they left the school parking lot, she noted increased traffic on the highway. She'd heard that Chief Saunders was having problems at the shooting scene because of gawkers coming in from out of town. During the short drive downtown, even this late in the afternoon, their Subaru was passed by communications vans from television stations as far away as El Paso.

"Guess we'll be seeing a lot of news media around here for awhile," she said, an attempt to draw Paul out.

"I guess."

"Honey, is something wrong? Is anything troubling you?"

"Mom, don't call me honey. Please?"

She had to smile. At least he wasn't behaving totally out of character. "Is it about what happened today, about what the Caldwell boy did? If that's bothering you, we can talk about it. It's natural to be upset about something like that."

"Yo, Mom, nothing's bothering me. Honest. Okay?"

"Okay, Paul."

One end of Main Street was cordoned off near the Town Hall and the hardware store. It had been more than eight hours since the shooting, yet there was still a lot of activity over there. On the outer fringe were people straining their necks for a better view. Next were the communications vans and the news crews, lots of microphones and cameras and hurrying about. Beyond this were at least a dozen official vehicles, many with their rooftop lights flashing.

She steered the Subaru into a parking space in front of the supermarket.

"Are you coming into the store with me?"

Paul picked up a science fiction paperback from atop the stack of textbooks he'd placed on the car seat between them. "I'll wait."

"Back in a minute," she said.

Naturally, it took more than a minute. There had been so many groceries and household supplies to buy when they first came to town that she'd managed to forget purchasing several items, and this was the first real chance she'd had to pick up what she'd missed. She'd kept a shopping list that had grown every day.

Russell's Market was not crowded, though business was brisk with people stopping off after work on their way home. The aftershock of that morning's shooting was palpable inside the store. These were local folk who knew each other. Robin couldn't help overhearing some of their conversational exchanges as she wheeled her shopping cart by. The slaughter on the streets of Devil Creek was the sole conversational topic. While she was in the produce department, she happened to glance out the plate glass window overlooking the parking lot. Mike Landware stood beside her car, talking with Paul.

When she pushed her cart out the door, she encountered Mike on his way in.

He smiled. "Hello, neighbor."

That smile, warm and genuine. A timbre of voice she found enticing, appealing. There was fatigue in the smile, a tightness at the corners of his eyes and mouth. And again she sensed the vague aura of sadness, of loneliness about him that was intriguing, so appealing. *Watch yourself, Robin,* she reminded herself.

She returned his greeting in kind with the best smile she could manage given the fatigue she felt. "Hello, neighbor."

"Paul and I were just talking sci fi," he said. "That's some sharp kid you've got there."

She looked beyond him to where Paul remained as she had left him, engrossed in his book, apparently unaware of their conversation. "Thanks. I like him too."

"You've done a good job raising him."

"It hasn't always been easy. Do you have kids?"

"Nope, no kids." His gaze drifted down the street to the congestion around Town Hall. "Quite a day for Devil Creek."

"Terrible. I imagine it's been keeping you busy."

He nodded. "The paper's a weekly so most people will know everything about it before they read it in the *Clarion*."

"Whenever I hear about something like this happening, I always wonder what could drive someone to do it."

"Well, as a journalist it pains me to say so, but I've got a hunch that's something we'll never know."

Robin thought then of something she had intended to ask him at the first opportunity, after last night's dream about the stairs and a hanging, swaying corpse; of staring into her own dead face . . . So much had happened in the real world since that dream, she'd almost forgotten. Almost.

"By the way, Mike. You didn't happen to see anyone around my house last night, did you?"

He frowned. "Why do you ask? Did you see someone?"

"Not really." She suddenly felt foolish. "I was having a nightmare. I woke up and thought I saw someone against the shade, in the moonlight. It was probably nothing."

"If there was someone, it could have been one or both of those Caldwell punks. Paul told me they'd been pestering you."

"I hadn't even thought of that."

"Look at it this way. If it was Bobby Caldwell, you don't have anything to worry about. As for his brother Tobe, Chief Saunders has him over in the jail right now."

"Well that's a relief, anyway."

"I'm usually up late nights, writing. I'm nocturnal by nature, always have been. Anyway, I can see your house from mine. I'll keep an eye on it. If you think you see or hear anything again, call me right away and don't worry about what time it is."

"I really do feel like an idiot now that I've said anything. I'm sure it was part of the dream."

"The offer stands just the same."

"Thanks, Mike."

"By the way, is something bothering Paul?"

"Why do you ask?"

"I don't know. We were talking about the book he's reading. Asimov is one of my favorites. I've sort of gotten to know Paul since you guys moved in. It's probably none of my business."

"No, that's okay, go on."

"It has to be what happened this morning. Everyone in this little burg is having trouble getting their head around that one."

She decided not to mention that Paul hadn't seemed himself even that morning, before the shooting.

"I'm sure that's all it is," she said. "Sometimes I think I worry too much about him. But that's a mother's job, isn't it? Well, it's been nice visiting with you, Mike, but I'd better be going. Like you said, it's been quite a day and I do have a growing boy to feed."

"Robin, I have an idea."

"And what might that be?"

"I invited you and your growing boy over for a barbecue

that first day when Mrs. Lufkin introduced us. You took a rain check, remember? Natural enough that you'd want to size me up first."

"I remember," she said, knowing where he was headed and, she hated to admit, pleased.

"Well, have you?"

"Have I what?"

"Sized me up. You must have made up your mind by this time whether or not I'm a jerk or a guy you might like to be friends with in addition to neighbors?"

She couldn't help smiling. "As a matter of fact, I have made up my mind."

"Please don't keep me in suspense."

"I think you know the answer. I think Paul's right about you. Yes, Michael, I think we can be neighbors and friends."

"Good. I'd like that."

"I'm certainly glad we got that out of the way."

"Then I guess the next question is, would you and Paul like to come over for a barbecue tonight?"

She felt a strong inclination to pull back. She shouldn't have been caught off guard by the invitation, but she was.

"Oh, I don't know, Mike. That's awfully nice of you but . . . it really has been a long day."

"I will gracefully take no for an answer, but I do feel compelled to point out that it's been a long day for all of us—you, me, and Paul. Maybe we could all use a little re-laxation with some pleasant company, to unwind. Care to reconsider?"

She liked the way he automatically included Paul in the invitation. She fought down her inclination to pull back. "I wouldn't want to make it a late night. Tomorrow is a school day."

"Fair enough."

"Okay then. Sounds great. I'll make a salad. What time would you like us to come over?"

"Say, sixish? That's a couple of hours from now. How does that sound?"

"That sounds just fine."

"One more thing. Please say you're not a vegetarian."

"I'm not a vegetarian," she said.

"Then you are in luck. I'll have the coals going and the burgers ready to go. You are in for a culinary experience. See you then."

"At six," she acknowledged.

With a wave, he continued on into the market.

She continued with the grocery cart toward the car, telling herself that she had done the right thing.

Chapter 16

It was a perfect night for a barbecue, cool enough to wear long sleeves but still pleasant. There was no breeze. The night was clear and starlit. The full moon emerged from behind the mountains, at first an oversized iridescent globe, every lunar crater seemingly close enough to reach out and touch as it gradually arced into the sky, diminishing in size but not iridescence.

Paul had a great time. The hamburgers were excellent. Also, he was glad to see that hanging out with Mike was just as much fun with Mom along. He'd come to think of Mike as *his* buddy. Mike knew a lot about science fiction. He was always fun to talk to. He didn't talk down to Paul just because Paul was a kid, but instead with an awareness of Paul's intelligence, the same way Mom did. But Paul had been concerned that he'd be cut out of the conversation once Mike and Mom started talking. It didn't happen that way, though. The conversation during preparation and consumption of dinner spanned subjects that all three of them had in common: movies, books, and food. It was an easygoing, relaxed time. No mention was made about the massacre.

At eight-thirty, when Paul said he wanted to go home and watch *The X Files* on TV, his mother made him promise to wash up and be in bed on time. Paul then left them there, sitting on the patio, Mike and his mom finishing their drinks and visiting. By bedtime, his mother still hadn't returned home. Looking out his window, Paul could see them next door in the light that spilled from inside

Mike's house onto the patio. They were still talking.

Paul had always been glad that his mother and father had gotten their divorce. They'd argued all the time, filling the house, filling his ears, with their rage. The arguments got worse toward the end, right before Paul and his mother moved out of their house. Before that, he used to hide in his room, seeking refuge in a closet where he could hardly hear them. But there was no escape. He'd heard them even there, crouched on the floor of the closet. He'd listened to his mother and father shouting, each cursing the other, and his stomach would tie itself into knots.

He couldn't recall ever spending time with his father. They'd never gone anywhere or done anything together when it was just the two of them, but Paul didn't care. It was the same way with most of his friends and their fathers. It was the same with their moms, too. His mother was different. Sometimes his friends in Chicago told him that they wished their parents were more like his mom, more interested in what they were doing in school and how they spent their time. As for his father, Paul didn't even like the man. His father was the cause of all the troubles that had torn their family apart and ultimately destroyed it. Paul had never even discussed the divorce with his father. His dad obviously didn't care even a little bit about Paul's feelings or what he thought about any of it. That's what had hurt most. Paul missed some of his old friends, but he honestly wouldn't care if he never saw his father again. The stomach cramps and bad dreams had disappeared soon after he and his mother had moved out of the house where he'd spent all of his life. But it was Dad's house. Anything was better than living there.

But today the pain in his stomach, the cramps, returned. He hadn't slept well last night after returning from his trip up the hill with Jared. And tonight, even though he was tired, he had trouble falling asleep.

He and Jared had spoken in the schoolyard during the noon recess, when no other kids were around.

"You didn't tell your mother, did you?" the pudgy boy had asked, first thing.

"No, I didn't tell anyone."

Jared sighed his relief, as if he'd been holding his breath all morning. "Good." He spoke with conspiratorial disapproval. "I thought I could trust you. I thought we were friends. You're smarter than all those idiots." He indicated the crowded playground. "I thought you'd think it was cool, what I wanted to show you. I didn't think you'd melt down and turn coward."

"I'm no coward," said Paul. "If you still want to be my friend, don't call me that again."

"All right, all right. Sorry."

"And I don't want to talk about last night anymore."

"Okay, we won't."

That had been the end of that topic. But it was not okay. What Bobby Caldwell had done that day was frightening, but it had happened in broad daylight. Right now, lying awake in his bed, alone in the silent house, staring at the dark ceiling of his room, Paul thought about something else. He thought about the previous night. It was difficult to believe that it was only twenty-four hours since he and Jared had spied on Bobby and Tobe and that woman. He still hadn't gotten over the impression of watching the brothers, real people—not people in books or movies—violently fighting with each other over a woman who would've let them do whatever they wanted to do to her anyway, to hear Jared tell it. And this had occurred no further away than the other side of the hill, up the road from his house. It wasn't so much the actual violence he'd witnessed that had been bothering him since his mother had gotten him up for school that morning. Instead, it was the dawning awareness of what realities, what dangers, the night could hold even in a supposedly safe community as tiny Devil Creek, out there within such close proximity to his own supposedly safe and secure warm bed. What Bobby Caldwell had done that morning only underscored this dawning awareness.

What else lurked on out there in the dark, so close to home, he wondered, *that no one knew anything about?*

Chapter 17

"Another beer, Robin?"

"No, I think two should be my limit. As you may have noticed, I'm sort of a cheap date."

"You don't look tipsy to me."

"I'm glad it doesn't show. And I should say that I don't think I've talked this much since I left Chicago. I'm giving myself a sore throat, and I'll bet you've got a sore ear."

"Not even numb. I wouldn't want you to break any self-imposed curfew, but I do have Coca Cola and 7-Up."

"I'll have a 7-Up. Thanks, Mike. And no, I'm not breaking a curfew. I decided before Paul and I came over tonight that I wouldn't have any preconceived schedule and right now, sitting here talking with a man who exhibits good taste in movies, books, music, and hamburgers seems exactly right. Thanks for a wonderful evening. And thanks for being a friend to Paul."

He opened the sliding screen door and stepped into the kitchen. "My pleasure. And believe me, it's been my pleasure having both of you over tonight. Thanks for accepting the invite."

"I'm sorry if I appeared stand-offish when we first met."

He returned carrying their soft drinks. "A woman has to be careful. And you have been busy."

She accepted a drink. "Until I gave myself this chance tonight to slow down, I didn't realize how much I needed a break." They clinked glasses. "To new friends."

"To new friends."

He'd been the perfect gentleman. An easy back-and-forth, give-and-take conversation had ensued after Paul left them to themselves. Among the topics discussed had been relationships. They spoke of the value of trust and how, if that was gone, everything was lost. Discussing that subject, Mike had referred to himself at one point as a one-woman man. She told him that she was divorced and that it had not been pretty, as divorces rarely are. She did decide to tell him about Jeff's two bizarre phone calls when she'd first moved in.

Mike had frowned upon hearing her relate the gist of the calls, permitting her to complete her narrative without interruption. When she was finished, he stroked his chin in a gesture she found appealing.

"So he didn't tell you where he was calling from?"

"That's right. I wish there was a way I could find out."

"Maybe there is," he'd said without further comment on the subject.

Now, as he returned to a patio chair facing hers, Robin said, indicating the soft drinks and in the spirit of their good-natured banter, "And I thought all newspaper men were heavy drinkers."

She knew she was prying, but she couldn't resist. During the evening she'd told him that she and Paul were from Chicago, and that this was the beginning of a new life. Yet while his conversation was substantive and open, Mike hadn't spoken of his own past. Nothing indicated that he was a heavy drinker. He'd only had soft drinks during her visit. She only hoped to get him to open up a little bit by turning the conversation in his direction.

He said, without inflection or hesitation, "Some reporters drink a lot, some don't. I did, but I don't anymore."

She instantly regretted saying anything. "I'm sorry. I don't want you to tell me anything that you don't want to tell me."

104

He sipped his 7-Up. "I was married to a woman up in Albuquerque," he said. That subtle, elusive sadness, which hadn't been present this evening, returned.

She regretted even more initiating this line of conversation. "Mike, really, it's nothing we have to talk about."

"You've told me about yourself. You have a right to know something about me. There's nothing I've been through that I can't talk about with you. I promised Carol that I'd give up drinking. That was her name. She pulled my life together when I was slipping over the edge and all she ever asked in return, the only real thing she ever asked me to do for her, was to climb out of the bottle and never climb back in."

"You still love her. I hear it in your voice."

"She's dead."

"Oh. I'm sorry. Mike, you don't have to go on."

"I want to. I'll admit to having been curious about you and Paul. So here's my story, the condensed version anyway. Carol's death is what brought me to Devil Creek. We were both teaching at the University in Albuquerque, but I couldn't stay around there after it happened. It hurt too much, being around the friends and the places we'd known together. Our friends did their best to help me heal. They meant well and it was good to have them around. But they couldn't help with the hardest part, when the only one you really want to be with is the one who's gone. I had to get away. I'd worked for a newspaper in Denver, but that's where I started the heavy drinking. There were too many old ways to slip into if I went back there. I looked around and I found Devil Creek. The cost of living is low, the scenery can't be beat and I've saved enough to spend a year on the book I'm writing. I guess it seemed like a good place to put the past behind me and start a new life." He stared into the night sky. "The West has always been like that. A place to start anew. A place to start again." He smiled—sheepishly, she thought—and his mood lightened. "So now you know the life story of Michael J. Landware."

"I'd hardly say that."

"I hope you know enough about me to feel safe in accepting another invitation."

Uh-oh, she thought. She finished her 7-Up and rose from her chair.

"Mike, I really did have a wonderful time, but I have stayed later than I'd planned. I'd better be going."

He stood with her, flashing an unexpectedly good-humored grin. "Relax, Robin. I assure you that I was not about to ruin a perfect evening by coming on to you. What I meant by another invitation is that Charlie Flagg's been telling me about some hiking trails into the mountains outside of town. I thought maybe you and Paul and I could think about packing a lunch and hiking a few miles in sometime. Do a little exploring, maybe this weekend if you happen to be free."

She laughed, feeling like an idiot for so misreading him. "I think that would be very nice. Mike, I'm sorry. I . . . I thought—" She faltered.

"All is forgiven. I'm a gentleman even if I am a writer, and I can certainly see where an attractive woman like yourself would have trouble with guys coming on too strong."

"It happens." She extended a hand. "Thanks again, Mike. Let's talk later this week about this weekend. Unless my workload from school is too heavy, I'm sure Paul and I would love—"

The ringing of his telephone interrupted her.

Mike frowned. "Kind of late for anyone to be calling. Excuse me."

He returned to the kitchen, where he took the call. She couldn't hear what was said. He returned in less than a minute, looking somber.

She said, "I hope that wasn't bad news."

"Not for me."

"What do you mean?"

"That was Charlie Flagg."

"Don't tell me there's been more trouble."

"No, not yet. Apparently things are happening down at the Town Hall. Charlie wants me to drive over and check it out for the paper. I'll walk you over to your house, Robin. Then I'm heading into town."

Chapter 18

Ben Saunders was trying to squeeze water from a rock, and he knew it. Tobe Caldwell could tell him nothing that Ben didn't already know. They were alone in Ben's office with the door closed. It was twenty minutes short of midnight.

Tobe was a mess. His stubbly beard was caked with dried spittle. His orange jail coveralls were soiled with sweat and he reeked. His hair was like a dirty wet mop. He sat slumped in a wooden chair.

"I tell you I don't *know* why Bobby done it. He just went plain nuts, Chief. Like out of nowhere. I was afraid he was going to shoot *me* next. That's why I got out of Dodge so fast, soon as he started shooting at them officers. We woke up this morning and he was all surly for no reason, and dressed up in them fatigues, Dad's M-1 locked and loaded and Bobby with all that ammo." The words poured from him, a torrent of traumatized shock.

"Tobe, how often did Bobby handle that rifle?"

"Aw, Chief, we're country boys. We'd shoot at tin cans or squirrels and rabbits maybe once a week, and uh, Bobby did get a little crazy when he heard that new teacher was coming to town. Uh, he used that rifle to shoot out her front tire that first day when she was driving into town so we could fun with her. But this morning, he looked kill crazy and I didn't know what to do about it. I was scared. He told me to drive him into town and I always done what Bobby told me to do, but I never thought in a million years that he'd go berserk like that. That's all I know. It don't make no more sense to me that it does to anyone else. Swear to God."

Tobe had been picked up by the Highway Patrol a few miles from town, as if he really thought that every cop in the state wouldn't be looking for him after he'd been seen speeding away while his brother went about his shooting spree. Ben had cleared it through the state authorities to have the prisoner brought to him for questioning when they were finished. The state and county cops had taken their time before finally packing up and leaving for the day. The curiosity seekers and the regional media people were also gone.

Ben sat on the corner of his desk, leaning forward, staring straight into Tobe's face from only inches away.

"Two of my men are dead, Tobe. I want to know why. You've got a triple count of Murder One staring you in the face. I'm sure you're aware of that. Since you drove Bobby into town this morning, you're an accomplice and will be charged with homicide. That's what those state cops have on you."

Tobe eyed him warily, a cornered, injured rodent sensing a possible way out. "I couldn't stop him, Chief. I yelled for him not to do it. But that brother of mine wasn't listening to nothing but what was inside his head." Tobe wrung his hands. "Jesus. Bobby wasn't much but he was all I had. Jeez. First Pa offs Mama for cheating on him, then they execute Pa. Now this. Bobby goes berserk and now I don't have nobody. Who's going to take care of me? Bobby, at least he did the cooking and took care of stuff. Now I don't have nobody." His pleading eyes sought out Ben's. "I'm telling you everything I know, Chief."

The office door burst open. One of Ben's deputies appeared. Ben looked around irritably.

"Dammit, Roy, didn't anyone ever teach you to knock? I

left strict orders not to be disturbed."

"I know, Chief. Sorry. That's why me and the boys held off coming to get you." Roy Rinehart was the most recent addition to the force, a local kid of twenty-two, fresh out of the Marines. At the moment his face was flushed.

"Get me for what?"

"Uh, we've got an . . . escalating situation on our hands outside."

"Say what?"

"Uh, you better come take a look. There's a crowd forming. They've, uh, got themselves an attitude—an ugly one."

Ben stood from the corner of his desk. "Okay. Let's see what you've got."

Tobe made a yelping sound. "Hey, what about me?" Now that the office door was open, crowd noises could be heard from outside. "They're here to get me because of what Bobby did, right?" His eyes swept the unbarred windows. "You ain't going to just leave me here, are you?"

Ben unloosed a pair of handcuffs from his belt. "Don't worry, Tobe. You'll stay put."

He held Tobe's arm. With a double flick of his wrist he handcuffed Tobe to a pipe next to the chair. Tobe's urgent protests followed them, echoing down the corridor. Ben briefly flashed back on trotting down this same corridor that morning, wielding a pump shotgun, seconds before discovering Perks and Chavez.

When he and Rinehart pushed through the double glass doors onto the parking lot, louder, angry shouting swallowed up Tobe's cries. It wasn't much of a crowd, but they were making plenty of racket aimed at his deputies who stood side by side, blocking access to the Town Hall. When the crowd saw him, he was met by a show of angrily raised fists to the accompaniment of displeased grumbling. Ben saw no weapons. He strode forward without hesitation, inserting himself into the center of this confrontation, positioning himself squarely before his deputies, facing the men who led the small mob. The parking lot was well lit by vapor lights, allowing him to clearly identify those closest to him. He addressed these men directly.

"Hello, Tal. Hello, Jay. A little late for you boys to be out carousing, isn't it?" These were men he saw in town nearly every day.

Tal Watkins was a small time rancher who usually dressed the part of a country gentleman, though at present one shirttail hung outside of his slacks while the other remained almost tucked in. "This ain't no party, Chief. We're here to see that justice is done."

"Don't tell me you're here to string somebody up."

Jay Seavers, standing next to Watkins, was a burly handyman and shade tree mechanic. He wore beer-stained bib overalls. "We're not here to lynch anyone," he said.

"I'm glad to hear that," Ben replied, his hand resting on his holstered sidearm.

Seavers said, "We just want to make sure things get done right."

There was muttered agreement from the men crowded behind him.

"So it's almost midnight, and you want to make sure that I do things right," said Ben. He shook his head. "The bunch of *you* should be home doing the right thing. You should be home with your wives and children. The bunch of y'all smell like a distillery. What did you do, drink out the stock over at *Ritchie's* and now you want to raise some hell?"

Seavers replied, drunk and surly, "Told you what we

want. We want justice. What's the difference if we had us a few? That don't change nothing. It sure don't change right from wrong."

"Slow down, Jay. Slow down. You boys are fixing to bite yourselves off a whole mess of trouble."

Watkins said, "Our gripe's not with you, Chief. Yeah, we had us some lubrication. Then we started thinking over what happened today. The more we thought about it, the madder we got."

"Drinking and thinking is kind of like drinking and driving, Tal. It don't mix."

"Everyone here knew Bill Perks and Sonny Chavez. We knew them and their families."

Someone in the rear shouted, "We want charges brought!"

Ben spoke to all of them. "Bobby Caldwell killed those people today. Then he killed himself. He's laying over there in the Garrett Funeral Home right now. You boys asking me to file charges on a dead man? That's pretty damn silly, don't you think?"

"We want charges filed against that idiot brother," said Seavers. "Everyone saw Tobe there when the shooting started."

"I was discussing that very thing with Tobe before I was so rudely interrupted," Ben said. "You fellas think I don't have a mad-on about what happened this morning? I worked side by side with Chavez and Perks every day."

"Then why aren't you doing something about it?" someone wanted to know.

"Like I said, friend, I was doing something about it. I was in the middle of interrogating Tobe just now when a bunch of peckerwoods interrupted me because they couldn't hold their liquor."

Watkins blinked. "Chief, that's no way to talk."

"Y'know, maybe you're right about that, Tal. And the way you fellows are behaving is no way for grown, responsible men to act."

Someone demanded, "Are there going to be charges filed against that punk or not?"

Ben ignored that. "I'm going to leave you gentlemen now," he told them. "I'm going back inside to do my job. Now, I know you boys. Some of you even came to my wife's funeral when Helen passed. So what say we forget this little bit of unpleasantness. The lot of you go on home and sleep it off and maybe your womenfolk won't give you too much hell about where you've been at this hour. Go on. There's nothing you boys can accomplish here tonight except to get yourselves in trouble."

The raised fists had been lowered. The angry muttering had ceased.

Watkins said, "I reckon maybe the Chief is right."

Ben nodded encouragement. "Now you're talking. You men go on home. It's natural enough that you should be grieving and worked up over what happened today and want to do something about it. But this is the wrong thing to do."

Watkins said, "We appreciate you understanding our side of it, Chief."

"Like I said, I feel the same way. It's tearing my guts out, what happened. But Deputies Perks and Chavez lived to uphold the law. This isn't the way to honor their memory or what they stood for."

Watkins turned to the others. "All right, men. Let's break this up. We were wrong, coming down here like this. Let's let the Chief get back to work, what do you say?"

This time the muttering was embarrassed agreement and

apologies. They began dispersing without further conferring among themselves; shadowy figures ambling away in twos and threes in different directions.

"Good work, Chief," Rinehart said when the parking lot was again empty.

Ben told his deputies, "Handling them was the easy part. Getting anything I can use out of Tobe Caldwell will be a might tougher. I'd best get back to it."

Then he noticed someone standing nearby. A man partially emerged from the shadows as the deputies drifted back into the building.

The figure said, "Uh, you don't know me, Chief—"

"I know who you are," Ben said. "You're the writer fella who rented that place from Mrs. Lufkin. Charlie Flagg told me he hired you to write for his newspaper."

The man paused some ten feet away, half in and half out of the shadows, projecting nonchalance as he stood there with his hands in his pockets.

"You keep close tabs on your town."

"Not close enough to my way of thinking. Not after today. I'm a busy man, Landware. What do you want?"

"Charlie called me. He asked me to come down. I'm wondering if you have any comment for the press on what just happened here."

"Frankly, I'd just as soon you didn't write anything about it. Fact is, I was glad the media was gone for the day and wasn't around to see what happened. And here you are, lurking in the bushes."

"I wasn't lurking, Chief. I was observing."

"Whatever. Point is, I don't want to embarrass those men and their families. They're good, decent, responsible citizens, most of them. Come morning, they'll regret what happened and that's good enough for me. What do you say,

Landware? I'll talk about it with Charlie in the morning."

"You won't have to. You're right. He'll feel the same way. There's been enough bad news for one day."

"Mighty decent of you," Ben said. "Appreciate it. Saw you around town today. Saw you and Charlie every time I turned around, seemed like."

"Just doing what Charlie pays me to do, trying to find some fresh angles on what happened."

"Any luck?"

"I found out how people in a small town like Devil Creek respond to a tragedy like this. City people shake their heads and put it behind them a few minutes after hearing about it. These folks take it a lot more personally because it is personal to them."

Ben nodded. "Oh, they'll squabble amongst themselves sure enough, believe that. But a thing like this makes everyone forget the small stuff. Reckon that's the up side of everyone knowing each other in a town this size."

"I just heard you tell those men that you're interrogating Tobe Caldwell. Anything new that we could make public?"

"Those media folks from out of town will be camped out on my doorstep first thing tomorrow, I suppose," Ben said. "I'll have a public statement then. I think it's wrapped up. Bobby snapped and went on a rampage. There's nothing more to it than that."

"I was telling someone the same thing a little while ago. I hope we're right."

Ben frowned. "Why wouldn't we be?"

"I don't know, Chief. The thought just came to mind."

"Heck, son. Didn't mean to bite your head off. This whole day's worn me down and now I've got two newshounds instead of one to deal with over at our town paper, and me just getting used to Charlie Flagg always standing around watching like he's taking notes on everything that's going on, which he probably is."

"Nature of the beast. He does have a newspaper to fill up once a week."

"Speaking of Charlie, where is he? Why isn't he here?"

"He sounded exhausted when he called me."

"Come to think of it, he looked a might peaked when I spoke to him this afternoon. Figured it was because he showed up right after the shooting." Ben felt his expression grow tight. "He saw what an M-1 will do to a man up close. Fella hasn't seen something like that before, it can shake him up."

"It can shake him up if he has."

"Amen to that. Well, good night, Landware."

"Good night, Chief."

Ben stood there and watched the other man walk to a Jeep parked on a side street adjacent to the parking lot. He found himself thinking about Mike Landware's neighbor, the new teacher in town. Robin Curtis reminded him of his own daughter, vaguely in appearance but mostly in spirit, and he realized that he felt protective of Robin.

The Jeep's taillights left the parking lot and were gone.

There was something about Mike Landware that Ben wasn't sure about. Nothing he could put his finger on but he was not sure what to make of this new man in town. Because of his protective impulse toward a hardworking single mom named Robin Curtis, who reminded him of his Val, he decided to do some checking on Michael Landware.

Whenever he got the time.

Chapter 19

The beast within awakens.

It's been building all day. He felt fine yesterday. Then, this morning, he awoke to the incredible pressure between his temples, pulsating. Strangely, the sensation was not at all unpleasant at first. The day is strange, so strange, the beating of drums constant inside his head.

When he hurried to the aftermath of the shooting to see what he could do to help, he saw death. Smelled fresh blood on pavement. Red red red blood. And God help him, he became aroused. Got himself a hard-on like a length of pipe. So wrong. So good. He doesn't understand.

No one seems to notice that he's . . . different. They speak of nothing but what the Caldwell boy did. They do not understand. He, on the other hand, does understand. He doesn't know why or how. He cannot tell anyone. But he knows. He understands the beast within. Tonight, the beast controls him. He exists only to fulfill the trembling need that pulsates through him, fueling his loins with fire.

He awakened after dusk. Got up off the couch. Went to the kitchen. After some comparison, selected the biggest and sharpest knife he could find. He left the house without being seen, stalking the night. The night temperature is crisp but he wears no jacket over dark clothes. He is a predator in its element.

He smells danger.

Mid-block is an alley, and this is where he goes. A street light at the next intersection only deepens and darkens the shadows here. He presses himself against a brick wall. Headlights sweep the front of the building. A police car cruises past. He sees the inky silhouettes of the officers inside, patrolling the night. They do not see him. The police car moves on.

He hears footsteps. Footsteps coming toward him through the darkness. The steady clip-clip of a woman's brisk walk. And he cannot recall where he is. Strange. He should know where he is. But does it matter? He could be anywhere. What matters is why he is here. The beast is hungry. Nothing else matters. The beast within him commands and he must obey. He wants to obey. He wants nothing for himself, only to serve the beast.

She walks past him then. Denim. High-heeled black boots. Short jacket zipped against the evening chill.

He emerges from the shadows, revealing his presence. She hears him. Turns to face him with a startled gasp of fright, and a sigh of relief when he steps closer.

"Oh, it's you," she says. "You threw quite a scare into me. Guess I'm jumpy after what happened this morning."

"I'm sorry."

She senses then that something is different about him. Something is wrong here. She says, "You're out late, aren't you? Well, I'd better be on my way."

No one else is nearby. No traffic. Adjacent buildings are completely dark, towering monoliths bearing mute witness.

He attacks. She tries to scream. Tries to struggle. He is too strong for her, has strength he never knew he possessed, summoned up now to yank her to him. His hand covers her mouth, stifling her scream. He drags her into the deepest shadows. She is young. She struggles wildly, forcefully, vibrantly. It only excites him more. During their struggle, her body grinds against his. She can feel his arousal. This makes her more frantic. The beast is too strong for her. He is the beast. He throws her to the ground. Throws himself atop her. His drool drips syrupy mucus into her face. The knife plunges. Again. Again. Again.

He moves hurriedly away from there. He encounters no one.

His breathing, his heartbeat, slowly return to normal the further he gets from the scene. He completes the return trip to his home at a leisurely pace, nothing more sinister than a solitary man taking a starlight stroll.

He will wash the bloody knife in his kitchen sink and replace it in the rack. He feels exhilarated. Within him, the beast is satiated.

For now.

Chapter 20

By the end of her first week in Devil Creek, Robin had almost managed to convince herself that moving to Devil Creek, New Mexico may well have been the single worst mistake of her life since marrying Jeff.

She had moved to this small, rural community to get away from crime, violence, and bad influences on Paul. And yet during the past week, in addition to the massacre, on the nights following the shootings something even more frightening was visited upon Devil Creek. More frightening because, unlike what Bobby Caldwell did, it represented the unknown. Bobby Caldwell's blood orgy of rage, for all its horror and the misery it wrought, could at least be understood for what it appeared to be: a random act of violence committed by a deranged gunman. The serial murders that began that night were different. A local woman going out to one of the town's convenience stores for cigarettes was the first victim, slain in the alley behind the laundromat on the edge of town.

The regional and national news media again descended on Devil Creek. This time, a contingent remained, housed at the local motel. The state police set up an office to assist in the investigation after an identical murder was committed the following night. A similar, as in *identical*, slaying had occurred on every consecutive night thereafter. Mrs. Russell, who ran the supermarket with her husband, was the second victim. She'd been stocking shelves and apparently let someone in through the back door after hours. The third victim was a rancher's daughter who had car trouble outside of town on the way home from her waitress job at *Donna's Café*. It appeared as if her killer had been the first person to happen along. The girl had trusted the person to assist her. The fourth murder victim made the most news because she was a media person from Albuquerque who had gone out for a stroll by herself along one of the dark streets of Devil Creek that paralleled Main, apparently thinking that there was nothing to be afraid of because she was street-wise from having lived in the big city. She'd even carried a .25 caliber automatic in her purse. The gun was still in her purse when they found her, stabbed to death like the others.

And now here it was, Saturday.

Identical slayings. The media, tabloid and otherwise, repeatedly referred to the murders as brutal and said they were sex-related, but were no more specific than that. They didn't need to be. Everyone in town knew that the victims had been stabbed, then raped. The grisly, nauseating details were common gossip.

What no one knew was the identity of the killer. The police were unable to uncover any leads. There was only one certainty. The killer was a resident of Devil Creek. The authorities didn't say this in so many words, but everyone knew it had to be the case. No drifters or suspicious characters had been sighted before or after the nightly killings began. Another indication that the killer was a local was that no real struggle appeared to have been put up by the victims, as if they'd been caught completely off guard after they'd allowed the killer to approach them.

Naturally, everyone in town was on edge. Robin could clearly see the birth of awareness in the eyes of Devil Creek's residents of what people in urban areas had long taken for granted. You could not trust your neighbor. No one was safe. She sensed a discernible, escalating paranoia among the townspeople, born of the knowledge that someone within their midst, someone they interacted with every day, was the one responsible for these awful serial murders.

Unless, thought Robin, the killer is someone from *my* life.

But realistically, how in the world could such a thing be? Take a perceived shadow fleeting across a bedroom shade, and two telephone calls from a surly ex-husband. Could that conceivably add up to having any connection whatsoever to what was happening in Devil Creek? But there were lingering doubts, even if she could not force herself to give voice to them. The more she thought about it, the more it sunk in how her ex-husband's treatment of women had always been abusive. With her it was psychological. She was never thin enough to suit Jeff. She spent too much on family expenses. That kind of thing. Additionally and perhaps more importantly, though, his sort of bang-every-bimbo-in-sight sex drive was more about predatory misogyny rather than the pursuit of anything approaching romance. Could that sort of profile fit someone who would perpetrate terrible crimes against women if he felt he'd been pushed too far, and snapped. Was that Jeff? Did he hate women enough to be a serial killer? And if so, how would that possibly benefit him regarding his telephoned threats to ruin her paradise? And how could anything so insane have anything to do with the massacre perpetrated by Bobby Caldwell?

She had arranged with the phone company for caller ID, but there had been no more calls from him.

Nonetheless, throughout the week Robin continued to have trouble falling asleep. She lost her appetite. She felt as edgy as everyone else did. At least there had been no reappearance of a silhouette darting across her bedroom shade, no further indication that a stalker lurked around her house. Maybe Mike Landware was right, she told herself. Maybe it had been that grubby psycho Bobby Caldwell.

And so here she was at 9:30 a.m. on Saturday, dressed casually in a new T-shirt and jeans she'd bought in Albuquerque on the trip down, wearing her favorite old pair of Reeboks, driving to school for a community meeting that had been scheduled to discuss the events of the past week. The public was urged to attend the meeting. The meeting had been scheduled to begin at nine o'clock. She'd been looking forward to sleeping in, but no such luck.

As she drove to the school, she tried to fight off the depression that wanted to draw her in. The day was overcast with a high gray haze, the first overcast day she'd seen in New Mexico. Back home she had always liked cloudy days. She loved the outdoors, but there was something special about those days when it was fun to stay inside on your day off, snug and comfortable with a good book or some music or housework. She wasn't sure what she thought of cloudy days in New Mexico. She decided to withhold judgement. This morning's clouds only made her feel gloomy. When she first decided to attend the meeting, she'd initially planned to walk to the school. It was largely a lack of regular aerobic exercise that was contributing to her moodiness, she knew. The exhaustion she'd felt at the end of the first day of classes had only been physical exhaustion. But by the end of this first week, she had felt completely drained on every level—physical, emotional, and mental. She'd taken extra paperwork home every night. She wasn't getting any exercise. And instead of spending her Saturday morning like any normal person should, at home or running errands, here she was dragging herself off to a meeting, feeling like a robot whose battery was about to give out; a meeting called because this little of corner of the world had decided to go totally berserk coincidentally with the same time that she and Paul had arrived here to escape their own madness. So she was driving to the meeting because she was too pooped to take the walk. And late to boot!

She slipped a reggae tape into the car's deck and hummed along to the music as she drove, a conscious effort to lift her spirits and her energy level. She'd fixed Paul breakfast before leaving the house, quickly preparing them each an omelet. As they were finishing, Paul's friend Jared showed up. Paul said they intended spending the rest of the morning playing video games. Paul was washing the breakfast dishes when she left. He seemed recovered from whatever had been bothering him earlier in the week. The children of Devil Creek knew all about the serial murders of course, about the crazed killer nightly cruising their streets for fresh victims. But life went on for children—usually, it seemed, far easier than it did for adults. Since no children had been victimized, and the crimes had all been committed at night, Robin did not feel overly concerned about leaving Paul at home, especially since he had a friend visiting. She saw other kids out playing in their yards along the way as she drove to school, which managed to reassure her that Paul would be okay. Stop worrying, she told herself. Those other kids' parents aren't overprotective and you shouldn't be, either.

Had moving to Devil Creek been the biggest mistake of her life? She reminded herself that moving here was not only intended as an escape, but also to prove something to herself once and forever. She did have doubts and insecurities about exactly how independent and self-reliant she truly was, and Devil Creek had seemed as good a place as any to find out. Sometimes, she knew she was stronger than some of the people in her life had given her credit for being. Other times, she feared she wasn't as strong as she liked to think.

In Devil Creek, she had intended to find out. There were many things about her life here that she already liked very much. Teaching was grueling and demanding, yet filled with rewards that made it worthwhile at a soul-satisfying level. She enjoyed getting to know the roomful of young faces that constituted her class. And there were the daily visits with Connie Silva, who was fast becoming a good friend. As for that new-kid-on-the-block feeling she'd experienced on her first day at work, she'd reminded herself of an old Robert Louis Stevenson quote that had somehow always clung to a corner of her mind: "There are no foreign lands. It is always the traveler who is a foreigner." That pretty much summed up her situation in the "foreign" surroundings of her new hometown. She would be fine. And then there was Mike, a nice guy who she was still slowly getting to know. And Mrs. Lufkin.

But there could be no denying the fact that, beginning with the Caldwell boy's rampage, life in Devil Creek had become a near-constant exposure to the violent depths to which a human could sink. Slaughtered victim after victim. That was the day-to-day reality of life in Devil Creek these days. That is what her "new life" here had become.

At least, she reassured herself, she had not been directly affected by any of it.

Chapter 21

In the gymnasium, the faint smell of the locker rooms mingled with the stronger scent of fresh wax. At the far end of the gym, opposite the double doors through which she entered, rows of metal folding chairs on the shiny floor were occupied by sixty or so people. They faced a podium where a small group of people sat including Mrs. Lufkin, whom Robin hadn't seen since the day she'd rented the house.

She'd been somewhat disappointed that she hadn't seen more of her feisty landlady whom she'd taken such an immediate liking to. During her visit with Mike Landware the night of their barbecue, Mike had noted that Mrs. Lufkin seemed to be not only one of the town's prime characters, as he put it, but one of its prime movers and shakers as well. The woman's presence on the Concerned Citizens Committee today was certainly proof of that. Robin recalled the older woman rushing off that first day to help with a church bake sale. Mrs. Lufkin was obviously just too active to stop by for idle chitchat, and of course, Robin had been extremely busy. But she intended to become better acquainted with the woman. She experienced a moment of fondness at first seeing Mrs. Lufkin here.

As Robin crossed the gym toward the rows of chairs, Chief Saunders was in the process of wrapping up his remarks from the podium.

"We've called in auxiliary deputies and I've increased the patrols," he was telling them. "Combined with the State Police, this means we'll have the community well-covered."

A woman close to the front called up irritably, "How can

an insane murderer elude the police in a town this size? We all know each other!"

Various voices were raised in agreement.

The Chief made a placating gesture. "We're doing the best we can, folks. In the meantime, please exercise extreme caution in whatever you do and wherever you go, especially at night. It's safe during the daytime, seems like, but after dark parents should know where their children are and you ladies shouldn't go out alone until this is cleared up. And don't let anyone you don't know into your house. Call us immediately if you see the slightest thing that looks out of the ordinary. Don't you worry, folks, we'll get through this if we stick together. Now, I'd like to bring on Mrs. Lufkin, the head of this Committee, who has a few things she'd like to say."

Robin looked around for a vacant seat and found one next to Connie Silva. Her spirits lifted as she and Connie exchanged smiled greetings, their attention remaining centered on the podium where Mrs. Lufkin prepared to speak.

Robin's landlady looked almost munchkin-size following, as she did, the heavy-set Chief of Police. Mrs. Lufkin cleared her throat.

"I just want to say that this town has plenty to deal with and that we'd better start doing a better job of dealing with it than we have been." Her voice was reedy, but underlying the words was the fiber of a reed strong enough to bend and survive countless storms, some worse than this one, over the course of her seventy-plus years. "There's plenty to be concerned about," she went on. "The fear, not knowing who to trust—but we must work together to deal with this. Otherwise, it will only get worse. We must openly discuss our fears with one another. They shouldn't be swept under the rug. I've spoken with Reverend Kroeger and we're going to establish a support group. An office will be set up at the Town Hall and beginning next Monday, trained people from Las Cruces will come to counsel adults and children who feel they're having trouble coping. The important thing is that we remain friends and neighbors to each other. We've weathered tough times before, and we'll weather these. Thank you."

This brought a round of applause, and Robin and Connie joined in. Robin tried to ignore a sense that, beneath the strength she'd heard in Mrs. Lufkin's words, she'd also had to lean closer, like others she observed in the audience, to hear the older woman. Mrs. Lufkin's speaking voice sounded weaker than Robin remembered.

As Mrs. Lufkin returned to her chair, Connie leaned closer to Robin. "You're renting from Mrs. Lufkin, aren't you?"

"That's right. She's quite a woman, isn't she? She certainly drew these people together and inspired them."

"Mrs. Lufkin is very special. I've known her since I was a little girl and most of the people here in town have had dealings with her or are her friends, or both. Everyone loves her. She's done a lot of good things for Devil Creek over the years."

Next up to the podium was Reverend Kroeger of the Community Presbyterian Church, a mild-mannered, middle-aged gentleman of slight build, nearing sixty, with a thinning thatch of white hair. Robin surmised that many of those present today probably were members of the Reverend's flock.

"My friends, Mrs. Lufkin is quite right. After the killer himself, the biggest threat to our community is fear. We must not let this get out of hand. Whenever there's a big unknown out there, fear can escalate to an alarming point."

Robin found herself only half-listening to the preacher. She had been raised in the Protestant faith. She considered herself a spiritual person, though not necessarily a religious one. She did, however, have a long-standing interest in the religions of the world. Her readings had led her to the conclusion that all religions basically addressed the same three fundamental human needs: the need to deal with the fact of mortality; the need for a moral code by which people can coexist in a society; and the need to personally relate to the majesty of a world which is so obviously greater than any individual.

But, rather than pledge her faith to a single religion, instead Robin had addressed these needs within herself by drawing on common threads of wisdom she'd found throughout her wide-ranged reading. She considered it her responsibility to pass on the wisdom thus gained to Paul mainly by example. She was not particularly partial toward getting a sore tail bone from sitting and listening to a man of the cloth drone on when she could be at home sleeping in, especially this Saturday morning.

Realizing that her mind was wandering during the Reverend Kroeger's remarks, at one point she happened to glance along the row of seats across the aisle from her. She spotted Mike Landware sitting there, three chairs in. Their eyes met and they exchanged neighborly smiles and short nods.

The Reverend was saying, "Fear has a way of feeding on itself. Fear eats away at the moral fiber of a community from deep within before anyone knows what's happening. Fear breeds suspicion. Suspicion breeds hate and hate turns neighbor against neighbor, family against family, friend against friend. We must not allow that to happen in our town."

He went on to enumerate steps that the Committee had implemented. There would be a community barbecue the following afternoon. Plans were under way for teen activities. In addition, the high school weight room would be open to the community three nights per week.

Reverend Kroeger was the final speaker. With the program completed, the audience rose and some impromptu conversations began. Robin was glad it was over.

Next to her, Connie stood to leave, her usual cheery smile brightening her face. "See you Monday. Time for me to head home."

"Don't be in such a hurry." Robin decided that this would be a good time to get to know Connie better outside the classroom. "Why not follow me over to my place? I baked a pie last night and if we're lucky, Paul and his friend left us a couple of pieces. What do you say?"

"Gosh, Robin, I'd really like to. Maybe one day next week after school, okay? My kids will be in daycare then. Today I've got a sitter watching them and you wouldn't believe the prices they charge."

"Oh yes I would. Well, let's do it soon. And bring your kids along."

"Sounds great. See you."

"See you Monday."

As Connie moved toward the exit, Robin next caught sight of Mike conversing with the man who owned the hardware store. On the stage, Mrs. Lufkin was saying goodbye to Reverend Kroeger. As Mrs. Lufkin stepped down from the slightly raised stage, Robin observed something tentative about her movements. The elderly woman placed a foot gingerly on each step, not at all the spry, confident old-timer Robin recalled. She intercepted her near the stage.

"Mrs. Lufkin, are you feeling all right?"

The woman replied with a wan smile. "Bless you for asking. Matter of fact, I did wake up this morning not quite feeling myself. It's nothing for a soul to fret about, though. I'm quite all right, thank you."

"Would you like me to drive you home?"

"Heavens no. I'm certainly well enough to drive. But you're a dear to make the offer." She rested her fingertips, feather-light, on Robin's arms. "How are you and Paul doing in your new home?"

"Oh, fine, fine."

A semblance of her former sharpness shone in Mrs. Lufkin's eyes. "There's something, isn't there, dear? I can tell. Now tell me. What is it?"

"It's nothing really. I, uh, was going to ask you about the history of the house. That can wait until you're feeling better."

"What is it you wanted to know?"

"Well . . . I want you to understand that it doesn't change my mind about the house. Paul and I are both very happy there. We like it a lot."

"I'm glad to hear that."

"It's just that, well, Paul told me something that he'd heard. I was curious to know what you could tell me about it. Do you mind if I ask how long you've owned that house?"

"I've owned it since it was built. What did Paul tell you?"

"That there was a murder and a suicide there. In the kitchen. One of Paul's friends told him about it at school."

This brought a weak smile. "Paul's friend is pulling your son's leg and yours, my dear. Nothing like that ever happened in that house."

"He said it was a soldier from the Korean War. The man

shot his wife, then killed himself."

"Well, there you are, you see. The house was built in 1961, years after the Korean War."

At that moment, Mike walked over.

"Hello, ladies. Uh, Mrs. Lufkin, are you feeling all right?"

"Lord, I must be a sight. Robin just asked me that same question. I'd better get home and fix myself a cup of tea and rest for a spell."

The three of them strolled together out to the parking lot.

"Why don't you let me follow you home?" Mike offered. "That will ensure that you get there safe and sound."

Mrs. Lufkin emitted what could only be described as a lady-like *harrumph* as they reached her Datsun. "Robin has already volunteered to nursemaid me, Mike. I don't much cotton to being fussed over."

Robin said, "All right then, we won't fuss over you." A glance passed between her and Mike, a private sharing of bemused affection for this woman. "But I will stop in on you later this afternoon, if you don't mind, to see how you're doing."

"I'll be doing fine," Mrs. Lufkin said tartly, "but company is always welcome. You drop in any time." She paused before opening the door of her pickup truck. Her hand resting on the door handle, she looked up at the hazy sky that had turned a darker shade of gray. Her eyes traveled to a bank of ominous clouds hugging the craggy mountain peaks that overlooked the town. "If I didn't know better," she said in a faraway voice, "I'd swear those were snow clouds moving in. But it's way too early for snow."

Then she was in the pickup cab. She switched on the engine.

Mike was observing her closely. "Are you really sure you feel well enough to drive home?"

"I'm fine. Really. I'm just feeling . . . I don't know." The older woman raised fingertips to massage her temples. "I do feel . . . tingly. A tad feverish. You're both dear souls for caring. I feel lucky to know both of you. 'Bye now."

She drove off, leaving Robin and Mike standing side by side, watching the Datsun turn slowly onto the highway.

"I'm glad you'll be checking in on her," Mike said. "She's a tough old bird, but maybe not as tough as we'd like to think."

"Don't let her catch you saying that."

"I won't. How's Paul?"

"My son and I are about to have a little conversation about not believing everything you hear."

"From your tone, I'd say Paul's in the dog house."

"It's nothing serious, but he and I are going to have a talk. One of those parent-child issues that comes up from time to time. He was disappointed when he heard that we weren't going on that hike because of this meeting. I told him we could do it next weekend, if you're free then."

He grinned. "For you two, I'll make myself free." He paused, and lowered his eyes in a way that she found appealing. He swallowed audibly, and his eyes met hers again and said, "I've, uh, found myself thinking about you quite a bit, Robin."

She'd known he was going to say something like that. A part of her wanted him to say something like that. Unfortunately, she hadn't quite gotten around to figuring out what she would say if this occasion arose.

She began by saying, "Mike—" and that was it. Further words wouldn't come, and she became acutely embarrassed, and tried not to let it show.

"I don't want to make you uncomfortable," he said quickly, lowering his voice for her ears alone, "and I don't want you to get the wrong idea. But, well, uh, I just wanted you to know. You've been on my mind since our barbecue." The corners of his mouth crinkled self-consciously. "I guess you've been on my mind some every day since Mrs. Lufkin introduced us." He drew himself straight up and met her gaze straight on. "There, I've said it. Hope you don't mind."

"I don't know if I should be saying this," she found herself saying, "but you've been on my mind, too. There's a nice comfort zone between us, Mike. I like you very much."

He chuckled, a sound she found pleasant. "Then would I spoil things if I suggested—"

And the old fear factor kicked in, making her say with a smile and a touch to his arm with her fingertips, "You might. For now, let's leave well enough alone, and let things flow."

The smile and the touch had their effect, and he was gallant enough to take the rebuff gracefully. "Right. Well, uh, that's more than I was hoping for, if you want to know the truth, so I'll take it."

She couldn't help chuckling. "Mike, you're fun. And funny. Thanks for making me smile. I think I need that more than anything at this point in my life."

"You make the world a prettier place when you smile, if I may be permitted to say so," Mike smiled with exaggerated courtliness. "Okay. Well then. Right now I'd best get over to the paper and write up this meeting."

"You mean this conversation we're having right now?" she chided.

"I see a twinkle in those eyes," he said. "You know what I mean. I have a feeling you might read me better than I read myself. Are you one of those women, Robin?"

"Depends on the man."

"Good answer. Talk to you soon."

"Good," she heard herself say.

He walked away, and she watched him walk away, liking what she saw, the way he moved. She felt drawn to this intelligent, introverted, creative neighbor of hers, and it had been fun to flirt. But she was wondering if she would regret it. With Jeff's phone calls, her SOB of an ex-husband had reestablished himself in her life in a way that was ugly and mean, and made her feel unclean. Given that, maybe it was too soon for her to harbor even the imaginings of romantic feelings for anyone no matter how attractive and available.

She walked to her car. The sky was growing more overcast by the minute. The temperature hadn't dropped much. It still felt in the mid-seventies. But observing where the clouds were darkest as they moved in, as they continued building behind the mountains, Robin decided that, despite what the calendar and the warm recent temperatures indicated, Mrs. Lufkin was right.

They did look like snow clouds.

Chapter 22

Charlie Flagg stopped by the *Clarion* office while Mike was putting the finishing touches on his article. There were dark purple pouches under Charlie's eyes. The eyes were bleary as if from lack of sleep or intoxication, or both. His red beard was unbrushed, his hair tangled and oily. His clothes looked as if they'd been slept in. He stayed for less than a minute, acknowledging Mike's presence only with a gruff grumble as he came in. Avoiding eye contact, Charlie went directly to his desk where he stood, his back to Mike, just long enough to glance through the morning's mail.

Initially, Charlie had seemed to Mike to be your average, friendly, good old country-boy type. Mike hadn't been able to place Charlie's accent exactly. It was Midwestern, not southwestern, he could tell that much. But the West was full of people who had moved from somewhere else. Charlie's manner at first had been amiable, pleasant. But during the course of the week, he'd become more and more as he appeared today: distant, introverted, and preoccupied. Much like everyone else in town, Mike reminded himself.

On his way out the door, Charlie finally spoke. "About those Indians, were you going out to check up on old Gray Wolf and that grandson of his today?"

"Matter of fact I was going to drive over there this afternoon."

"Great." Charlie paused in the doorway. "Uh, look, Mike. Sorry if I've been out of sorts around here lately."

"Forget it. This is some bad stuff that's going on around here. Everyone's been thrown off by it."

Charlie nodded. "Think I'll go home and get drunk. Do the same if you want. The hell with following up on those Indians. The hell with everything."

"Thanks for the offer, boss. Think I'll stay on the job." He was talking to the door that Charlie had already slammed shut on his way out.

When Mike left the newspaper office ten minutes later, there was a subtle bite to the wind coming down off the mountains, a nip that penetrated the light shirt he was wearing. He decided to stop home and change into something more suited to the changing weather before driving out to see Gray Wolf and Joe Youngfeather. At home he changed into a flannel shirt and blue jeans and decided, as long as he was there, to fix himself a quick ham sandwich. He washed it down with a Pepsi, grabbed a denim jacket, and was out of the house and halfway to his Jeep when he heard raised voices from the patio of the house next door.

He heard Robin saying testily, "I don't care if your friend Jared was bored playing video games. With everything that's been happening, I wouldn't have gone to that stupid meeting if I'd thought you were going to be here alone."

"Mom, I can't help it if Jared wanted to go home." Paul's response was plaintive and defensive.

"The point is, Paul, we'd agreed that you wouldn't be here alone, that you'd be with your friend. I get home and you're here alone."

"Aw, Mom, you're just mad because I told you what Jared said about those people being killed here. I thought it was true when I told you."

"I'd give that boy a piece of my mind if he was here. Filling our heads with that talk!"

"Maybe that's why he went home before you got here."

"Don't you get sassy with me, young man. I think you'd better go to your room and stay there for awhile."

"Aw, Mom—"

"Go to your room. Right now."

Pretending not to overhear any of this, Mike noted out of the corner of his eye that Paul obediently went into the house. Sliding his key into the ignition, Mike next realized that Robin had seen him. She was walking in his direction.

She wore the same loose-fitting T-shirt and jeans as at the assembly, and she looked as good to him now as she had that morning. That was to say that even in a T and jeans, this woman was a knockout. The wind played attractively with her chestnut hair. He was suddenly very glad that he had never touched the whiskey bottle stored in his kitchen cabinet. A woman like this would have no use for a drunk. There was something about her that made him feel good, made him feel things he hadn't felt for another woman . . . since Carol.

"Hello again," he said.

"Hi, Mike." She smiled self-consciously. "I hope you didn't overhear too much of that disciplinary tirade, and I hope I didn't sound like too much of a bitch."

"You sounded like a mom giving her kid a talking to. I caught plenty of the same from my mom when I was Paul's age."

"One of Paul's friends told him a tall tale about a murder and a suicide that supposedly occurred in our house. Paul told me, and I guess I let it get to me more than I should have. Then today at school, Mrs. Lufkin told me it never happened."

"I don't know if it's my place to say this, Robin, but that doesn't really sound like Paul's fault."

She grinned. "I should've known you'd side with him.

But as a matter of fact, you're right. These things that have been going on, this helpless feeling of not knowing what to expect next, of not knowing who's going to be the next victim, not knowing who's committing the murders I . . . guess I'm feeling stressed."

He reconsidered his plans for the afternoon. Charlie Flagg had given him the afternoon off if he wanted to take it.

"I could take Paul off your hands for awhile, if you'd like," he said. "He and I could hike up one of those trails. The three of us could, for that matter."

"That's a very nice offer to make. But your first instinct was right. What I think Mom needs most right now is some down time at home. As for you and Paul . . . Mike, I don't want to impose my troubles on you."

"You're not. And you'd better let me know what you think, because here comes Paul."

Her son was walking across the yard, toward them.

Speaking in a more neutral tone than she'd used a few minutes earlier, Robin said, "Yes, Paul, what is it?"

The boy exchanged a brief nod with Mike. "Mom, I just wanted to say that I'm sorry for wising off. I know you're upset. I just didn't think I'd done anything wrong."

"You didn't," she admitted. She placed an arm around him, gave him a hug. "We're pals again."

"Great." With that settled, Paul turned to Mike. "Hey, dude."

"Hey, buddy."

Robin said, "Mike was wondering if you'd like to take off and do something with him this afternoon."

"Sure!"

Mike said, "How'd you like to go for that hike we were talking about?"

Paul brightened as if a switch had been flicked. "Sounds great! Is that okay, Mom?"

"It's okay." Robin raised her eyes to the overcast sky. "But take a jacket with you." As they watched Paul race back to the house, she said, "Thanks, Mike."

"Forget it. I could use a little getting-away-from-it-all myself."

Then Paul was back, radiating enthusiasm. "Ready?"

"Ready." As Paul climbed aboard the Jeep, Mike told Robin, "We'll be back in a couple of hours. Maybe we'll stop in town for a cone at *Donna's* on our way back."

"Have fun, you two. I'll go with you next time."

"Bye, Mom!"

Mike slipped the Jeep into gear.

She waved. "Bye, you guys."

The gravel road to the highway was washboard-rough in places, bordered on one side by irrigated pastureland where cattle grazed and noisy cicadas prattled ceaselessly. Opposite, the terrain climbed to the tree line and rolling foothills beneath a steep mountain slope. They were less than a quarter mile from the convenience store-gas station at the intersection of the road and the highway when Paul pointed at a figure walking toward them.

"There's Jared. Can we stop? He's on his way to visit me."

"Sure."

Mike braked the Jeep to a stop directly alongside the red-haired boy.

"Hi, Mr. Landware."

Paul had introduced Mike to Jared earlier in the week. "Hello, Jared. I hear that imagination of yours has been getting you in trouble."

Jared looked apologetically at Paul. "When you called a

140

little while ago and told me your mom was having a melt-down about what I'd told you, you sure sounded mad at me. That's why I was coming over. Are you mad at me?"

"I guess not," Paul groused. "Just don't do it again. Jeez, what a bonehead thing to do, telling that story about the soldier and his wife."

Jared grinned. "Hey, I don't know. I thought it was kind of funny myself."

Paul grinned a rueful grin. "Maybe I would too, if it wasn't *my* mom that was yelling at me."

The eyes behind Jared's thick glasses shifted uncomfort-ably in Mike's direction, then he said, "Hey Paul, there's another reason I was coming over. Can we talk? I mean, alone? Is that okay with you, Mr. Landware?"

Mike chuckled, mostly to himself. "Don't trust anyone over thirty is alive and well, I see. Naw, I don't mind, guys."

Paul stepped from the Jeep. "I'll be right back." He fol-lowed Jared beyond Mike's hearing range, then demanded impatiently, "Well, what is it?"

"You've got to keep your voice down," Jared said. "I've got something to show you if you want to come see it with me. Something really cool."

"Jared, you'll just get us into trouble."

"No, I won't. Listen, this is for real. It's way cool."

"What are you talking about? I'm not going to sneak around with you and watch people . . . doing private stuff."

"It's nothing like that."

"Then what is it?"

"I, uh, I don't know. It's the army or the FBI or some-thing. I'll bet they're here to investigate those serial killings. They've got a van and electronic surveillance stuff and sen-tries and everything. You ought to see it. It's up the mountain, but it's not hard to get to if you know the way like I do."

Paul found his curiosity sparked in spite of himself. "How did you find them?"

"I told you I like to go up the mountain a lot to find a place to read where no one can bother me. Sometimes I go way up the mountain. That's where they are. I was just walking along a trail when I heard voices. I moved in real slow and I saw them." Jared's eyes gleamed. "So do you want me to show you or not? I know a shortcut from here. I was there this morning, after I left your house."

"Jared, if you're feeding me a line of crap again like that bit about the soldier killing his wife—"

"This is for real. They didn't see me, and they won't see us."

"Okay, but what if they do catch us?"

"What can they do? They'll call Chief Saunders and turn us over to our mothers and maybe we'll get grounded for a couple of days. Big deal. But that won't happen. I know my way around up on that mountain. You'll see."

Already Paul was having second thoughts. "I don't know. I think I'll go on with Mike."

"Well, I'm going back to check those guys out some more. You should see the guns they have."

"If I do go, I'll have to tell Mike."

"Tell him we're going to my place. He'll never let you go if you tell him the truth."

Paul considered this. It wouldn't be right. But it would be fun, going to spy on soldiers and a secret van. Jared was right. What harm could there be? Besides, he reasoned, *no one* did what they were supposed to do *all* the time.

"All right. Just a sec."

He returned to the Jeep.

"What's up?" Mike asked.

"Is it okay if I go with Jared instead?"

"Sure, Paul, if that's what you want."

Paul hadn't expected it to be so easy. "Thanks!"

He started to turn away. "See you!"

Of course, it wasn't that easy.

"Whoa, partner," said Mike. "First we drive to the convenience store and give your mom a call. She has final say."

"Oh. Yeah. I guess so."

"I'm assuming Jared would rather you called home. The other option is to go back and ask your mom in person. That way Jared can get his serious talking-to for that tall tale."

Paul laughed. "You're right." He called, "Hey, Jared! Come on. I've got to call home first."

The chubby red-haired boy registered no outward response to this. The boys climbed into the Jeep.

They continued on. The clouds overhead continued to thicken, nearly blocking out all trace of the sun by now, the purple of the cloud-line over the mountains deepening to black.

Chapter 23

In the parking lot in front of the convenience store, Mike sat in the Jeep with the engine idling. For a full minute, he watched Paul and Jared trudging off. A random gust of wind blew through the covered Jeep, crisp and cool. Mike rolled up his window. He slipped the vehicle into gear and turned left onto the main road, driving north on the highway, away from town.

He'd offered the boys a lift to Jared's. They declined, telling him that they wanted to stop on the way there to pick up another friend who lived on the way. Paul called his mother from a pay phone. Cell phones were all but useless in this remote, mountainous area. Mike then spoke briefly with Robin to confirm that the change in plans was acceptable to her. And so he and the boys had parted company.

He decided to resume his original plan for the afternoon, yet he had to admit that he wasn't driving out to the Indians' property solely to write an article for Charlie Flagg's newspaper. He was making the trip because of a nagging suspicion—a feeling he didn't quite understand himself— that somehow Joe Youngfeather and Gray Wolf might have something to offer about whatever the hell was happening in Devil Creek.

This time, when he steered onto the isolated piece of land that overlooked the dry creek bed, everything at first appeared much as it had on his previous visit. The truck and the Harley were parked exactly where he remembered them. Once again there was no sign of anyone in or near the small adobe hut. Last time, though, the sun had been shining and birds singing from the juniper trees. Today, the sky had only grown darker since he'd left town. No birds sang today.

He tapped his horn, two short taps, a common practice in the West when visiting a rural home uninvited. He shut off the Jeep's motor and waited, debating with himself the advisability of turning around and driving away. After three minutes, he stepped from the Jeep, looking around, buttoning his jacket. The wind coming down off the mountains carried a sharp bite in these open spaces.

"Hello! Anybody home?"

He couldn't hear the old man chanting as he had last time, or maybe that was because of the wind. He walked toward the outcrop that overlooked the creek bed, recalling that last time, Joe Youngfeather had gotten the drop on him from behind because he hadn't been careful enough. He did not intend for that to happen again. He stood upon the same spot, gazing at the spot below where this time there was no sign of Gray Wolf. He did not see Joe pressed against the ground directly beneath the outcrop until it was too late. Strong hands gripped his ankles and yanked him off his feet. He landed on his backside with a jarring thud, the back of his head painfully rapping the ground. Then he became fully aware of the figure swooping down upon him.

As before, Joe wore black from head to foot. His black hair was braided. His harsh warrior eyes glowered.

"Wait!" Mike managed. "I don't want trouble!"

His words were choked off. He was pinned to the ground. The wide-bladed combat knife, freed of the buckskin sheath Joe wore at his chest, was held to Mike's throat.

"You were told to stay away from here."

Mike let his reflexes take over. He brought his left hand up as fast as he could, which was fast enough, gripping the wrist holding the knife. At the same instant he managed to position a knee between himself and Joe. He kicked with enough strength to send Joe tumbling away. Mike leaped to his feet. Joe assumed a crouch, an angry snarl upon his face, the knife held steady. He started to close in. Mike executed a snap kick, an automatic movement, instinctively summoned from his combat training. The toe of his boot connected with Joe's wrist. Joe grunted, the knife flying from his fingers.

Mike said quickly, "Joe, *stop,* damn it! All right, I'll leave. I wanted to speak with your grandfather, not you. I'll leave. We don't have to kill each other."

Joe bent over and retrieved the knife. Mike made no move to stop him. Joe hefted the knife a few times as if testing its balance then returned it to its sheath. "As long as I've made my point."

"You've made it."

"You fight well. Where did you learn to fight like that?" Joe asked.

"Fort Bragg," Mike said.

"Special Forces?"

"Uh huh."

"Nam?" Joe asked.

"I was there."

"You weren't hard to take," Joe said, with a slight grin.

"I'm a little rusty."

"I was Special Forces. Two tours in country. And I'm not rusty."

Mike massaged the sore spot at the back of his head where he'd smacked the ground. "I hear that. So can we be friends?"

"No."

"Guess that's clear enough. But why the attitude, Joe?

It's been a long time since the war. Why all the stored-up hatred?"

"It's got nothing to do with Vietnam. My grandfather raised me. My father was killed in a rig accident in the oil fields. My mother died when she was seventeen, when I was three. I don't even remember her."

These statements caught Mike off guard. He said, "You're a grown man now. What does any of that have to do with hatred?"

"From before I can remember, Gray Wolf told me stories. Stories from the old days when our people ruled this land. When he was a young man, my grandfather rode with Geronimo. They raided the cavalry posts, stole the horses and ran them south across the border and sold them to Mexican bandits. But within a decade we were driven from our land, driven beyond the fringes of your society with the hope that we'd wither away and die."

"That was long before anyone living today was even born, Joe."

"If you were one of us, you'd understand. It's no different today. My grandfather shunned your world and life on the reservation. And after what I saw in the service, I felt the same way."

"Can I speak with your grandfather?"

"He may speak to you, but you will never speak to him."

"What does that mean? Where is he?"

"He dwells with his ancestors. To you, he is dead."

"I'm sorry. I didn't know."

"No one knows, except for you. Now everyone will know, but it won't matter. No one cared about the old man when he was here. For sure no one will give a damn now that he's gone."

"You could be right. Right now most everyone in town

has their hands full with whatever evil it was that your grandfather was chanting to keep away the last time I was here."

"You were skeptical. Are you going to tell me that you've come to believe that there are spirits, good and evil?"

"I want to get a handle on whatever's going on here. You said Gray Wolf was a magic man. You said he was chanting to drive away evil. The next day a kid goes berserk and blows away several people before he kills himself. Then a serial killer opens shop. I'm not so sure about spirits, but I know evil when I see it. And right now, Devil Creek's got more than its share."

"And you think there's a connection between that and what Gray Wolf foresaw?"

"I'm here to try and find out."

"If your friends in town knew you even thought such a thing, they'd never stop laughing."

"I doubt it," Mike said. "No one's in a laughing mood. Maybe you're the one who's wrong. You told me, the last time I was here, that nothing could stop this evil. I don't believe that."

"There's nothing I can do to help you," Joe said.

"I hoped you might have some ideas."

"I don't. You're on your own. The town is on its own."

"Because of what happened between the Indians and the whites before any of us were born?" Mike made a dismissive gesture. "That's crazy, Joe. You're an intelligent man. I can tell you're a good man. But you're letting hate twist your head and your life. I thought magic men were wise men. Gray Wolf didn't teach you to hate, did he?"

"No, he counseled me to banish my hatred. But I can't."

"Listen to me. People are dying in Devil Creek. Every

night a woman—someone's mother, sister, daughter, wife— is murdered with the kind of savagery I haven't seen since Vietnam."

"It happened over there all the time," said Joe. "It still does."

Silence descended, an invisible wall separating them. The only sound for several moments was the breeze whispering through the juniper trees.

Mike said, "You can't be this callous."

"I'm not callous. I'm stating fact."

"So there's nothing you can tell me that will help?"

"If there was, I'd tell you."

"Then I'll have to be satisfied with that."

Joe's dark eyes glittered like the black waters of a deep well. "Do you think I'm a part of what's happening?"

"If I thought that, I'd have gone to the authorities."

"Then what did you think my grandfather could tell you?"

"You said he was certain that something was going to happen. I wanted to ask Gray Wolf what he knew that made him so sure."

"My grandfather moved between planes of reality as you or I step from one room to the next. I can only tell you that he knew because he *knew*. Now get out."

"Guess I don't have much choice. But before I go . . . may I ask what happened to his remains?"

The unreadable eyes narrowed. "You are a ballsy, persistent sonofabitch, aren't you?"

"So I've been told."

"I broke the law," Joe said. "I'll deny everything if I have to. I'll say he just moved away. No one will give a damn. I didn't report his death. I built a funeral pyre for my grandfather and cremated him, as he wanted me to. Gray Wolf's ashes were carried away on the night wind. Now his spirit soars and he is strong again."

There was nothing Mike could say to that. He returned to his Jeep and drove away from there.

Chapter 24

Mrs. Lufkin's house was a modest two-level structure, an older home, well maintained; white clapboard with a peaked roof and an adjoining garage on an acre of land. An ash tree grew in the front yard. Robin parked at the curb, and approached the front porch.

If her intention had been to relax after Paul left that afternoon, then things had hardly gone according to plan; not after the phone call from the convenience store only a few minutes after Paul drove off with Mike. She would've preferred that her son had stayed with Mike, but she hadn't felt like getting into a battle of wills over who Paul should or should not spend his time with, at least not as long as he and Jared were at Jared's house playing video games.

At first she passed her time alone comfortably ensconced in a stuffed chair by the window, reading her Edward Abbey book on the Southwest, a cup of hot chocolate on the window ledge. But every few pages her eyes would wander out the window at the gathering dark clouds, at the trees across the road swaying in the wind, and she would begin to think about other things. She had to admit in retrospect that it was amusing, the prank Jared had played on Paul with that tall tale of murder and suicide that had been effective enough to give her a nightmare. She decided to go easy on Jared when she saw him again.

A serial killer on the loose, not to mention her hectic week at work, had both combined to overload her, Robin realized. She'd become fond of the chubby red-haired kid with the thick glasses who came over to play with her son.

Kids *were* kids. She was no angel when she'd been that age. And Jared didn't have the greatest home life. She could not be harsh with him for the joke he'd played.

Children that age naturally formed their own social strata, with its own secrets that were kept from the adult world just as adults kept their secrets from children, or at least tried to. She tried not to be overly protective with Paul. She hardly needed a child psychologist to tell her that a possessive mother rarely had a positive impact on a child's overall development. She had successfully struggled against the impulse to call the Philbin house and make sure that Paul and Jared were there together, safe, like they were supposed to be. She would not be overly protective, she told herself.

Through the window by her chair, she saw Mike return to his home an hour after he and Paul had initially departed. He glanced in her direction as he strode from his Jeep to his house. They'd exchanged a neighborly wave. She had continued trying to focus on reading for another half-hour or so, then decided to drive over and check in on Mrs. Lufkin.

Another matter that kept distracting her from her book was her memory of how pale and fragile her landlady had appeared at the school meeting that morning.

She stepped onto Mrs. Lufkin's porch, next to a colorful flowerbed of snapdragons, petunias, and pansies bordered by sweet alyssum that emanated a fragrant, honey-like scent. She knocked lightly on the front door. There was no response. She knocked again with a little more strength. The door was ajar. It opened inward several inches.

"Mrs. Lufkin, are you home?"

There was no reply. She repeated herself, somewhat louder. No response. The branches of the ash tree scrab-

bled across the overhang of the porch. The sound was un-
settling, scratching at her nerve ends. A big fat bumblebee
sailed past at eye level, either wholly oblivious to her or un-
concerned, its buzz an industrious drone as it settled on one
of the alyssum.

She went around the side of the house. The backyard
was a well-tended quarter acre of lawn surrounding a colorful flower garden. No one was there. She returned to the
front porch. A pervasive sense of worry consumed her.
She'd never been here before, but Mrs. Lufkin had assured
her that she would be welcome. She opened the door and
stepped inside, into a carpeted, old-fashioned foyer of oak
paneling and potted plants.

"Mrs. Lufkin?"

She raised her voice loud enough to carry through the
house. She was expected, after all. She called the woman's
name again. Again, no response. Complete and utter silence. Leaving the foyer, she moved deeper into the house.
For some reason, she wasn't sure why, she left the door
open behind her. She passed a sitting room, then a dining
room, the kitchen archway, and a short hallway. She
reached a set of stairs. The stairway was a lovely piece of
work, the stairs and banister of polished mahogany leading
up into impenetrable shadows.

Robin froze where she stood.

She had seen these stairs before. *Exactly* the same. In her
dream. In her nightmare.

Thunder rumbled in the distance and she almost let out
a startled cry.

But she made no sound. She did not understand this. As
in her dream, her body seemed to move of its own volition,
without mental command, carrying her toward those stairs
as if she were sleepwalking. She started up the stairs, as-

cending slowly with one hand gliding along the banister, the other hand drawing the collar of her jacket tighter around her throat to ward off a chill. An eerie feeling slithered through her.

Exactly like in her dream, the dark at the top of the stairs was like a magnet, drawing her inexorably onward.

There was a landing at the top of the stairs. A hallway extended the length of the house, with the doors along the hallway closed except for the one directly opposite the top stair where she stood. This door was open no more than a few inches, not enough to allow her to see inside. *In the nightmare, there had been no landing. No hallway. Only a dark, high ceilinged room, barren of any furnishings. Dark wood-paneled walls. A body twisting slowly at the end of a rope . . .*

"Mrs. Lufkin?"

Robin's voice sounded faint, weak even to her own ears; sounded fearful, resigned. Slowly, she glided toward that partially-open door, reaching for the doorknob . . . somehow knowing what she would find.

Chapter 25

Paul was glad his mom had reminded him to take a jacket. The surrounding forest blocked much of the wind, but the air was growing colder. Sometimes a wayward gust would stab through the trees to where he and Jared lay, stretched flat upon the ground, side by side on their stomachs on a carpet of fallen pine needles. The cold was beginning to numb his nose and ears. He still felt bad when he thought about not staying with Mike, but what Jared had brought him to see really was something. He'd lost his bearings three times during the hike from the road to this spot. There were places where the trees rose so high, their branches formed a natural ceiling that blocked out the sky and any point of reference. Jared knew the way, though. Jared was overweight and gave the impression of being slow and clumsy in town but somehow, up here on this mountain, he moved through the forest with what could only be described as a graceful ease. It was a revelation, seeing how at home he was up here. He'd led them around the small clearing, to their present position where they could look down from slightly higher ground, barely parting blades of wild grass, without having to lift their heads.

Several hundred feet below, a van was parked in a clearing. They'd been observing the van, and the pair of military sentries posted near it, for several minutes now. The van, without markings, was painted green. Camouflage netting was draped across it, making the van, and the sentries standing near it, invisible to airplanes or helicopters. A tent had been pitched nearby, also camouflaged from the air. An antennae dish extended from the roof of the van, aimed at an angle down the mountainside. The dish was aimed in the direction of Devil Creek.

Four men were down in the clearing. Three soldiers wore camouflage fatigues. The two sentries were armed with rifles. They appeared relaxed, as if they had been stationed here for some time and had grown bored and careless. The third soldier sported a blond crewcut and was armed with a pistol instead of a rifle. He and a fourth man had emerged from the van moments earlier.

This fourth man was not a soldier. That is, he didn't wear a uniform, but he was quite obviously the man in charge. In his early sixties, he was lean and wiry with a narrow, angular face highlighted by a pinched mouth that was more of a gash across the bottom half of his face. He had severely close-cropped hair and moustache and rimless glasses. A high, intellectual brow accentuated by a receding hairline, and a white smock made him look like a doctor or scientist. There was an undeniable air of authority about him and even from this distance, Paul detected an air of arrogance about the man.

Jared said, close to Paul's ear, "What'd I tell you? Cool, huh?"

There was no chance of the men below hearing them, thanks to the distance, the precaution of whispering, and the wind cutting through the forest.

Paul nodded. "It's cool. But I've got a feeling they wouldn't like it very much if they caught us up here."

"I bet they've got sensors in places where hikers would pass, coming from town. It's a good thing we live a ways out of town. We came here from the opposite direction. See, they're not so smart. They didn't expect a couple of nosey kids."

"I wonder why they're here, doing what they're doing."

"That dish on top of the van, that's high-tech equipment," said Jared. "It's a listening post. They're listening in on what's happening in Devil Creek. Maybe watching, too."

"Jeez, what an imagination. You'll make a great writer when you grow up."

"I'm already a great writer."

Paul stared as the men below conversed. Their words did not carry across the distance. The blond-haired one and the one in the doctor's smock did most of the talking. The sentries did the listening.

Paul whispered, "I just don't think they'd be acting so secret if they were up to any good."

"So what do you think they're doing?"

"I don't know. But I think we'd better get back. I don't want my mom to worry. You know, with the murders and everything."

"Stop sounding like a baby."

In the clearing, the blond man issued instructions to the sentries. They nodded and hurried off, disappearing into the dense green wall of trees. The blond-haired man and the man wearing the white smock remained by the van.

Paul said, "We should get out of here." He tried not to sound afraid. "What if those sentries are circling around behind us?"

"They're commandos. They'd charge straight up here and grab us if they knew we were here. What could we do?"

"Grab us?"

"You know what I mean. They'd take us into custody. I'll bet they're Green Berets."

"You're crazy. What would Green Berets be doing in Devil Creek?"

"They're here to take out whoever's causing all the trouble in town because the police can't. These guys are some secret government commando outfit, like in the movies. They're here to catch the serial killer who's murdering those women."

"I guess you're right about them not knowing we're here."

"So why don't we stick around? I bet those sentries won't be gone for long. Let's see what happens."

"Okay. I just hope it won't be long."

It wasn't long before there was movement from the spot in the tree line where the sentries had disappeared, and the men clad in fatigues re-emerged with another man walking between them. White Smock and the blond-haired man stood waiting as the three approached.

Paul studied the red-haired, bearded man being led into the clearing. "Hey, that's Mr. Flagg. Charlie Flagg."

Jared nodded. "The man who owns the newspaper."

Mr. Flagg looked different, nowhere near as confident as he had a week earlier when he'd stopped on the highway outside of town to help when Tobe and Bobby Caldwell were bothering Paul and his mother. That was the first and only time Paul had seen the man. Now Mr. Flagg wore a sullen expression. His appearance was unkempt.

"What do you think he's doing down there?" Paul whispered.

Jared shrugged again. "I don't know. But I'd sure like to find out."

"What do you mean?" Paul knew very well what Jared meant.

"We could sneak in for a closer look."

"Then they'll catch us for sure."

"No, they won't. Just step where I step. We won't make

158

any noise. Then we'll go home."

Without another word, Jared belly-crawled back from the ridge. He crouched and moved away at an angle that followed a drop in the terrain, concealing himself from view of the men in the clearing as he moved closer to them.

"Jared, come back."

It was a whisper, and of course Jared didn't hear Paul. Or he pretended not to. And Paul pretended he did not hear the apprehension in his own voice.

But he could not leave without Jared, and so he followed.

Chapter 26

They crept in as close as they dared, concealing themselves in dense tree growth and foliage no more than fifty feet from the clearing, allowing them to clearly overhear most of the conversation between Charlie Flagg and the other men.

Paul's throat was dry. His stomach felt queasy. The hairs at the nape of his neck stood on end and his flesh crawled.

"What is the meaning of this intrusion?" the man in the white smock demanded of Charlie Flagg without greeting or preamble. He glared at the sentries who had accompanied Charlie into the clearing. "Hickey. Taylor. Was there any sign he was followed?"

"No, Dr. Bittman," one of the men replied promptly.

The other snickered and gestured with his rifle. "Would've taken care of any problem like that, Doc."

The man named Bittman returned his glare to Charlie. "Explain your presence," he snapped curtly. "You were to report tonight at 2200 hours as usual, not before."

The soldier with the blond crewcut stood with his feet firmly planted, scrutinizing Charlie with narrowed eyes, his hand on the butt of his holstered side arm. "He shouldn't be here," he said to Bittman. "It looks bad, him not being in town."

"You may be right, Mace," Bittman nodded. Then, to Charlie, he said, "Report, as long as you're here. Update me on those new arrivals in town, the teacher and the writer."

"There are three new arrivals, remember?" said Charlie.

"She has a son. His name is Paul. You know that from my reports."

Paul felt his stomach muscles spasm at mention of his name, and he heard Jared gasp beside him.

"The child does not concern me," Bittman was saying. "You were instructed that the man and woman were a Class A Priority. Robin Curtis. Does she represent any manner of potential complication?"

"Doc," said Charlie, "I believe that's the basic nature of woman."

A tic caused Bittman's left eyelid to flutter. "The facts, please."

Charlie snorted a humorless laugh. "Okay. Robin Curtis is sharp. She's intelligent. But she's a single parent school-teacher doing her best to make ends meet and raise a kid. I said it before and I'll say it again. She in no way poses a potential complication for you or anybody else, unless we're talking about that next door neighbor of hers. Maybe they'll fall in love. Heck, maybe they already have. Why should that concern you, Bittman?"

Mace spoke. "The man and woman could be a plant. Having the kid along for camouflage would be a nice touch."

Jared emitted the slightest chuckle, which he did a pretty decent job of muffling. The man below gave no sign of having heard him. Paul reached across and clamped Jared's arm in a silent admonition to quiet his friend.

Bittman was saying to Charlie Flagg, "You will appreciate that there is inter-agency rivalry even at this level, on a project of this magnitude. Especially at this level, I regret to say. On the other hand," he nodded to Mace, "the Major is a born pessimist. Do not concern yourself, Mr. Flagg. As you know, we have accessed every telephone in town. We

have the whole of your bucolic little community under surveillance." He indicated the van. "This is a state-of-the-art
mobile unit programmed for continuous data collection.
You are my eyes on the inside, so to speak. The data you
supply is vital to my success. And so, kindly continue. The
man, Landware."

"I've got my eye on Landware," said Charlie, "but he's
nothing for you to worry about either. If I was you, Doc, I'd
worry about me."

"I think I understand," said Bittman. "You have your
doubts about this project, about whether it is truly government-
sanctioned. You have gone beyond merely verifying my credentials, haven't you, Mr. Flagg? You've taken it upon
yourself to investigate me."

"Something like that."

"Indeed, I would wager that you have sought to backtrack this project through by searching for a paper trail in
the government bureaucracy. Yes, you see, I know that. I
know everything."

"Maybe you do at that. Then you'll also know that I
could only check so far back before I hit a solid bureaucratic brick wall and no one would tell me anything, and I
think that's because they honestly couldn't. You are connected, Doc. You've got credentials that check out. And yet
there's no trace of you beyond a certain point. That's kind
of strange."

"You were fully briefed on the Top Secret classification
of this project at the outset. You were advised that I am in
total control of it. All relevant information is compartmen-
talized strictly on a need-to-know basis."

"You're right, you did tell me that. I just didn't think I
was going to be having those second thoughts."

"I am an accredited scientist," Bittman said sternly.

"Major Mace here is attached to a highly-classified government security agency. And you are being well paid for assisting us."

"Yeah, I'm being well paid. I don't sell my soul cheap." Charlie ran his fingers through his hair. "Bittman, I showed up early because I can't take it anymore. I want some answers. I want to know what the hell's going on. Who gave you people the right to use the citizens of this community as guinea pigs? We'll start there."

Bittman's eyes turned frosty behind his rimless glasses. "I was under the impression that everything had been explained to your satisfaction the night you came sniveling to me, so distraught following the unfortunate incident involving Robert Caldwell."

"Unfortunate incident? That little weasel mowed down innocent people!"

As he hid there beside Jared, listening to this exchange, Paul felt his breathing grow shallow. His heartbeat seemed to reverberate, through his clothing, against the cold ground.

"I am a man of science, not emotion," said Bittman. "Forgive my apparent callousness. That was also the night you sent Landware to report on those citizens who showed up at Chief Saunders' office, instead of going yourself. That was exactly the sort of thing you were contracted for, Mr. Flagg. As I explained to you that evening, the government was not involved with that in any way."

"Right. Just like my government's not involved with a serial killer running around town cutting up women."

"Precisely. I do appreciate how it could appear otherwise."

"Could appear? *Could?* Pal, it *does* appear otherwise, and I do mean big time."

"And we have discussed that as well, have we not? Really, Mr. Flagg, our background check on you was extensive and, frankly, suggested a far more stable and reliable personality than you have exhibited of late, if you don't mind my saying so."

"You had Devil Creek wired, but you needed the human factor," Charlie said. "Someone who could take the pulse of the community, monitor the feelings and emotions that your cameras and your telephone taps couldn't pick up. Well, Doc, I've been keeping an eye on things for you, like you contracted me to. What better front than as owner of a weekly newspaper? That's how you played it and I've been playing ball right along with you. But I'm here early today to advise you that what I've been observing has made me sick. That's right. I'm calling in sick, Doc. I'm bailing out."

"It has already been explained to you—"

"Yeah, right. The Caldwell kid blowing the town to hell. Some pervert running around killing women. Yeah, it's been explained to me. It's all one big unfortunate coincidence. It's got nothing to do with this government project of yours, right?"

"Correct. We are here to observe and document the day-to-day life of a small, isolated rural community. Nothing more, nothing less. Nothing sinister, I assure you now as I have in the past."

"Why is this study being conducted? Tell me again."

"I suspect such a study will be useful in everything from preparations for crisis management in the event of a national catastrophe like a terrorist attack to such prosaic matters as budgetary allocations for municipalities. Certainly you by now appreciate that individuals, not to mention an entire community, behave differently when they know they are being observed. Once again I reiterate, these are matters well removed from my sphere. Need to know, Mr. Flagg. Remember? Need to know. I am merely the man on the ground, charged with accumulating data for this study."

"Uh-huh. Well, I'll tell you, Doc. I don't think I've slept more than two hours a night for the past week. I've done some thinking. Another woman's just been murdered and I'm starting to have trouble with the way this thing smells. I believed what I wanted to believe about you and your 'project,' and now four women are dead, butchered, and I haven't been able to sleep because something tells me that, God forgive me, I'm a part of it."

"You were to be an impartial observer," Bittman said, with obvious disapproval. "Instead, you became involved even before the project commenced, the day you observed the Caldwells interacting with that new teacher and her son. You chose to intervene, counter to your instructions."

"They were hassling that poor woman. What was I supposed to do?"

"You were supposed to obey my orders."

"I'm going to start obeying my conscience," said Charlie. "I was stupid to sign on with this crazy whatever-it-is, government or no government."

"Mr. Flagg, you're becoming hysterical."

"No, I'm not. I'm just getting pissed off. The people in this town are my friends. This insanity has got to stop."

Bittman assumed the air of a superior, not without sympathy, whose patience has run out. "Believe me, sir, when I tell you that we are wholly committed to doing everything we possibly can to avert the atrocities taking place in your town. We are of course routing every report, every piece of data gathered, to the proper authorities. Surely you cannot truly believe that our government has anything to do with the violence that is occurring here. That wretched Caldwell boy and what he did, these unfortunate serial killings, they *are* coincidental. They have absolutely *nothing* to do with this project. If anything, they will most likely render our findings utterly useless. These are hardly normal circumstances under which to evaluate human behavior."

"God knows I want to believe you," said Charlie. "I want to with all my heart and soul. This is driving me crazy."

"What do you intend to do?" Mace asked quietly. "These local yokels find out you're with us after what's happened, they'll run you out of town."

Bittman concurred with a nod. "The fact that your accusations against us would be proven groundless would hardly soften your fall from grace in the community, I daresay. No one likes a spy."

"If it comes to that," said Charlie, "I'll take my chances."

"Of course, Mr. Flagg. Of course. But then, this conversation is strictly academic, is it not?"

"I hope so. You tell me."

"Very well, I shall tell you. Would your mind be sufficiently set at ease if I were to supply you with irrefutable, verifiable authorization of this operation from a higher source than you could ever imagine?"

"That would help. How high a source?"

"The White House. The President's Cabinet. Would that be sufficient?"

"Doc, you'd make me the happiest man in the world if you could pull a rabbit like that out of your hat."

This time it was a gasp that Jared quietly sounded, and Paul's clamp upon his arm tightened. Jared was starting to realize that this grand lark had turned into something else, something ominous. These men were discussing things that were a lot scarier to Paul than watching the Caldwell brothers beat on each other.

The corners of Bittman's gash of a mouth had crinkled in what could have been the trace of a smile.

"I will arrange it, then," he told Charlie, "and have such authorization when you arrive here to report tomorrow. And now, Mr. Flagg, you may as well file the rest of today's report."

Charlie hacked up a wad of phlegm and spat it upon the ground before he got around to saying, "Not much to report. And what there is, it breaks my heart to see."

"Save the editorializing for your newspaper, sir. I want only facts."

"These are facts. Until not long ago, this town was a mighty fine piece of paradise, off the beaten track with the same problems you'd find in any town, gossip and the like. But yeah, a piece of paradise where life was good and simple, and people got along."

"It's changed, has it?"

Charlie nodded. "With every murder. The people, they don't know what to think or who to trust. They *watch* each other instead of *seeing* each other. Yeah, that's what it is. It's like what China or someplace must be like, with everyone spying on their neighbor. Everyone's afraid. Afraid to be friends, to interact with each other. It's a paranoia you can smell in the air; a cancer eating away at this community. They've all got good reason to think that one of them is a mass murderer."

"I see."

"As a matter of fact, Landware is checking up on that crazy old Indian and his grandson that you wanted me to keep tabs on, damned if I know why."

"This too has been explained to you. There are few variables in the demographic composition of Devil Creek. Those aborigines qualify, and so need to be monitored."

"There is something else going on in Devil Creek these days, and I'd draw your attention to it."

"Truly? And what might that be, Mr. Flagg?"

"There's a *goodness* in these people that is refusing to die. Sure, they're afraid. They're paranoid. They're sleeping with the doors locked, which no one used to do. They're not always at their best. But Doc, the basic *decency* of these people is stronger than anything that could work against it. I'm seeing that, too. I'm not going to let down people like that. They're being held hostage in their own community and they don't like it. They're binding together to get through it, and they're becoming stronger as a community than they ever were before."

"Inspiring. And have you anything else to report?"

"No, I guess not. Not at this time."

"Very well then. I do believe we are finished with you, Mr. Flagg. You see, I regret to say that all of your suspicions regarding this project are in fact one hundred percent correct. Furthermore, I'm afraid that you pose far too serious a security risk to be allowed to leave here alive. I am sorry." Bittman turned away, saying under his breath, "Major."

Mace, who had angled around behind Charlie, moved with extraordinary swiftness. His knee went to the base of Charlie's spine as his forearms vised Charlie's neck. There was a cracking sound like a branch being snapped, louder than anything Paul had ever heard.

Paul's senses reeled, and he sensed Jared grow taut with shock and agitation.

Mace released Charlie's body, allowing it to fall. Charlie's head was twisted into an unnatural position. Mace studied the corpse with detached disdain.

"What a moron. Why'd he come up here and sound off like that? Didn't he think we'd whack him?"

"He had his doubts," Bittman said, "but he wanted to believe that we were government sanctioned."

Mace made a contemptuous sound. He kicked the corpse. "Moron."

It was as if Paul could not breathe.

Beside him, Jared leaped to his feet.

"I'm getting out of here!" Jared's eyes were wide circles. If he'd been a child actor, he'd have been accused of over-acting.

"Jared, no!" Paul whispered harshly.

Too late!

Jared bulldozed his way through dry underbrush like a frightened rhino with no regard for the ruckus he was causing or anything except blind flight.

Mace snarled. "Damn."

He and the sentries, Hickey and Taylor, were already bolting toward the sounds, coming after Paul and Jared.

"Get them!" Paul heard Bittman's command. "Whoever they are, they saw everything. Do not let them escape. Kill them."

Chapter 27

Paul would remember the loud, sharp *snap!* of Mr. Flagg's neck breaking for the rest of his life. His life! The full realization of their predicament smacked him between the eyes with the same abruptness as the snapping of Charlie Flagg's neck.

The men in the clearing were racing uphill, straight in their direction.

Paul followed Jared as fast as he could away from there. But he'd lost sight of Jared. He slipped, in his panic his ankles becoming tangled in the undergrowth and he almost fell, but managed to maintain his balance and keep running. Behind him, he heard shouts, the men scrambling from the clearing in hot pursuit. Then he caught sight of Jared, up ahead. He sprinted faster. He'd never run so fast. Then one of the sentries emerged from a break in the trees up ahead, having left the clearing at an angle to intercept Jared. The man held his rifle as if ready to fire.

"Jared, look out!"

It was all Paul had time to cry out before he realized that the other sentry was rushing at him. And for one instant Paul could not believe his eyes. This sentry was aiming his rifle directly at him! For one horrific instant, fright and confusion rooted Paul to the spot. The man fired a short burst. Angry flashes flickered and spat from the rifle's muzzle. Bullets slapped into trees, severing branches close to Paul; very, *very* close. He threw himself to the right, running away deeper into the forest. The ground sloped downward. The rifle fire stopped. He did not look back. He pushed on, angling sideways down the slope, the bottoms of his sneakers slipping and sliding in places, one time badly enough for him to throw out a hand to steady his balance. Dirt and rock scraped the palm of his hand raw. He heard the man coming after him. He thought of the blond-haired commando who had killed Mr. Flagg. Where was that one?

He heard Jared screaming, "Paul! Paul, *where are you?*"

He'd lost sight of Jared again, but the frightened scream carried clearly from somewhere nearby. He started to shout a reply. But that would give away *his* location. But he could not leave Jared behind. Before he could do anything, there came another hammering of gunfire, muffled through the wall of trees but again extremely close. At first he thought they were shooting at him. No bullets came near him. The gunfire ceased. There was no more sound from Jared.

Paul reached the bottom of the slope and kept running. Branches clawed at his face. He tore headlong through the forest, knowing only that he was going downhill, that he must get off the mountain. *They got Jared!* They killed Mr. Flagg. They killed Jared. And now they were after him! The ground funneled down to become a projection of rock that clung like a natural path to the base of a steep incline. Within a foot of the other side, the ground dropped away like a cliff. He scuttled along the outcrop, past juniper trees that seemed to grow from rock, their roots thick and gnarly, deeply embedded where erosion had eaten away at the path over the years. Across the shelf of stone, the ground sloped more gradually with more trees. He could find cover there, Paul told himself. He was halfway across the projection of rock when he heard the man with the rifle rushing down the incline behind him. He did not stop. He did not look around. They were going to kill him. He kept on running.

Automatic rifle fire stammered loudly behind him. A

burst of pain exploded in his right side like a strong fist, striking with enough force to spin him around, sending him off balance. He tumbled from the path, toppling over the edge of the sharp drop.

Chapter 28

At first Mike didn't hear the rapping at his kitchen door. He was writing at the table, and the clacking of the typewriter enveloped him. This was the first work he'd done on his novel since Bobby Caldwell had gone nuts. A preoccupation with that and the serial killings had diminished the urge, not to mention the focus, to create fiction. What were lines of type across sheets of paper compared to the tragic, real, senseless loss of human life? He'd reached the end of a paragraph and stopped typing. That's when he heard Robin tap-tapping on the glass of the door. He let her in.

She wore a white skirt and a blue sweater and, framed in the doorway, in the fading light of the afternoon with the purple mountains and the darkening sky behind her and the breeze playing with her chestnut hair, she should have been a picture of flawless beauty. But there was a flaw. Her features were drawn taut, a mask of stress and concern.

"Robin, what is it?"

"Please, Mike, can I come in?"

"Of course. What's wrong?"

She stepped inside. He closed the door against the cold breeze.

"It's Paul."

"What happened?"

"I'm worried about him. He's not at his friend's house. He should have been home by now."

"Have you spoken with Jared's mother?"

"Jared's mother is drunk. She's barely coherent. I called a few minutes ago, when I got home. All she could tell me was that she hadn't seen Jared or Paul all day. The last time she saw her son, or thinks she saw him, was when he left on his way to visit Paul. After you left them, they didn't go to Jared's. So I'm worried. It's going to be dark soon and, well," she bit her lower lip, "it's been a terrible day. Did you hear about Mrs. Lufkin?"

"No. What?"

"She's dead, Mike. She committed suicide in her home this afternoon. I was the one who found her."

"Robin, I had no idea. You should have come right over and told me." He instinctively reached down, lightly touched her wrists, giving them a squeeze, gazing into her eyes. "My God, that must have been terrible for you. How are you doing?"

"The police kept me there for awhile. Chief Saunders was very nice. But it was awful."

"I wish I'd known earlier . . ."

"It was so strange. It was like . . . like a dream I had last week. Exactly like in my dream. I don't understand it."

He tried fighting off the numbness he felt from this unexpected news. "The poor woman." He knew his words were inane. What *could* you say at a moment like this, dealing with news like this?

"I only saw her for a few seconds before I looked away. I couldn't stand to see her like that." Her words came listlessly, numb with shock. "The Chief told me the rest later, when I asked him. There was a mantle in front of where she . . . where she did it. There was a photograph on the mantle. She must have been looking at it for a long time before she . . . hung herself. The photograph was a family portrait. Mrs. Lufkin and her husband and her son, from a long time ago. She'd told me her son was killed in Vietnam. Then her husband died of cancer. She missed them so much. So much. More than any of us realized. She was always so . . . so full of life."

Mike made himself think clearly, through his emotion. "About finding Paul," he said. "Let's call that video arcade in town where the kids hang out. I'll bet he's with some new buddies and they just forgot about the time."

Her eyes cleared of their mist. "He knows I'd worry about him. He'd call if he was going to be late. I guess I came over here because I thought—" the forced steadiness in her voice faltered. "Well, I thought you might have heard from him."

He hated to say, "I haven't seen him."

"Then something is wrong. I knew something was wrong."

"Take it easy. We'll take this one step at a time."

They were still touching, sort of holding hands. She withdrew from his touch.

"I didn't mean to bother you. I'd better go home and wait for him. I'm going to call the police."

"That's a good precaution for you to take. But don't worry, Robin. I'm sure he'll be home soon." The reassurance sounded hollow and phony to him.

"Thanks, Michael."

"For what? I'm just being a good neighbor."

He held the door open for her.

She paused on his doorstep, looking back. "You're more than a good neighbor. You're a friend."

"If there's anything I can do."

"You could keep me company while I wait." Her lower lip trembled. "I am having one hell of a rotten day. I really could use some company. Or does that sound terribly uninviting?"

He didn't pause to grab a sweater or jacket. "Let's go over to your place and call the police."

Chapter 29

Robin was waiting for Chief Saunders at her front door when he arrived. When he stepped inside, the Chief's eyes sharpened when he saw Mike standing there in the living room.

Robin said, "Thank you for responding so quickly, Chief."

Saunders stood with his hat in his hands in the manner of a western gentleman. "Got here fast as I could. I'm sorry to see you again so soon under official circumstances. Ma'am, the first thing I have to ask is, are you sure there's reason to be concerned about your boy? I mean, it isn't even sundown yet. You'd be surprised how often children his age take off playing and forget how late it's got and throw a scare into their parents. We get a half dozen calls like that a month."

"You don't know my son. This is very serious, me not hearing from Paul with night coming on."

"Believe me, ma'am, I understand. That's why I'm here. When did you last see Paul?"

"He left the house with Mr. Landware at about four o'clock this afternoon."

Saunders looked at Mike, his eyes asking a silent question.

Mike said, "Paul and I were going for a hike." Mike told Saunders about him and Paul meeting Jared, and of their calling Robin about the change in plans.

"And when was the last time you saw the boys?"

"Out front of the convenience store. I sat in my Jeep and

watched them walk toward town."

"Did anyone see you?"

"See me sitting in my Jeep? I guess so. They know me at the store. Mr. Barva or one of his daughters is always working the counter. They'd have seen me unless they were busy."

Robin's expression clouded. "Why are you asking if anyone saw Mike?"

"Just routine, ma'am."

"He knows something about me," said Mike. "Don't you, Chief?"

Saunders paused a moment to mull over his response, then he nodded. "I put through a background check on you. Had to. Matter of fact, it was routine. New man moves into town, single fella with no family, no job, then bad things start happening. I had to check."

Robin was staring at Saunders. "You don't think Mike has anything to do with . . . anything?"

"If I thought that, ma'am, right now I'd have him under arrest. And I wouldn't have come out here alone. Mr. Landware appears to me to be a man who knows how to handle himself. If I'd come to arrest him, I'd have some backup."

"I'm no tough guy," said Mike.

Robin turned inquisitive eyes on him. "I don't understand. What's he talking about, Michael?"

Mike looked her straight in those uncertain, inquisitive eyes. This was the moment of truth. However she judged him now would dictate everything that happened between them from this moment on.

"I dropped Paul and Jared off at the convenience store and that's the last I saw of them. I'm as worried about them as you are."

Their eyes held.

"I believe you," she said. "But there's more. I want to hear all of it."

Mike felt Saunders' cop eyes boring into him.

"I told you that my wife died in Albuquerque," he told Robin. "But you're right. There is more to it. Carol was murdered. I was teaching a night class at the university when it happened. She was raped and stabbed in our apartment off campus. She was five months pregnant."

Robin flinched as if physically slapped.

"Oh, Mike—"

Saunders continued the story. His flinty stare never shifted from Mike. "A car was seen driving away at a high rate of speed. A witness wrote down the license number. A man was arrested. He refused to make a statement. He was the handyman at the apartment complex; had sexual misdemeanors and a history of mental illness that they didn't know about when they hired him. It's important to tell you, ma'am, that there was no physical evidence linking Mr. Landware to that crime. I spoke with the detective in charge of the investigation."

"Lieutenant Ordway," said Mike. "Yeah, he interrogated me. He suggested that I could have made it from my classroom to the apartment while my students were taking a test I'd given them that night. Funny, I don't remember much about Ordway. I was still in shock from . . . seeing Carol. From seeing her body. They were damn brutal about the way they showed her to me for the first time."

Saunders told Robin, "They held the handyman in jail on suspicion. He was scheduled for a hearing the next morning. But he never made it. On his way to the hearing, he broke loose from his guards and threw himself over the railing of the walkway from the jail to the courthouse. It was a three-story drop. He broke his neck. The police and most everyone wrote off the handyman's suicide as confession of his guilt. But the case was never officially closed."

"I didn't murder my wife," said Mike. "I haven't killed anyone since before I came home from Vietnam and that was more than twenty years ago."

Saunders' gaze softened slightly. "Trust me, son, I want to believe you."

"Well, I believe him," said Robin. "And I want to know what we can do about my son," she said to Saunders. She heard the wind outside. She shivered. "Paul and his friend are out there. What can we do to find them?"

"As soon as your call came in, I put through a requisition for a search and rescue at daybreak, if the boys are still unaccounted for."

"Daybreak?" Robin's voice rose an octave. "But they could be lost! I heard a weather report on my car radio. It might snow tonight in the mountains."

"Ma'am, it takes time to initiate search services. I have to follow the book. I'm doing everything I can."

"I know. I'm upset. I'm sorry. I don't want to take it out on you, Chief. But I do want to play some part in your search, if it comes to that."

"Wouldn't have it any other way." Saunders still held his Stetson in both hands, and became momentarily distracted with rotating it in slow circles. "I'm, uh, sorry to both of you for any embarrassment I may have caused, bringing up what happened in Albuquerque. But you'd best be advised, Mr. Landware. There are people in this town who don't know anything about any of that, but they're drawing conclusions of their own because bad things did start happening as soon as you moved here. I wish I could keep people from thinking and talking like that, but I can't."

"Doesn't make a man feel too welcome," Mike said.

"It's not the way these folks are normally, believe me. They're good people. Decent folks. But everyone in town is under a lot of pressure right now, with all these things that've been happening. I mean, we can even count Mrs. Lufkin's suicide in that list."

Mike said, in a metallic monotone, "I did not kill Mrs. Lufkin."

"Of course you didn't. No one is thinking that. I just meant that it's all building up, like steam in a pressure cooker. What's going on, it's eating away at this town, eating down deep into the bones, into the soul of the town."

"Is there a chance that everything that's happening could be related? I know that sounds crazy."

"I don't rightly figure how that could be," said Saunders. "Who'd stand to gain from something like that, and how could everything be connected? There'd have to be some thread linking it all together. Bobby Caldwell killed himself after what he did. His brother Tobe is cooling his heels in the county jail, so he's not a serial killer. And what could Mrs. Lufkin have to do with any of it? That old lady used to give my family pecans from her orchard when I was just a pup. She was one of the finest, most generous people this town will ever know. She couldn't be part of anything like what's been going on." Saunders shook his head. "This here's a situation I don't know what to make of. Never seen so many ills visited on a community this size in so short a time. But I'll tell you what. I intend to put a stop to it, and I reckon that's the business I ought to be about right now. I'll do what I can to get helicopters out tonight to fly over the mountain to look for those boys, ma'am. They'll show. But if not, well . . . you just look for us along the highway, most likely near the Philbin boy's house. In the meantime, you give me a call first thing you get word from your boy, would you please?"

"Of course. Most of me expects Paul to walk through that door at any minute."

"Well, good night, folks."

"Good night, Chief."

"Night, Chief."

They stood side by side at the front door, watching Saunders back his police car out of the driveway and drive off.

"I can leave, too," Mike said. "If you want to be alone—"

"I don't want to be alone." She crossed her arms before her, clasping them tightly as if trying to retain body warmth. "It was me *needing to be alone* that sent Paul out of here this afternoon. I was so selfish. His safety and well being are my responsibility. He's only twelve years old! And I, quote, needed some space, unquote."

"Robin, stop it. Don't think like that."

She moved to a couch that faced the window, looking out across the patio, at the mountains that she and Mrs. Lufkin had admired and talked about only, what was it, only seven days ago? So much had changed. She sat, staring out at the gathering gloom. He sat next to her, sideways upon the couch, facing her. And she told him about her nightmare that night in this house, after Paul had come home with his wild story of murder and suicide. She told Mike about the dream of being awakened, of walking up a staircase to a room of shadows at the top of the stairs where she had seen her own dead face strangled at the end of a rope. Exactly as she found Mrs. Lufkin.

When she was finished, she asked in a quiet voice, "Mike, how can such a thing be?"

"I don't know."

181

"Where's Paul? Why hasn't he called? Why isn't he here?"

"Something's not right. We both know that. So does the Chief. But, Robin, you've raised a tough, self-reliant kid. I don't know what's going on either, but that boy of yours is a survivor. You're the reason he's that way. He'll be all right."

"It's nice of you to try and make me feel as if I don't bear responsibility for him being out there."

"It isn't your fault. We both thought he was going to Jared's. You acted responsibly."

"I think I made one hell of a mistake moving here," she said, "you know that? I should have never left Chicago. I'm very good at making very big mistakes. I made one with Paul's father. I should have seen the way Jeff was before we ever got married. My parents tried to warn me. They died before I ever got the chance to tell them how right they were."

"Robin, don't sink into self-pity. You don't owe that to Paul or to yourself."

"I'm just saying that when I make a mistake, it's a doozie. My parents met Jeff when we were in college. He'd asked me to marry him and I said yes, so of course I wanted him to meet the folks. Dad was a career military man, and he and Mom didn't take to Jeff from the start. We went out to dinner and the evening ended in a terrible argument about something, I forget what. Vietnam. After that I only spoke to my parents on the telephone. I felt they weren't giving Jeff a fair chance, that they were letting some difference in politics stand in the way of our love and happiness. At that age, I guess their disapproval only drove me closer to him. They didn't come to the wedding. I never saw them again after that night. They were killed in an automobile accident that winter. But they saw something in Jeff during that one evening that I didn't. So you see, I can make very big mistakes. And thinking that I could start a perfect new life by moving to Devil Creek, New Mexico, definitely ranks at the top of the list of real big mistakes."

"I hope you don't think you're making a mistake, trusting me."

"I don't think I'm making a mistake."

"That picture the Chief painted . . . I can understand how someone could draw the wrong conclusions."

"The Chief doesn't believe those things."

"Maybe. Maybe he's just waiting. Waiting for some solid evidence to come along."

"You've told the truth," she said. "Now I'll give you some of my truth. I hadn't planned to, but here it is. Mike, you're not like any man I've ever known. Jeff is, was, the only man I've known, and he's like too many of the others out there; not a man at all, just an insecure little boy in a man's body, trying to prove to everyone that he's a man because he's hustling other people out of their hard-earned money or bedding every bimbo who comes along. You're a real man. You don't have to prove anything to anybody, including yourself. Including me. You just *are.* You're confident. You're strong and you're tender. You're compassionate. I sensed those things about you the day we met and nothing I've seen or learned about you since has changed my estimation of you. From your friendship with Paul to your being at the community meeting this morning, to the way you always treat me with friendship and respect, the way a woman likes to be treated—my heart tells me you're a good man, Michael, and that I'm not making a mistake about you. I sensed your sadness when we met. Now I know what you've been through. You've been through a living hell and you've hurt like no one should have to, yet you've emerged intact, the strong good man that you are. I'm trusting you." Robin gave a humorless, self-conscious smile. "Stress can make for compulsive chatter, I'm told."

"I have done bad things in my life, Robin. That is truth."

"I know. Vietnam. But that was war, Michael. I told you, my father was a soldier. I understand. War is obscene, brutal, dehumanizing. But a soldier follows orders and does what he has to do to survive, both for the ones who depend on him in combat and for the ones back home who love him, so he can return safely to them." Again the smallest trace of a humorless smile. "You see, there aren't a lot of perks to being an army brat, but one can learn a few things."

His mouth was a grim line. His eyes were somber. "After Vietnam, I swore on my parents' graves that I'd never kill again. I wanted to break that vow after what happened to Carol. I wanted to find whoever did that to her and strangle him with my bare hands. But I never got the chance."

Robin looked deeply into his eyes. "The fact that you made such a vow tells me all I need to know," she said. "Just like the way you didn't come on to me that night at the barbecue the way you could have. You don't know how much I appreciated that. But the fact of the matter is, well, it just made you all the more attractive to me. I'm lucky to have you as my friend, Michael. I want to feel sorry for myself and cry, but I can't. Not now. When I do, it will be later, after it's over and Paul is back. Right now, I'm going to sit right here and wait for the telephone to ring or for my son to come walking through that door with one whopper of an excuse for causing all of this concern."

"And I want to stay with you," he said, "until one of those things happen."

She rested the back of her head against the back of the couch. She contemplated the ceiling, not really seeing it. "I wanted to be independent and never need anyone except Paul."

"Flesh and blood is good," Mike acknowledged, "but even with that, everyone needs someone."

"God," she blurted with an intensity that surprised her, "I want to be part of a couple tonight." She felt as if she were venting aloud, more than talking to him. "Until we know what's going to happen next . . . Mike, I need to be held."

He situated himself with one movement that allowed one of his arms to encircle her waist, and he drew her to him with a strength that was inviting, not forceful, and she yielded, feeling the contours of her body press against his chest. It was the first time a man had held her like that since Jeff, and she couldn't remember the last time that was. Years ago.

"So tonight we are a couple," said Mike, making no attempt to kiss her. But he held her like that, and his strength was the tender embrace she needed.

Her face was inches from his. She said, "You make me feel safe."

"It might sound funny coming from me," he said, "but, lady, holding you makes me feel the same way."

Their first kiss lingered and was many things, by turns sweet and tentative, the brushing of her moist lips to his leathery ones, and then his arm, the one encircling her waist, clutched her tighter, not brusquely, but not gently and the unbidden mewing from her throat harmonized with the masculine growl from deep in his chest that sounded like a waking bull, and the tentative kiss became hotly compressing lips, plenty of heat and the progression seemed so natural that her tongue darted into his mouth like a fiery wet serpent to entwine just once with his tongue before she felt wanton and ended the kiss, drawing back but remaining in his embrace, gasping for breath.

"Well," she said.

They were both smiling like silly high school kids.

"You're a good kisser, lady."

She started to smile and mouth a pert response when everything washed across her consciousness again and their moment was lost. But she did not withdraw from his embrace.

"And if we're a couple for tonight," she asked, "what about *after* tonight?"

"Why don't we take it one night at a time?"

She laughed despite the circumstances.

"Spoken like a true man." The laugh was a brief one, and her expression became serious again. "You're good company, Mike. You're welcome to stay and wait with me if you want to."

When he did not move to get up, she guided one of his arms around her shoulder and nestled against him with her head on his chest. And so he sat with her on her couch, with his arm around her, staring at their reflection in the window now darkened by nightfall. He listened to her breathing. She must have fallen asleep instantly. He had not held a woman like this since Carol.

And then he realized for the first time that he had fallen in love with Robin Curtis.

Chapter 30

Mike snapped back to full consciousness as if a switch inside his brain had been flicked on and for a single instant, he flashed back to Nam, to when he'd grab shut eye whenever he could on those penetrations behind Charlie's lines. *After forty-eight hours at a stretch, with nothing but paranoia and bennies to keep going, after the heat and the humidity and the physical exertion of hacking through the endless jungle, after the team was flat-ass worn out and couldn't, just plain couldn't, push on one more step, then a security perimeter would be established. Then he'd catch some z's, trading off with his buddies— until the snap of a twig or a bird call from a treetop kicked him wide awake from the deepest black of dreamless sleep.*

His first conscious thought was anger at himself. He'd realized he was growing drowsy, but he certainly hadn't intended to fall asleep. Yet he'd drifted off to dreamland there on the couch, an arm around Robin, her head resting against his chest, the scent of her—not perfume, not soap, just the natural, pleasing womanly scent of her—lulling his senses. Now those senses awakened as in the old days.

She stood at the window, her back to him, staring out into the night.

But it was not like Vietnam at all, because it was not her rising from his embrace that had awakened him. Robin had been up for awhile. She wore hiking boots, jeans, and a down jacket over a flannel shirt. Lightning ripped across the sky, followed by rolling thunder. The thunder had awakened him. That, or the night wind whistling and moaning around the house, louder than before.

He joined her at the window. "Guess I was more tired than I thought."

"I woke up in a panic," she said in a small voice. "It's four in the morning and my son isn't home. I can't just sit here and wait for daylight. I've got to get out there and *do* something, or try to."

"Let's go, then. But where to start? Do you have someplace in mind?"

"I woke up remembering a trail Paul pointed out to me last week when we drove past it. It leads up the mountain about a quarter of a mile north from Jared's house. Paul told me that Jared knows those trails. They could have gone up that way, and gotten lost. I know it's not much, but if those kids are lost up there and are trying to find their way back, we can call out to them. They'll hear us."

He nodded. "It's worth a try. I'm betting Paul found a place to lay low until this weather blows over if they are up there. We talked about wilderness survival. He learned things about it from those western novels he read."

"It's the only thing I can think of to do. I've left a message on the machine in case he calls while we're gone."

"I'll get my jacket."

They took his Jeep. Halfway to the main highway, it began to rain. Not a heavy rain; tiny droplets whipped by the wind. As they turned onto the highway, he switched on the wipers. Their *snick-snick* was the only sound in the vehicle. The headlights turned the raindrops ahead into millions of cold shimmering diamonds. Eventually, Robin pointed out the spot where she wanted him to pull off the main road. He did, cutting the Jeep's engine and lights. Rain pattered on the tarpaulin roof like tiny drumming fingers.

"You are a trusting soul," he said, "driving with me out

here into the night, without telling anyone, while the whole town is cowering behind locked doors, scared to death of a maniac killer."

"I told you why I trust you. Don't I make sense?"

"We can make sense some other time. Right now, let's look for those boys."

Other than drawing their jacket collars tighter, neither acknowledged the swirling, bone-chilling rain as they stepped from the Jeep. Mike produced a flashlight. Its beam clearly picked out a foot trail.

Robin said, "Paul told me that this trail branches off into other, smaller ones up ahead. This is going to be like hunting for a needle in a haystack, isn't it?"

"As a writer, I couldn't have chosen a more moth-eaten cliché." He wanted to lighten her up if he could, so she wouldn't be so wound up that she'd lose it if they didn't find the boys tonight. He was rewarded with an involuntary, barely audible chuckle. *Good enough,* he thought. "And you were right," he added. "This does beat the hell out of sitting back there doing nothing."

They followed the trail, the flashlight beam guiding them as the path began to climb. Although tall trees sheltered them in spots, the path cut across open stretches where windblown rain stung them like pinpricks. The wind moaned eerily. They started calling the boys' names, alternating the names and the direction in which they shouted. There was no response except for the howling of the wind. They trudged on, calling the boys' names, over and over. The rain had thoroughly soaked their clothing by the time the flashlight illuminated a spot where the trail narrowed.

Mike swept the forest around them with the beam. There was no sign of other trails. The one they were on dwindled to nothing.

189

The tip of Robin's nose, her ears and her hands were numb from the cold. In the flashlight's beam, she saw something else: the wind-driven droplets of rain becoming windblown flakes of snow. Her heart sank, as it had been sinking in the half-hour since they'd left the Jeep. She should have known from the outset that this was hopeless.

Mike said, "We're not doing those boys any good. We'll be of far more use tomorrow during an organized daylight search."

"Michael, what could have happened to them?"

"We'll find out tomorrow. We have to have faith in Paul. He can take care of himself. I know he can, and so do you. Trust what you've taught him."

"You're right. I know you're right."

They started back down the mountain, still calling out the boys' names into the vast, rainswept darkness.

Chapter 31

Paul heard the voices.

Voices from somewhere far, far away, separated from him by miles and miles of fog. There was fog inside his brain, fog from the pain and nausea that came and went. The voices didn't sound real. They called out names. He knew the voices. Worried voices. Real worried. Worried about him.

He passed in and out of consciousness there in the small space he'd found, where he had dragged himself to escape the wind, the rain that was turning to snow, and the men who wanted to kill him.

When the bullet had struck him, there on the stone shelf that had formed a path above the drop-off, it had felt like a fist pounding into his side, knocking him from his feet and over the ledge. It hurt when he tumbled down, rolling over and over, the world spinning around his head like a merry-go-round gone berserk. He'd come to a stop in tall grass from where he overheard the men on the ledge above.

"Did you get him?"

"Yeah, I got mine. What about yours?"

"I think so. He fell off here and rolled down there some-where."

"I don't see him."

"He's down there."

"Better go down and make sure. Mace won't like it if one of those brats gets away."

The footsteps had moved off. He understood what was happening. They were following the stone shelf to the more

191

gradual slope, intending to work their way down and look for his body. That gave him maybe a minute. He'd been up, lurching away from there, continuing downhill. His right side, where he'd felt the punch, was starting to hurt, so he'd looked down and saw the torn material where the bullet had grazed him. The material around the tear was soaked with blood. Panic had washed over him and he'd almost tripped, but he kept running through the encroaching dusk that began cloaking the forest. He lost all sense of direction, knowing only that he must keep heading downhill, down off the mountain. He'd heard the men calling to each other behind him, trying to determine which way he had gone. He ran and ran until he could run no more, until he had to stop, the pain in his side throbbing, the world reeling and darkening before coming back into focus a little slower each time. He could not go on. He had to rest. The rain blowing against his face was the only thing that kept him barely conscious, kept him going. He felt himself growing weaker by the second. The men behind him would not slow down. They wouldn't stand around trying to decide what to do. They'd killed Jared and they would kill him if they caught him.

He saw the crevice beneath a large rock; a tight, narrow crawl space worn away by erosion, barely wide enough to squeeze into. A bush of some sort grew in front of the crevice. The fallen branch of a dead tree lay nearby. He found that he could actually lie down against the ground inside the crevice. The rock protrusion angling out above him made it a dry spot away from the rain and the wind. Dragging the branch with his left arm, he positioned the branch lengthwise so that it hid the crevice and the overhang from anyone passing by. Hardly enough to pass close inspection by someone looking directly at it in daylight, but he had some chance of avoiding being found tonight.

Paul never learned if his pursuers came near his hiding spot because those were his final rational thoughts before the pain and the fog overtook him. He grew dizzy, unsure of sound and sensation. He could not be sure what was real. He lost track of time.

At one point, he heard the voices calling for him and Jared. Yes, he knew those voices. His mother and Mike. Calling his name. Calling Jared's name. Didn't they know Jared was dead? The voices were not real. He would miss Jared. Jared. Jared had been his only friend in Devil Creek, except for Mike. The voices calling his name faded back into the fog. *I'm here, Mom! I'm here! Help me!* Something in his brain tried to make him speak. He could not speak. He grew sleepy. The bullet wound throbbed where he pressed his jacket against it to stem the flow of blood. His world was the wind and the cold and the pain and the darkness.

I'm here, Mom.

Mike, I'm here.

His mind slipped into the darkness.

Chapter 32

Mace entered the van, allowing a trace of windblown snow into the warm interior. Bittman was at the computer console. His thin, bony fingers sped dexterously across the keyboard, monitoring, sorting, and filing data as it was received. He did not look up. Mace drew the door shut behind him, against the elements. As always, the windowless compartment basked in the glow of the computer screens.

"Report."

"We've only found one body. The other one, Taylor swears he winged him. The kid's out there somewhere. If he's not dead, he will be soon."

"The police have been notified that the boys are missing," said Bittman. "Helicopters will overfly tonight."

"We're covered. They won't spot anything."

"See that Taylor and Hickey are so advised. What about the boy you did kill?"

"He's with Charlie Flagg in Flagg's Bronco at the bottom of that lake near here."

The man in white stopped typing and watching the screens.

"Two young boys, Major. Not even teenagers, and they breached your oh-so-careful security. When you were hired, I was given to understand that I was buying the best."

"Those kids were a fluke. You can't foresee something like that."

"You should have. And now there's a young boy out there on the mountain tonight who witnessed two murders."

"First off, that brat's not going to make it off this mountain, wounded, with the temperature getting down to freezing. He won't live to tell anybody anything. But just in case, I say we haul out of here tonight. You must have enough by now."

"Ah, but I don't." Bittman's eyes shone behind his glasses. "And it is just now becoming really interesting, don't you see? What with the children in the equation, this exacerbates everything. It is of extreme importance and interest to me personally, and to the integrity of the project."

"Integrity. Yeah, right. But what about the search and rescue tomorrow morning? They'll be fanning out from a base camp no more than a couple of miles from here."

"True, but they won't reach anywhere near here until at least early afternoon."

"We should withdraw now, under cover of darkness."

"And risk the boy surviving? Telling everyone what he saw and, more than likely, what he heard? We must proceed on the assumption that the child now knows everything about us. We must take every step possible to insure that this boy is rendered as dead as the first."

"What do you suggest?"

"Ah, I detect condescension and sarcasm. Admittedly, I am not a very pleasant example of the species. I am a man of science, Major, with little regard for the social niceties that bond the pack mentality of the common man."

"That makes two of us, so at least we agree on something. But I still want to know what we do about this situation."

"If you want the remainder of your retainer, which is considerable, you will follow my instructions. That is what we will do, Major."

"I know the arrangement. The second half goes into my

Swiss account at the completion of the mission. And you determine when the mission is completed."

"Precisely. This may be a paramilitary operation to your mind, Major, providing security, hiring those ruffians who work under you. To me, it is a sacred mission that must be, *will* be fulfilled."

"So how close are we to being fulfilled? It'll be dawn in a few hours."

"At first light, you will instruct your men to reconvene our search. Resume where you last saw the boy. I will accompany you."

"That's a change."

"I prefer to review data as it comes in. But the retrieval system is automated. As you quite correctly point out, locating and nullifying the boy must be our top priority."

"He can't have gone far."

"We will allot ourselves ninety minutes to search for him."

"The search and rescue parties, the helicopters . . . it'll be chancy.

"I thought you and your men were the best."

"Okay, Doc, okay. We'll find the boy. And if he's not dead, we'll make sure that he is."

"If we cannot find him, then it is highly unlikely that the search parties will, either. After ninety minutes, we will return here and break camp."

"We take the same way out as we came in?"

"Of course. The trail leads to the highway in the opposite direction from where the search parties will be. We'll take the highway to the Interstate. You and your men will have shed those ridiculous paramilitary fatigues you insist on wearing and will be clad in appropriate civilian attire. In the unlikely event that we are stopped, we will pass as representatives of the news media." Bittman nodded to the computers. "There is enough here to substantiate such a cover story. But no one will stop us. We will disappear, and our mission will have been fulfilled."

"All right, Doc. You're the boss."

"Indeed. I am the boss. And you will not be paid if anything happens to me; if I do not survive. You do recall that stipulation in our arrangement, don't you, Mace? You getting paid depends on my survival."

"Don't worry. You'll survive. After some of the hell holes I've pulled duty in, I'm not worried about these country bumpkins."

The man in white did not respond. Bittman returned his attention to the computer console, his glasses reflecting the glow of the monitors. His fingers danced across the keyboard, as if Mace was not there.

Chapter 33

Mike steered the Jeep back onto the paved road.

"It's stopped raining," Robin noted, for something to say.

"Wind's died down, too."

She loosened the collar of her jacket, withdrew tissue from her purse and dabbed away the moisture left by the rain across her forehead and around her eyes. The Jeep's tires hissed along the wet pavement. The rich aroma of damp earth and pine was dense on the air. She stared up at the murky shape of a mountain.

"I wonder what the weather's like up there." Then she realized something. "This isn't the way back to the house. Where are we going?"

"I'm hungry. How about you?"

"Yes. Yes, I'm hungry. I haven't thought about food in so long, I can't remember the last time I ate. But I can fix us something at home. What if Paul—"

"If Paul's there, he'll answer the phone when you call. If he's trying to call you, he'll leave a message on your machine."

"It's been more than an hour since we left."

"There's a phone at a rest area three miles from here."

"That will do, I guess. But where can we eat at this time of night, or morning? *Donna's* is closed."

"How about the truck stop?"

"But that's on the Interstate. That's fifteen miles."

"That's why I want to go there. I need to make a phone call, too."

"I don't understand."

His eyes stared straight ahead as he drove. His knuckles were white, like polished ivory, gripping the steering wheel.

In a gesture of some intimacy that managed to remain wholly natural, she used a fresh piece of tissue to dab away moisture from his forehead, too.

He said, "Something's all wrong."

"I know you work for the newspaper, Michael," she said in a weak attempt to be droll, "but that's not exactly news."

The dabbing job completed, she withdrew. The gesture of intimacy passed unacknowledged, he was so preoccupied. He said, "Whatever is happening is big and very strange. I don't have any idea in hell what it is, but if it's as big as I think it is, unless I've gone totally off the deep end, I'm not so sure we can trust the phone lines in Devil Creek."

"What if Paul leaves a message on our machine?"

He patted the metal dash. "This baby is supercharged. We can be anywhere in or around Devil Creek from the truck stop within ten minutes if we have to. You keep calling home as often as you want. They won't block your calls."

That got her attention. "They? What do you mean, *they?*" She studied him. "My only concern is for Paul and Jared."

"They're my only concern, too. But we do need to eat, right? And I've got to leave town long enough to make a call."

"Can you tell me who you're calling?"

"An old friend."

"And it has to do with Paul? Wait a minute. Did you just say that someone is tapping my home phone?"

"I'm suggesting that someone is tapping most of the

phone lines in Devil Creek."

"That's some suggestion. And why would you think that?"

"Be as skeptical as you want. I'd prefer to see you poke holes in my theory. But I think Chief Saunders is right. It is incredible that so many strange things should happen all at once in such an isolated little community. You and I each moved here because it *is* isolated. Maybe that isolation is the reason these things are happening."

"It's strange, no denying that," she said. "But it's a mighty big leap in logic to say that it's all being orchestrated. That is what you're saying, isn't it?"

"Let's let our logic leap around and see where it takes us."

"Okay."

"For the sake of argument, what if there is a connection? What if the disappearance of Paul and his friend has something to do with everything else that's been happening?"

"Mike, that's cruel. Paul and Jared are lost. That's all there is to it. Stop trying to scare me."

"You know I'm not trying to do that. Sometimes the truth is cruel and scary. What if it *is* all tied in somehow, and what if Paul in some way did manage to become involved? Isn't that chance, no matter how slim, worth a telephone call to probe beneath the surface?"

"But what you're suggesting is so farfetched. The Caldwell boy, the massacre, the serial murders, Mrs. Lufkin . . . to say that these things could all somehow be part of a *plan?* I don't know, Mike."

"Neither do I. But there are only two possibilities. Either the occurrences are *not* orchestrated, are completely coincidental and unrelated to each other. In that case we'll quickly learn nothing. *Or* . . . there *is* a thread. And if so, I just might be able to dig up a lead on what happened to Paul and Jared. That's how it breaks down."

"But who would stand to gain by orchestrating all of these terrible, vicious things?"

"That's something else I can't tell you . . . yet. I don't have a clue. I couldn't begin to tell you who could be behind something like this. But I want to find out if the quiver I'm picking up has any credence. So Robin, are you in or out? I can understand you wanting to be home, for Paul." He reduced their speed. "Tell me if that's what you want and I'll take you home."

"When I was home, I had to get out and do something."

"I was going to point that out."

"Why do you think someone has the telephones tapped?"

"Because something this big, involving the deaths of all those people . . . if there is a guiding hand, they'd want to keep a close tab on things. Monitoring communications would be a basic step. That's why, if this far-out scenario of mine *is* the case, and we're trying to get a handle on it, we cannot trust the phone lines in Devil Creek."

"Everything linked together," she said slowly. "I'm having trouble with that. Mike, I know how strongly you feel about Paul. I hope you're not overreacting."

"If that's the case, no one will be happier than me."

"You've got to admit, your scenario sounds paranoid."

"A placid little town, a beautiful setting, miles from nowhere, and all of a sudden, in one week's time, all bloody hell breaks loose." His frown deepened. "How many people dead? A town pulled apart at the seams by festering, debilitating fear and distrust. Does that just happen?"

"Sometimes."

"Robin, my gut tells me that things like this, *this* concentrated and intense, don't *just happen.* An old Indian who isn't around anymore thought there were evil spirits coming to Devil Creek. It's beginning to look like he was right."

"Now that is stretching it."

"That's what I thought. What I think now is that it's stretching it to think that this string of tragedies is nothing more than a freakish coincidence. My gut tells me that something here is way out of whack. Maybe I was a newspaperman for too long. Or a soldier for too long. But I put a lot of stock in what my gut tells me."

"I've noticed."

"And if there's one chance in a million that Paul's disappearance is in any way connected with what we're talking about, my way of doing something is to find a phone that isn't tapped."

"How do you know you can trust the phones at the truck stop?"

"If someone has the town under surveillance, they've been able to do so and avoid detection even with all the heavy attention Devil Creek's getting from the authorities and the media. That means they've got a small, concealed listening post." He tugged thoughtfully at an earlobe. "Whoever's monitoring the phones would want a contact inside of the community. Someone no one would suspect. Someone to monitor that human factor; the sort of things telephone taps don't reveal." He slapped the palm of one hand against the steering wheel. "I can't get over the vague impression of some kind of crazy experiment going on. I mean, in terms of a behavioral study, Devil Creek offers almost laboratory conditions because it is so isolated."

"This person on the inside," Robin said. "It would have to be someone that everyone in town knows and trusts; someone at the center of the social and business scene."

Lines of concentration appeared, etched into Mike's expression. "Most folks around town were born and raised here. I don't want to agree too much with the folks who suspect me, but they've got a point about one thing. It could be someone who's been around here just long enough to be trusted."

Her gaze moved to the night being probed by the headlight beams. "Mrs. Lufkin told me that you and Paul and I were the first people to move to town since Charlie Flagg moved here a year ago."

"Charlie's been acting stranger and stranger ever since this began."

She thought about that. "So has everyone else in town. No, it can't be Mr. Flagg. He came to Paul's and my rescue that first day when we got here, when we were being hassled by the Caldwells. Charlie Flagg is the one who sent me to Mrs. Lufkin to rent that house."

"And I work for Charlie. I know what you mean. I like the guy. Everyone does. Maybe that's my point. I'm not sure, either."

A light flickered deep within her subconscious, and she found herself saying, "There was one strange thing that I noticed when Mr. Flagg stopped to help Paul and me. I guess I just never gave it much thought, but now—"

For the briefest moment his eyes left the road, studying her. "Tell me. We're grabbing at straws here. Anything could help."

"It's just that, well, I haven't thought about it since it happened, but . . . Mr. Flagg was driving from the direction of town when he stopped to help. He got rid of Bobby and Tobe. And then, after he helped us, he made a U-turn and drove *back* into town. That's kind of strange, isn't it?"

Mike nodded. "Almost as if he was watching you from a

distance, maybe with binoculars from higher ground. When he saw what was happening, he made a point to drive out and assist you." He repeated the gesture of striking the steering wheel in frustration with an open palm. "I really don't get any of this."

"Mike, I just want Paul to be waiting at home when I call, to tell me that he got lost or he's sorry but he met some new friends and they were playing video games or watching some stupid movie and they forgot about the time. Maybe he met a girl. Maybe my son is falling in love."

"Robin, stop. Don't lose it now. We can't afford that. You know if that were the case, Paul would have called home before this. As for you and me, if we don't know who to trust except each other, that means we're going to have to depend on each other."

"You're right." She inhaled a deep breath, tried counting to ten but got impatient by five. "I'm sorry. So okay, we're giving serious consideration to an experiment and or a conspiracy. If people like that got their hands on a child after the things they've already done . . . Mike, are *we* going crazy? Can any of this really be happening? Maybe you and I are in the grip of the same distrust and fear and paranoia you were just talking about."

Up ahead was the turnoff for the rest area. Picnic tables, black and slick in the rain, were near rest rooms and a pay phone under a single amber light.

"Call home," he urged. "If Paul's not there, we'll get something to eat, I'll make my call and you can keep trying home from the truck stop,"

"I don't know if I can eat. My stomach's in knots." He brought the Jeep to a stop beside the pay phone.

"Robin, you should make yourself eat. You're running on adrenaline now, but tomorrow you'll want to be wide-awake for the search, and running on empty won't take you very far. If you can't get a night's sleep tonight, at least give your body some fuel to run on."

"I'll try." She stepped from the Jeep. "After I call home."

Chapter 35

At five-thirty, Ben Saunders met in a Town Hall conference room with his deputies and the local men and women who would lead the volunteer search and rescue teams. A light dusting of snow had fallen on the mountains during the night. The sky had cleared to the north with patches of red tinting the blue here and there amid gunmetal gray clouds. Sunlight pouring in through the conference room's eastern windows did nothing to alleviate the chill of the room, nor did the smell of coffee from a percolator.

Ben stood at the head of the conference table. A forest service map of this corner of the county was spread out before him. The others stood clustered around while he finished using a red felt-tipped pen to mark off and assign the search grids.

"Volunteers will be showing up at the base camp at 0600. We'll be there and set up by then. When the volunteers start arriving, divide them into the proper-size groups and aim at having everything operational by 0700."

That was about it. People finished their coffee, slipping into their coats and jackets.

Ben caught sight of Myra Kartchner in the doorway. He went over to her. "Myra, what is it? You look upset."

Myra Kartchner was the small-town version of a society matron: in her sixties, wide of girth, rosy-cheeked, given to wearing prim ankle-length skirts and white blouses. She had taken the dispatcher job after the last of her children left home for Brigham Young University in Provo. She and her husband owned acreage west of town. At the moment, her normally rosy cheeks were ashen and her eyes were sad.

"There's been another one."

"Oh, hell. Every available officer I've got is out there covering the streets. When we got past midnight, I thought we'd made it through a night. Well, who was it?"

"Connie Silva."

"Oh, no."

"A neighbor just reported it."

"I'll get Ray and we'll roll. Notify the proper agencies."

Myra's normally rosy cheeks were alabaster white. "I know the agency numbers by heart. But, Chief, there's something different this time."

"What?"

"There's a witness. A neighbor says she saw the killer leaving the Silva house."

"Do we have an ID?"

"The neighbor says yes, but she wouldn't tell me over the phone. She sounded extremely reluctant to say anything. You'd better hurry."

The witness was a jowly, fifty-eight year old woman named Mrs. Rogers. Her hair had been in curlers, her vastly overweight form wrapped into a threadbare terrycloth robe. She had a voice made raspy by years of whiskey and cigarettes. But her eyes had been sober, troubled, and unsure when they'd spoken minutes earlier.

Ben had taken one look at what the killer had done to Connie Silva, then had turned away and leaned against a tree to take in large gulps of oxygen. He hadn't puked, but he'd come close. Then he'd crossed the street to see Mrs. Rogers while Rinehart checked in on the neighbors Mrs. Rogers had left Connie Silva's children with after finding the body.

"When I heard the sound of breaking glass from the direction of Connie's house, I looked out my window," the neighbor lady told Ben. "At first I thought maybe I hadn't heard anything after all, but I watched the house for awhile anyway, and that's when I saw him. He left Connie's house. He passed under the street lamp. He was walking fast, but I saw him clear enough. There wasn't anybody stirring in the neighborhood except for me and him."

Ben hoped he was doing a professional job of concealing his impatience. "And who did you see, Mrs. Rogers?"

"There's just one thing more, Chief Saunders, and you'll understand when I tell you."

Ben did a marvelous job of not reaching out with both hands and throttling the old biddy. "Yes ma'am, and what would that be?"

"I want you to promise me you'll be the one to get him," said Mrs. Rogers emphatically. "I want you to promise me you won't turn this over to them outside police fellers with their fancy suits and them modern cars that you can't tell apart. Devil Creek has always looked after its own. That's the way it ought to be now."

"Yes ma'am, I promise. Now who did you see?"

Reverend Kroeger's wife had passed away ten years earlier. The Reverend maintained the home they'd lived in, a ranch-style house on a lot adjacent to the church grounds. Ben braked the police cruiser to a stop behind a late model New Yorker parked in the driveway. He and Rinehart stepped from their car. The yard was splashed with cool sunshine that burnished the well-trimmed lawn and shrubbery in shades of gold.

Ben touched the hood of the New Yorker. "Not even warm. This car hasn't been anywhere."

They crossed to the house. The frost had melted, leaving the grass with a spongy texture. No one was in sight. A few cars were parked in the church lot, most likely staff or some of the congregation showing up early to get things ready for Sunday services. A kid pedaled past on a bicycle, tossing newspapers into yards.

No one responded to Ben's knock on the front door. Rinehart's hand was on his holstered pistol, his eyes watching their surroundings. Ben scanned the house. The draperies were drawn. The doors were shut.

He said to Rinehart, "You take the back. I'll take the front. I've been here a couple of times. The Reverend's wife and my wife were friends. There's a hall that runs straight from the front to the back door. We'll be able to see each other."

"Funny," Roy said. His eyes were diamond-hard and unemotional, with all the humor of a marine caught in the middle of a killing field. "I've known Reverend Kroeger since I was a kid. My folks aren't church people, but I've seen him around town so often I guess I never gave him a thought. That old gal, Mrs. Rogers. You think we can trust her eyes?"

"I looked into her eyes," said Ben. "I believe her." He drew his service revolver. Rinehart did the same. "Be ready for anything, son."

"I am," said Roy. "You know what really pisses me off?"

"Tell me."

"It's going on 0600. The search and rescue is kicking off for those boys on the mountain. Instead of helping out over there like we should be, we have to deal with this scumbag."

"So let's make fast work of it."

Rinehart crossed the driveway, passed the New Yorker

and disappeared from sight around the side of the house.

Ben held his pistol down as unobtrusively as possible against his leg. He looked through the glass window set in the door, down the length of the hallway bisecting the Reverend's house. Seconds later he saw Roy, who returned his nod from beyond the glass of the rear door.

Ben rapped his knuckles sharply on the Reverend's front door again.

"Reverend! This is Chief Saunders. I have a deputy with me. We need to speak with you. Please open the door."

Then he heard for the first time the weird, ululating moaning sound that could have been mistaken for last night's wind that had rattled every window in town as it moaned down off the mountain. This was a human sound, a primal moaning, unidentifiable as either animal or human, coming from somewhere within this house but sounding distant, as if it came from the bottom of a pit far, far away.

Ben tried the door. It was unlocked. At the rear of the house, Roy also let himself in. They advanced cautiously and met in the living room. The interior of the house was sparsely furnished, meticulously maintained. There was an immaculate, antiseptic feel to the interior, as if no one really lived here. The whimpering sound was louder inside the house.

Ben followed his ears, which led him down a short corridor past a step-in closet opposite a room with a washer and dryer, beyond which were the stairs to the basement. The moaning—painful, plaintive, mournful—came from down there, at the bottom of those stairs.

Rinehart watched Ben for instructions. Ben silently motioned for Roy to follow. They started down, descending step by creaking step into the musty, close, dank smell down where a faint light burned. From somewhere beyond their range of vision, beyond the bottom of the stairs, the moaning became a weeping.

A desperate voice was crying, "I'm sorry . . . I'm so sorry . . ." over and over again as if in fervent prayer.

Ben reached the bottom step, setting foot on the dirt floor of the cellar, his pistol held in a two-handed Weaver grip, ready for target acquisition. Rinehart held a similar position several paces away, covering him. It was a typical cramped basement: a musty clutter of old boxes crammed with junk beneath a low ceiling.

Reverend Kroeger was kneeling near the furnace. He wore clerical black.

Rinehart gasped. "God in heaven."

"More like hell on earth," said Ben. He lowered his pistol.

Kroeger was beating his thin, willowy chest with his clasped hands, his features a bright purple, his entire body trembling, his eyes clamped shut. In a voice racked with pain, he resumed the anguished moaning that sounded to Ben, even in the confines of the basement, like that night wind. Then the moaning became words again.

"Forgive me, God. *It* made me do those things . . . the beast . . . Forgive me, Father. *Forgive me!*"

The Reverend then began mumbling the Lord's Prayer; breathy, gasping, anguished. The front of his trousers were soaked with fresh blood that glistened in the faint glow of the bare bulb suspended from the ceiling. Two things were on the dirt floor near him.

A steak knife, slick with blood.

And Reverend Kroeger's raggedly severed manhood, lying there like a small, strange dead animal.

Chapter 35

Paul awoke with a sob.

His first thought was that he hoped no one heard him. The jolt of pain that woke Paul also made him smack his head against the low rock overhang where he'd spent the night. He bit his tongue, not making another sound. He told himself that he must get his bearings. The whistling of the wind had been constant throughout the night, the wailing of the wind hurting his ears and making the cold worse, even beneath the rock formation that provided a windbreak.

He delicately parted his jacket and shirt. He didn't want to, but forced himself to look at his wound. The gash where the bullet had grazed his side was redder than it had been last night. The area around it was an ugly purple color. The blood was caked black. It hurt more than anything he could remember, even more than that time back in Chicago when he'd lost control of his bicycle and scraped his hands raw when he'd slid across the gravel. That pain had been bad, but this was much worse. He stretched his legs. At first, his calves ached from having been held in one position throughout the night. He scissored his legs back and forth as much as he could in the narrow space beneath the overhang, wiggling his toes in his sneakers. He fluttered his fingers. He hadn't gotten frostbite.

The call of wolves had carried to him while he'd tried to sleep, and twice something else had tugged him from restless sleep: a rumbling sound he knew from the movies. The rotors of a helicopter! A searchlight had swept within fifty feet of where he hid.

He had not left his hiding place.

The men who killed Jared and Mr. Flagg were after him. He'd seen movies where the bad guys worked for secret U.S. agencies that no one knew anything about, buried deep within the government. What if the men who had killed Mr. Flagg and Jared were with such an agency? If they and the man in the white smock were with the government, they wouldn't want any living witnesses to what they'd done. They'd call in helicopters to look for him, to find him and kill him. So he stayed where he was both times when helicopters had flown by. He had not gone out and waved to them like everything within him wanted to. His only hope was to try and make it down off the mountain on his own.

He should never have gone with Jared. He should have learned his lesson last week when Jared had taken him to spy on the Caldwell brothers and that girl. Yesterday, he should have gone hiking with Mike, like they'd planned.

When he was pretty sure there was no one around, Paul moved aside the branch he'd used to conceal his crawl-space. The pine needles, long dead leaves and even his own body scent gave the narrow little hiding space a snug feel that part of him did not want to leave. But he had to.

The daylight seemed brighter than usual. He was surprised to see snow, although there wasn't a lot. No more than a quarter inch in spots. Brown earth and rock and scattered pine needles shone through in places that had been shielded from the wind during the night, and what snow there was had a glaze that sparkled in the sunlight.

He crawled out from the crevice, the pain from the wound like a knife blade ripping into his side. Then he was standing. At first he weaved back and forth on his feet.

Crawling from the space had taken most of his strength. He almost fell, but managed to stay upright by bracing himself against a rock. With effort, he planted his feet firmly on the ground, maintaining his balance.

If he headed downhill, taking a southwesterly course, he'd reach the highway before too long, most likely at a point near town, maybe not far from the convenience store near his home. He'd call his mother from the first telephone he saw. She would be home, anxious, worried, waiting for him to call or show up. Mom was the only person he could trust. She would know what to do.

Paul left the rock formation, moving downhill across snow that in many places was little more than a shellac-like covering of frost. He left footprints in the snowy frost. There was nothing he could do about that. He wanted to run. He could not. It was difficult enough to walk, awkwardly moving sideways to keep his balance, carefully negotiating the terrain. Before he'd gone very far, the sun started to feel warm. Too warm. Hot. The sun was too hot. He could feel fresh blood, soaking the shirt and jacket around his wound. He paused on a level shelf of ground and removed his jacket. In the short time this took, the pain in his side flared, making him dizzy. The world swirled around his head. Take deep breaths, he told himself. He did, and the sharp coldness of the air snapped at his lungs and the dizzy spell went away.

He became aware then for the first time that he had already traveled below the snow line. *Loss of blood making me dizzy. Hurts so much. Can't stop. Don't stop. Keep moving. Have to keep moving. Have to! Have to get down off the mountain. Have to get home.* He plodded on, one foot in front of the other. Every step brought more pain. His sneakers were soaking wet from trudging through the snow. Had he guessed wrong? Taken the wrong direction? He was going to die up here, and the wild animals would feast on his body.

Then Paul saw the house.

A cabin in the middle of a clearing, no more than one hundred feet away. Telephone wires stretched from it to a pole, and a line of telephone poles continued beyond the cabin, disappearing from sight down the side of the mountain. There were no cars in sight. No smoke rose from the chimney on this frigid morning. The windows of the cabin, reflecting sunlight, looked from this distance like shining squares of gold.

Everything suddenly began to merge together for Paul—the sun, the bright blue sky, the emerald green of the forest—tilting around his head faster and faster, becoming a blur of color, slowing his forward movement.

Don't stop, his mind screamed. *Can't stop. Stop and you're dead, like Jared and Mr. Flagg.*

He pushed on, blindly taking one stumbling step after another. He had to make it. Had to call Mom. Had to survive. The sky began growing dark, but there were no clouds. He was going to pass out. If that happened, he knew he would die.

Chapter 36

There were two pay phones side-by-side at the entrance to the truck stop restaurant. While Robin called home, Mike used his credit card and dialed a number from memory.

Gil Gilman had been Mike's CIA control officer in Vietnam. They'd met when they were both assigned to a Special Forces base camp in the Central Highlands. Mike's Long Range Reconnaissance patrol had staged regular insertions deep into enemy territory, and the men's friendship began the time Gilman accompanied Mike's team on one such mission. This was not something a lot of Agency men chose to do. Most CIA control officers tended to resent the military they depended on for the data that was monitored by Saigon before being forwarded to Washington. This resentment stemmed mainly from the fact that the information coming from the recon patrols in the field nearly always fell short of what Washington expected to hear. Most of the CIA guys were either eager beavers just starting their careers or cynical old-timers on their way out. Either way, they viewed their assignment in country as banishment to the armpit of existence, and cared only about getting out, not unlike a whole lot of the GI's they handed out missions to.

But Gilman was different, as his accompanying Mike's unit into the bush demonstrated on more than one mission; into the mud and the blood, the muck of a dirty war in a jungle of blinding green during the day or pitch black at night, where the smells of jungle rot and death and fear permeated; where the flash of weapons fire at anytime from anywhere could mean you or one of your guys lying there, screaming for a medic. That's what it was like out there. But Gil Gilman honestly gave a damn about more than the success or failure of a mission. He *cared* about the men he sent out to risk their lives. Mike and Gil had taken enemy fire together. Combat forges strong bonds between people like nothing else, and theirs was a friendship that had outlasted that war and withstood the quarter century since.

Gil had been a rambler and a wanderer well before Nam, and so had looked up his buddy in Denver after rotating back to the States a few months after Mike, whereupon the two had resumed their friendship as if it had never been interrupted. When he left Denver, Gil had been vague, too vague, about why he was moving on and what he'd be doing for a living. They were tight enough for Mike not to push it, but he knew somehow, without a doubt, that Gil was going back to work for the Central Intelligence Agency. Occasional postcards from far-off, usually Third World countries, unsigned but with private jokes that only Mike would get referring to some past misadventure, confirmed the suspicion.

And of course, there had been Mike's "recruitment" as an on-site "civilian backup" for his old friend on those occasions in Honduras, Peru and Cuba.

Gil maintained a mail drop in a small town in East Texas and a telephone number that he said only a handful of people knew. He told Mike that the number would get a call through to him wherever he happened to be. Judging from his own three isolated experiences in his friend's world, and from the postmarks and the kinds of things that went on in those places, Mike was willing to bet that Gil's work was every bit as dirty as the war they'd fought together out of Base Camp 112 all those years ago in Vietnam. They hadn't discussed Gil's work the handful of times they'd gotten together in the States for fishing trips over the years. He and Gil had last seen each other at Elephant Butte Lake, south of Albuquerque, four months after Carol was laid to rest. Gil had, as always, phoned out of the blue. At first, Mike hadn't wanted to go on a fishing trip. He hadn't wanted to live, much less go fishing. Yet he now looked back on that trip as the turning point in his being able to accept and deal with his loss. Surrounded by the rugged, spacious, arid beauty of the Southwestern landscape, sitting in a rowboat on the tranquil surface of a blue green lake, he regained the strength to finally accept his loss, to dig down deep and dredge up the inner strength to face a future without Carol. It was during that fishing trip that Gil had read Mike's sketch for a novel. It was Gil who had connected Mike with the literary agent in New York who had gotten him the advance on his book.

Gilman answered on the first ring. That is, he picked up his receiver. He said nothing, waiting for the caller to speak.

Mike said, "It's me."

"Well hey, buddy. What a surprise."

Gil didn't sound surprised. He sounded his usual cool, affable self. They exchanged a minimal amount of banter, during which Gil mentioned that it was late afternoon where he was, which placed him somewhere on the opposite side of the world. The call had gone through effortlessly. Gil's voice was as clear as if he were standing beside Mike.

Mike briefed him on the extraordinary occurrences taking place in Devil Creek, New Mexico.

As he spoke, Mike watched Robin redial her home number. Worry lines at the corners of her eyes and mouth told him that there were no messages on her voice mail. No Paul.

Mike said to Gil, "I'm behind enemy lines, buddy. I don't know who to trust except for the woman standing here next to me, and her son. He's the one who's spent the night on the mountain."

Gil smiled across the connection. "Sounds like hell's popping in that little burg. And I thought they played rough over here where I am. Okay. So you think this Charlie Flagg is tied into something, is that it?"

"It's a real long shot," Mike said, "but it's the only angle I've got. I'm playing my gut on this one."

"Your hunches were always on target in Nam and in Denver, not to mention when it comes to finding where the fishies are biting. So what do you need?"

"I need someone who's plugged in. That's you."

"I'm plugged in, huh?"

"You and me talking to each other, with you wherever the hell you are, is proof enough of that."

"Most of the world doesn't even know about this little country I'm in," Gil said, "and I can't help thinking the world's better off for that. But yeah, okay. I'm plugged in. You want background on Charlie Flagg?"

"Affirmative. Gil, I'm sorry, but I just can't go to anyone else, and I need it as fast as you can get it to me."

Another smile crackled across the connection. "Hell, I don't even have to leave this handy dandy little laptop I'm toting. Okay. I'll background Flagg through my channels which, if I may say so, are considerable. I'll backtrack the guy and cross-reference anyone or anything that's even a little bit out of sync."

"There, uh, is one other thing," said Mike. He recalled the night of the barbecue at his place, when Robin had told him about the strange phone calls from her ex-husband. It had been haunting the back of his mind ever since. "As long as we're grasping at straws, there's a guy in Chicago I want you to check out. He's just gotten a divorce. The wife is living here in Devil Creek. Her name is Robin Curtis. I regret to admit I don't know if she kept his name for her son, or if it's her family name."

"You've given me enough. I can track him down. What do you want to know?"

"He made some harrassing phone calls to his ex-wife about a week ago. I want to know where he was when he made those calls, and where he is now. Can do?"

"What do you think?"

"Hotshot," said Mike with a laugh. "How's about I grab a bite with the lady and give you a call-back?"

"That'll work. I should have it before then, but I can wait. Excuse me while I get to work."

Gilman broke the connection.

Chapter 37

They chose a booth in the rear.

The well-lit and airy truck stop restaurant was doing a fair business considering the early hour. Around them was the murmur of conversation, the clink of silverware from other tables, and low-volume country music twanging from a jukebox in the corner.

A toothy waitress brought them glasses of water and menus, then moved on and it was during this time, after they had studied and closed the menus, but before the waitress returned, that Robin realized that she and Mike were holding hands—both hands!—across the table. Robin was mildly surprised by two things. One, that she and this man across from her were holding hands so naturally that it had taken her a few moments to realize this and, two, that she had no overwhelming desire to withdraw her hands from his.

The need to be with someone this night had not gone away, but grown. If she had been left to herself to worry about Paul, Robin knew she would have been a stark raving basket case by now. It was his presence that held her together, even if she felt like it with all the strength of Scotch tape against a hurricane. But she knew there was more to it than just Mike's presence. There was that easy, comfortable camaraderie when they were together, even in this time of crisis. His nature was peaceful, yet supremely competent. And he had already gone more than the distance expected from a neighbor, friend, or even a lover, insisting on being at her side as he had, just to help her. She thought of how

Paul and Mike had taken a liking to each other from the first. She'd tried to fight it, but she felt the same. Maybe she was still fighting it. *And if so,* she reminded herself, *perhaps with good reason.*

"Mike, are we falling in love?"

He fixated on his water glass, lifting and setting it down repeatedly to leave a design of wet circles on the Formica. "For your part, I think you have to answer that one."

"And what about your part?"

He lifted his eyes to hers. "What makes you think I haven't already fallen in love with you? Robin, I honestly never thought it would happen again. I loved Carol so much and I lived with that mindset ever since. And here you come along, competent, a good mother, attractive as all get out. And here's the best part, you're interested in *me*. I never had a chance."

"You can add fragile to that list of adjectives, Mike, because right now that's how I feel. Waiting to find out what's happened to Paul, I feel like a wineglass on a window ledge, and all it needs is a gust of wind to tip over and shatter into a million pieces. I can't trust my heart at a time like this."

He gave her hands a squeeze. "You're the one who brought it up. We agreed to be a couple for the night, remember? That was as far as your commitment went."

The trace of what could have been a smile touched her lips. "Thanks, Mike." And then more words poured forth from her before she could stop herself. "Oh God, I feel so guilty about what's happened. My son is my responsibility, and he's *missing!*" And she realized that tears were rolling down both of her cheeks. She reached for a napkin and gave her nose a healthy blow just as the waitress reappeared.

Mike ordered a ham and cheese omelet with hash browns and coffee. Robin declined to order at first, then gave in to his gentle prodding and ordered a salad. She excused herself and took her purse to the women's rest room to freshen up. She settled for reestablishing a semblance of being presentable, then rejoined Mike at their table.

He said, "You must know rationally that none of this can possibly be construed as being your fault."

"Thanks, Mike. But being a mother isn't always a rational condition. We have to find Paul."

"And we will."

Their food arrived, and they barely spoke during the meal as if by silent mutual agreement. Robin pecked at her lettuce, tomato, and cucumber listlessly. Twice, she left the table without a word, looking more wound up each time.

Mike watched through the window as she went to a pay phone and dialed, and each time she returned without saying anything, to resume pecking at her salad. Around them, the world was stretching, slowly coming to life. Bleary-eyed truckers rubbed shoulders with fresh-faced travelers getting an early start after a night at the Best Western next door.

Mike paid their tab at the register and they left the restaurant, each returning to a pay phone. Mike dialed Gilman.

Again, Gil answered on the first ring. Again, he said nothing.

"Scrambler on?" Mike asked.

"Always." The response was cool, affable, across the connection from somewhere far, far away. "I've gotta say, pal, you do retain the knack I remember so well for getting yourself eyeball-deep in very peculiar stuff."

"What did you find?"

"Enough to tell you that you are not, repeat *not*, paranoid. You, compadre, are an acute observer of the passing scene. It kept you alive in Nam, it made you a good reporter and, buddy, it's got you wired into one hell of a live one this time around."

Robin had dialed her number again. She hung up and began pacing, staring at the ground. A grossly overweight trucker waddled over to use the phone she'd given up. Mike said, "Okay, Gil, let's hear it."

"Patience," Gil said. "Let me tell it my way. I accessed Charlie Flagg's telephone records after he moved to Devil Creek. One number called matched a name that gave me that out-of-sync handle we were looking for. Have you ever heard the name Bittman? Dr. Horace Bittman?"

"Negative. Should I have?"

"Not if a certain government agency operating out of Langley, Virginia has anything to say about it."

"CIA?"

"Originally it went deeper than that. So deep that no one inside the Agency even knew about it until it was too late."

"Too late for what?"

"Too late for three hundred and forty people who offed themselves after Dr. Horace Bittman messed with their minds under a fully sanctioned, highly-classified experiment that our government will never, ever admit took place."

Mike was stunned. "Three hundred and forty people?"

"Don't be incredulous. You must've read about the CIA pumping LSD into human guinea pigs plucked from the Army back in the '60s. There was a ton of lawsuits over that. Some of those guys were dosed so heavy on acid, they were screwed up forever. The U.S. government settled on it, but experiments like those are still going on. You remember Jonestown, don't you, all those people going down there to join a religious commune and it ended up a mass suicide with hundreds dead. There were those who thought that was a large-scale CIA mind-drug experiment gone awry. They were wrong, but only about Jonestown, not about experiments being conducted under government sanction, dating back, as I say, to the '60s. That's where Bittman comes in. He was in charge of one such, uh, *experiment*. Of course, the agency conducting the experiment never existed."

"What do we know about them?"

A pause. Gilman said, "Uh, may I offer you some advice at this juncture, old buddy? Do not push in that direction. Don't even try."

Mike lowered his voice so the truck driver on the phone next to him could not possibly overhear. "Tell me about Bittman and three hundred and forty dead people. How does that tie in with what's happening here?"

"Bittman was a Harvard psychologist. His key interest was mind-altering drugs. Sort of a Timothy Leary-type, only dangerous nuts instead of just goofy. Back in the day, Bittman supervised LSD experiments on GI's. His specialty was using drugs to control members of an isolated social group, to alter their behavior destructively in order to study the ripple effect such altered actions had on the rest of the group."

"And these three hundred and forty dead folks?"

"This agency that never existed recruited and sanctioned Dr. Bittman a few years ago to conduct an experiment on some New Age cult flakes who were holed up down in the Brazilian rain forest. One day the cult's guru decided to instruct all of his followers to off themselves and that is what every last one of the idiots proceeded to do. Three hundred and forty men, women, and a handful of kids."

"Jesus."

"Enough to make Jesus weep. It was easy enough to shut down the Brazilian end. The cult had previously instructed its members to sever all social and family ties before going south. Of course that was the CIA covering its butt. There was a scattering of missing persons reports here and there in the States, but no one ever drew the threads together and, sure as hell, no one ever tied it to the U.S. government. The agency that never existed was dissolved. Heads rolled. But that was hushed up too. I'm confident, by the way, that Bittman's authorization did not come from the CIA or anywhere near White House level. The agency conducting the experiment was a maverick outfit deep down."

"So what happened to Bittman?"

"He was paid off with a humongous sum of the taxpayers' money and told to go far, far away and never come back."

"Simple as that?"

"More or less. Hell, what were they supposed to do with him? I mean, from their point of view, what would you do? Admit that tax dollars funded a loopy mind control experiment that went haywire and left three hundred and forty people as wormbait?"

"I'm amazed they were able to contain something that big."

"Bittman cooperated totally, since it was his bright idea in the first place to 'experiment' on cult members without the cult knowing about it. He messed with their leader's head, used some sort of radical mind drug that taps through normal intellectual and moral restraints. The leader snapped, ordered everyone to kill themselves, and it was over. Bittman was supposed to have had the leader under control. If the thing had surfaced, Bittman would have been drawn and quartered in public and no doubt would have taken the administration down with him."

The trucker at the next phone completed his call, and was immediately replaced by Robin again dialing her number.

Mike was trying with difficulty to absorb the overload of information he was hearing. "You said they paid Bittman off. They kept track of him, right?"

"They tried to. The earth seems to have opened up and swallowed the good doctor shortly after the deal was cut and the check cleared; enough money for Bittman to live several lifetimes in splendor. You could say Dr. Bittman retired rich. Thing is, he didn't retire. I accessed central CIA computers and made a search. Here's what I came up with. About ten months ago, Bittman showed up in El Paso trying to recruit professional mercenaries based there, to provide security for what he called an 'experiment' at an undisclosed location. Claimed he was sanctioned by a secret government agency. The FBI has the merc community down there pretty well wired. They put Bittman under surveillance."

"Put him under surveillance? Why didn't they jump him?"

"They intended to terminate. But because of the sensitive nature of those dead folks down in Brazil, the CIA stepped in and pulled rank with a reason for the FBI to stall. That provided a window for Bittman to pull another vanishing act before the Agency hit team arrived. Bittman appears to be hung up on making his name in science. Sees himself as a Nobel contender. Claims his work can benefit mankind, though I suspect those in Brazil might disagree if they could speak. The deal in El Paso suggests that he hasn't gotten any less insane. He is considered extremely dangerous."

At the next phone, Robin emitted a squeal. She stood clutching the receiver with both hands. Her eyes, wide with excitement, connected with Mike's. She was nodding vigorously as she listened to the receiver.

Mike said, "Look, Gil, things are breaking fast. I've got to run. So the important thing is that Charlie Flagg called Bittman."

"More than once, to the number Bittman had under an assumed name before the FBI tumbled to him in El Paso."

"Any idea on how they first connected?"

"Your guess is as good as mine. Before he moved to Devil Creek, Flagg and his wife owned a bed-and-breakfast in the Ozarks. The marriage fell apart after their last kid left for college. Midlife stuff. Charlie moved to Devil Creek and bought that weekly paper for a song from an old-timer who'd been trying to sell out for a year. A few months later the calls to Bittman show up on his bill."

"Care to interpret?"

"I'd say Bittman or one of his people made the initial contact with Flagg in Devil Creek. Flagg didn't come in with a lot of money. He had to take a loan to buy the paper. He'd fit the profile Bittman was looking for. The Doc would want someone on the inside. A local guy running a newspaper would be ideal. They gave Flagg time to think it over and after he did, he called Bittman in El Paso to sign on."

Next to Mike, Robin hung up her telephone and rapidly fumbled another coin into the slot and redialed. He found his attention sidetracked. *Paul must have left a message. She was calling back to listen again.*

He said, "Gil, I've got to go. Bottom line me."

"Okay, here it is. For my money, Bittman is your man. And if he is looming around there, he's got himself some professional muscle for back up, sure as hell. We're talking paramilitary. So watch your ass."

Robin stood as she had before, clutching the receiver with both hands, clasping it tightly to her ear, concentrating on every word and nuance she heard.

"Bittman also happens to be an electronics genius. He's most likely got the town wired if it's small enough. He's found a spot on high ground for a listening post where no one is likely to find him."

"I'm going to find him. What about that ex-husband?"

"Name is Jeff Lovechio. Businessman, successful but shady, says here. Plenty of reports to the Better Business Bureau but nothing that's landed him in court so far. I hacked into his phone records. An eight-year-old could have done it, Mikey."

"So next time I'll get an eight-year-old. Right now, Gil, I'm talking to you."

"All right. I'll dispense with the levity," said Gilman. "He placed those calls to Robin Curtis from his business phone in Chicago. Not the brightest bulb on the chandelier. Likes the ladies and the white go-powder too much is the scuttlebutt, but that's just preliminary. You want more?"

"What I want is to put some hurt on this guy," said Mike in a chilly voice. "I don't like what he did to a woman I care about, scaring her with those calls. And I want to keep him distracted."

"Distracted from what?" Gil's frown was as audible across the connection as his smile had been.

"I'm not sure," said Mike, "but I'd consider it a favor."

Gilman sighed. "You don't have to remind me. When I needed you, you were there. Consider it done, Mike. I can cause this boy Jeff a world of pain and he'll never know where it came from. He'll think the gods of slicksterism have all turned against him to tear him down. That what you want?"

Mike thought of the fright those calls had instilled in Robin. "That should do," he said.

"I'll start by taking his credit off at the knees. Our boy Jeff is about to enter the Valley of Feces big time."

"Thanks, Gil. I owe you."

This time it was Mike who disconnected. Robin terminated her connection by depressing the telephone's bar, then handed her receiver to Mike.

"It's Paul! We have to find him. Listen."

She fed in another coin and punched the number, watching him with keen, excited eyes.

He listened. It didn't sound like Paul at first, and it wasn't just the answering machine recording across the line that altered the boy's voice. There was desperation and pain, and weariness bordering on physical and emotional collapse.

"Mom, it's me. Are you home?" The boy's words tumbled in a torrent. *"Mom, something terrible happened. Jared . . . he's dead, Mom. So is Mr. Flagg. They were killed by men who looked like soldiers. They . . . shot me. Don't worry! It hurts, but it's not serious. A bullet grazed me and burned my side, is all. I'm okay. I spent the night on the mountain. Mom, I'm calling from a cabin somewhere near town. I can see power lines on the edge of the property. I can see down to that landing strip at the edge of town. But I don't know exactly where I am. There's a driveway that goes down to a dirt road, but there's no name on the house and no number on the telephone. I don't know where I am. Mom, when you hear this—No, wait. Wait! I see them. The men from last night. They've seen the cabin. They're coming this way. I've got to go, Mom. I'm going to hide. I love you! I'm sorry I made you worry."*

The connection clicked, replaced by the humming of the dial tone. Mike replaced the receiver.

Robin's eyes gleamed. She was out of breath. "What should we do?"

"We'd better contact Chief Saunders. He'll know where Paul was calling from."

"No," she said. "We can't go to the police, not if what you think is true about everything being connected."

"It's true. A crazy scientist named Horace Bittman is using Devil Creek for a mind control experiment."

"Crazy scientist? Mind control experiment?"

"I know it sounds nuts. I'll fill you in on the way back to town." He clasped his fingers through hers. Hand in hand, they hurried toward the Jeep. The parking lot of the restaurant was nearly full. The new day had begun.

"About Saunders," said Mike. "I'd like to think we could trust the Chief of Police."

"Michael, I don't think we should trust anyone but each other. You didn't think we could trust Charlie Flagg, and now he's dead. Dead." Her eyes caught his, flickering with uncertainty. "I don't understand any of this."

"Paul and Jared somehow stumbled onto Charlie getting his payoff for selling out the town."

"Aren't we putting a lot of faith in what your friend told you?"

"It's faith well-placed. If you believe anything, believe that."

She made an impatient flutter gesture with both hands. "All right all right all right! I've told you how I feel about you. Mike, I do trust you and I'll trust your mysterioso telephone friend. But I won't trust anyone else."

"Robin, if we don't go to the authorities, we're going to

need someone else to help us find the cabin Paul was calling from."

She considered this as they boarded the Jeep. The morning smelled clean and fresh after the nighttime rain. Sunlight made the wet slickness of the parking lot asphalt shine like polished glass.

She said, "I guess that means we do need to bring one more person into the circle, doesn't it?"

"That's what it means. We need someone who knows the area, fast."

"Is there someone we can trust?"

Mike thought of Joe Youngfeather. "There is. But it may not be easy to get him to help us."

Robin gave him the kind of icy glare he hadn't seen since his last Clint Eastwood movie.

"I'll make it easy. My child is on that mountain. He's been shot." Her voice trembled. "And with everything that's happened to him, that tough little guy of mine apologizes for making me worry. Let's go."

Chapter 38

As soon as Paul hung up the telephone, which was next to a window, he drew away from the window, hoping that the cabin's windows continued to reflect the sunlight as they had when he'd approached the cabin. If that was the case, the advancing men would not have seen him.

Upon finding no one home, the first thing he'd done was to break a windowpane at the side of the cabin. He'd reached in, unlatched the window and raised it, then climbed inside. It was painful, causing him to groan aloud. The cabin was paneled in pine, with throw rugs and comfy-looking furniture and a musty, unused feel. He'd found the bathroom and looked inside the medicine cabinet, hoping to find antiseptic or at least aspirin. The shelves were bare. He'd returned to the living room and the telephone. Picking up the phone, he'd given a nervous, happy laugh when he heard the dial tone. He dialed, heard his home phone ringing, and the connection was made. His heart had dropped when he heard the message his mother had left on their answering machine: *"Paul, honey, I'm out trying to find you. I'll be checking this machine every twenty minutes. Tell me where you are, honey, so Mike and I can come and get you. I love you, Paul."* She hardly sounded like herself. She spoke fast. She sounded terrible. When he heard the beep, Paul had left his message on the answering machine. It was the first time he'd spoken since he'd been shot and each word increased the pain in his side. Then he forgot about the pain and everything else when he saw the four men emerging from the trees into the clearing.

The three who wore camouflage fatigues were advancing on the cabin. The fourth was the wiry thin man wearing glasses who had worn a doctor's white smock yesterday at the van. This morning he wore a fore-and-aft billed cloth cap that made him look like Sherlock Holmes. He remained stationary, observing. The others—two with rifles, the blond-haired man gripping a pistol—were advancing fast.

Paul exited the living room through a curved archway, searching desperately, frantically, for a place to hide. Would they keep on going? Would they pass the cabin? The snow had melted around the cabin, so he hadn't left any tracks leading directly to it. But that was nothing but wishful thinking, he knew. Naturally they'd search the cabin. He raced to the back door and glanced out. A sun deck overlooked the gravel parking area and driveway. The ground beyond dropped away, a steep, rocky incline. But he would never make it that far, much less to the driveway. They'd see him for sure. He had to hide here, somewhere inside the cabin.

A clothes closet between the living room and the kitchen held nothing more than a pair of ancient, battered cowboy boots tossed into the corner. No place to hide there. Next was the upstairs bedroom. He painfully hobbled as fast as he could up the stairs. There was a bed and a dresser and pegs on the walls for hanging clothes. He started hobbling back down the stairs. He would try to make it to the back door. He would hide beneath the sun deck. Maybe they wouldn't look there.

As his foot touched the bottom stair, he heard the front door open. He stopped where he was, hunching at the foot of the short flight of narrow stairs. Holding his breath, listening.

They hadn't forced the door. Men like these used passkeys to open any lock. They entered the cabin. Another man stepped onto the sun deck. Of course. They had seen the broken window. But they couldn't be absolutely certain that he was still in here. If he could find someplace to hide inside, they'd continue on down the mountain in search of him. The back door opened and the man from the sun deck came inside.

There was no more time. Within seconds, they would meet in the center of the cabin, at the bottom of these stairs where he now crouched.

He retraced his way back upstairs. He pressed himself flat against the bare floorboards beneath the bed. The bedspread draped over the sides of the king size bed, nearly touched the floor. The world under the bed was stuffy with a thick layer of dust and dust balls. His sinuses ached. He wanted to sneeze. Paul pinched his nose, breathing through his mouth. The pain of the wound had returned with a vengeance. The world underneath the bed began to waver and grow dim.

Footfalls ascended the stairs. Came to a stop in the bedroom doorway. Floorboards creaked, every sound magnified beneath the bed. Boots walked across the floor, toward the bed, halting next to it the toes of the boots inches from his face. Then the lower part of the bedspread was suddenly whipped back and he was face to face with one of the men, one of those armed with a rifle. The man was kneeling down to look under the bed, the bedspread held in one hand, the rifle gripped in the other.

Paul opened his mouth to scream because he knew he was going to die.

The man quietly extended a black gloved hand, his index finger touching Paul's lips before he could make a sound. The moment held, suspended for what seemed like an eternity. Then the gloved finger left Paul's lips. The man shook his head to indicate that Paul should not make any sound.

Puzzled, Paul nodded.

The man let the bedspread drop back into place. The dust and the stuffy closeness reclaimed the universe beneath the bed.

Chapter 39

The Jeep flew along the straight stretches of the highway, becoming airborne during those occasional, brief moments when Mike would take a dip in the road without slowing. Even with the seat belt securing her, the gravitational pull as Mike took the curves at high speed compelled Robin to grip the roll bar with one hand and the dashboard with her other. She had confidence in his driving abilities. He handled the road and the speed seemingly without effort. They encountered little traffic.

As he drove, Mike told her in detail what he'd learned from his friend over the telephone. He sounded like some friend, this man Mike did not name or identify; another piece to the enigma of the guy. And what Mike told her was incredible. But she believed it. She believed every unbelievable bit of it about a mad scientist using Devil Creek for a mind control experiment.

"They dosed selected people in the community without those people knowing it," Mike said. "Highly-visible members of the community. Important in one way or another. Then Bittman observed how the drugged ones reacted, and the ripple effect of their actions on the collective psyche of the community. That's what his 'study' is all about. There are holes to fill in, for sure, but I'll bet that whatever drug they used won't show up in an autopsy; a drug that affects everyone differently, depending on what's buried deep inside their psyche."

She nodded, picking up the thread of thought as she'd agreed to. "That's why Bobby Caldwell went berserk and killed those people and himself? That's what turned someone else into a serial killer?"

"That's what I think. And I don't believe in coincidence. I think Mrs. Lufkin was dosed with the drug, too."

"My God."

"Remember how she was feeling under the weather at the school meeting? What we saw was the drug she'd been administered first beginning to take effect. After she left us, she went home and committed suicide."

Robin said again, "My God. If only we'd known. If only I'd insisted on going home with her, like I offered to, maybe . . ." She heard the despair in her voice, and let the sentence taper off.

"Robin, we have to deal with what is happening," he said in a steady voice, "not with what could have happened."

"I know." She forced her mind to push on. They had to push on. They could not dwell on "what if's." They must focus on the *un*answered questions. On strategy. She said, "The serial killer. Whoever it is, wouldn't people around him notice that something was wrong, the way we did with Mrs. Lufkin?"

"Maybe, maybe not. Assume the drug brings to the surface whatever dark impulses each one of us carry buried in our subconscious. The drug causes people to act on those impulses. With Bobby Caldwell it was sheer naked aggressive violence and self-destruction. It awakened Mrs. Lufkin's grief over the loss of her family, a grief that never did heal over the years. Now, the serial killer . . . those impulses are rooted so deeply within him that, even with the drug, he managed to keep it under wraps from those around him. I'm making this up as I go along, by the way. How does it sound so far?"

"The jury is still out," said Robin. "How could such a

drug be administered?”

“Bittman has men working for him, professionally trained soldiers who sell themselves to the highest bidder. Trained commandos who could move around freely and easily under cover of darkness. These men are trained for stealth. A town like Devil Creek would be nothing for them. They could slip into a person’s house while the person slept. Something colorless, odorless, tasteless, added to the morning orange juice. In Bobby’s case, make that his morning beer. Simple, and the drug has been administered.”

She said, “That night when I thought I saw someone outside my window—”

“Remember Charlie driving out from the direction of town to help you and Paul, and then doing his U-turn and driving back into town? I think they had us both under surveillance because we were newcomers and therefore an unknown element in Bittman’s little experiment, worth keeping an eye on. We weren’t ‘pure’ locals. That’s probably why they didn’t dose us. That prowler you saw could damn well have been one of Bittman’s guys, or maybe Charlie himself, keeping tabs on us.”

“And these are the men who are after my son.” She spoke through clenched teeth.

He didn’t take his eyes from the road, but he grunted an approving sound. “You’re pissed off. Good. That’s the best motivation there is. Stay mad.”

“Don’t you worry about that. Can’t we go any faster?”

Mike white-knuckled them around another curve. “I’m afraid this is it.”

“Fair enough. And, uh, there is one other thing, Mike.”

“What’s that, Robin?”

“I want to fall in love with you too.”

He glanced at her. "Want to?" he asked.

Robin was staring straight ahead, steadying herself against the swaying of the speeding Jeep and saying nothing. Mike returned his attention to the road ahead. That line of conversation was done for now.

Minutes later, they raced across the bridge that spanned the dry creek bed. Then Mike was slowing a little as they tracked onto a dirt road that was hardly more than a two-wheel, rutted path running parallel to a creek bed. The Jeep stormed on, jarring, bouncing as the washboard road climbed and dipped, leading them farther and farther from the highway, deeper and deeper into a seeming nowhere land of scrub brush. The trail topped a rise, dropped back down, and she saw a cleared parcel of land adjacent to the dry creek bed, the adobe hut with a very old pickup truck parked in front of it.

Sunlight shone off the chrome of a Harley Davidson motorcycle next to the truck. A man, clad completely in black, stood securing a bedroll and a backpack to the rear of the motorcycle. As Mike braked to a stop, the man turned toward them. He was a Native American. Lean-muscled, he wore a knife in a sheath at mid-chest. His black hair was worn in long braids. He left the motorcycle, striding forward with no sign of greeting, his face a stern mask, his eyes dark and impassive.

"Better wait here," Mike suggested to Robin.

"Like hell," she said.

She left the Jeep with him, to stand at his side.

The man in black did not acknowledge her. He walked straight up to Mike. They stood there facing each other, toe-to-toe.

The man in black said, "You're mighty stupid, mister."

"I don't have time for macho bullshit, Joe," Mike said.

"This is Robin Curtis. Robin, Joe Youngfeather."

Robin said, "Joe, Mike says you're the only person in town who can help us."

"Your friend is wrong." Youngfeather didn't break eye contact with Mike. "The last time your friend was out here, I thought we came to an understanding that he wasn't coming back again, ever, or it'd be his last time."

Robin reached out. She gripped Youngfeather by the arm, catching him by surprise and with enough strength to force him to face her.

"Dammit, mister, *I'm* talking to *you*."

He tugged the arm free. He indicated the Harley. "Everything I own is on that hog over there, except for my butt. And that's where my butt is going to be in one more minute: on that bike, hitting the road. Sorry, lady. I don't know what you came here for, but there's nothing I can do for you."

"You listen to me, damn you." She indicated the mountains in the near distance. "My son is somewhere up there. He's been shot. There are evil men who want to kill him. He's only twelve years old. You can help us save his life."

Youngfeather said to Mike, "What the hell is she talking about?"

"There's no time, Joe," Mike said briskly. "Believe her. Her boy called home and left a message on the answering machine. He's holed up in a cabin. We need you to help us pinpoint his whereabouts."

"Why don't you call the cops?"

"Because all of the weird things that have been happening in Devil Creek are connected, and we don't know who to trust."

Joe said softly, more to himself than to them, "Gray Wolf."

Mike nodded. "Right. You told me you believed in the spirit world."

"Gray Wolf dwells there now."

"The evil he fought against has manifested itself, and it's about to take the life of this woman's son. I never met your grandfather. But from what you've said about him, I think he'd want you to help us."

"I don't need you to tell me what Gray Wolf would want. He told me already, last night in a dream."

Robin's impatience bristled to the surface. "We can't afford to stand here talking. We came to you because you're an outsider in the community. We don't know who to trust in the community."

For some reason, that seemed to be all it took to win Joe's cooperation.

"You're right," he told Mike. "In my vision, Gray Wolf told me that I would carry on his fight. I told myself that it was just a dream."

Mike said, "The boy wasn't sure where the cabin is exactly that he was calling from. He said power lines ran along the property, heading down the side of the mountain. He said he could see the town and the landing strip."

"Could be two or three places."

"These two or three places," Robin said. "You mean in one area?"

"Right. Most likely one of the hunting cabins up on Missionary Ridge." Joe surveyed the mountain range. "Yeah, it would be one of three places. I know that country. Been hunting up there." He turned eyes, like laser beams, on Robin. "What the hell's this about men wanting to kill your son?"

"We'll fill you in," Mike said, "if you're coming with us."

"I'm going with you. The lady already knows that. Don't you, miss?"

"I hoped I would find a good man here," Robin said. "I knew that if I did, he would help us."

"Guess I don't really have a choice. I told you what Gray Wolf said to me in a dream." Joe strode to his Harley, reached into the pack and returned with a pistol that he handed to Mike. "Sounds like you could use some fire-power."

Mike accepted the weapon, but with a frown. He slipped the gun into his belt.

"Let's do it," he said.

They hurried to the Jeep. As they boarded, Robin said to Joe, "Aren't you taking a gun?"

Joe nodded to the Harley. "What I'd like to take is that hog. But a bike's no good for sneaking up on folks." He patted the wide-bladed knife worn on his chest. "This is the only weapon I'll need."

"Where to?" Mike asked.

"Back past town. A dirt road. The cabins are about a half mile up. It's a steep climb."

"Hang on."

Robin grasped the roll bar and the dash. She thought, *my God. A mad scientist and Indian mysticism. Stay safe, Paul,* she thought, fighting down the panic that would take hold if only she'd let it. *Mom is on her way.*

The Jeep kicked up a cloud of red dirt, rocketing back along the washboard road back toward the highway.

Chapter 40

The command center for the volunteer search and rescue was a dozen or so official vehicles of every description parked alongside the highway, flanked by dozens of civilian vehicles driven by the volunteer searchers. The temperature was gradually returning to normal as the sun crested the mountaintop.

Ben Saunders sat behind the steering wheel of his cruiser, listening to the police band, staring at the short wave radio in his hand as if doing so would somehow summon up news that the boys had been found.

The area crackled with activity. Rooftop lights flashed. Police radios chattered. Personnel from several agencies moved about grimly. There were satellite dish-topped television vans from Albuquerque and Las Cruces. Enterprising reporters had continually broken through, pointing microphones in Ben's face. They all wanted to know the same thing. Was there anything that hadn't been made public yet about the missing boys? The search teams continued to fan out, all in radio contact with the base camp, making good time. But there was no sign of Paul Curtis or Jared Philbin, on or off the record.

When Ben saw Roy Rinehart approaching, he stepped from the cruiser. He could see, over Roy's shoulder, where Mrs. Philbin, Jared's mother, was being cared for at one of the ambulances that were waiting to give immediate attention to the boys if they were found. *When* they were found, Ben corrected himself. It was only a matter of time. That's what he'd told Mrs. Philbin when she showed up, drunk as a skunk at seven-thirty in the morning. She was a gaunt woman who looked older than her thirty-eight years. She was overwrought; had screamed into Ben's face, berating him in slurred words reeking of whiskey, accusing him of not doing enough. Her son was lost and it was his job to find Jared. He was failing in his duties. He was a sorry excuse for a policeman. Why wasn't he up there helping the others? Ben had motioned to Roy with a silent nod to escort her to the paramedics.

"Thanks," he now greeted Rinehart. "I sure feel sorry for that woman. Must be hell on earth."

Roy nodded, his eyes sympathetic. "At least she's in good hands. That's all we can do for her, Chief. Anything new come in on the radio?"

"The choppers reported in. They haven't seen a thing." Ben lifted his eyes to the sky above the mountain. "I wish I was up there with them."

"Don't let what Mrs. Philbin said get to you, about not doing your job and all. We're doing our best. We got the Rev sedated and under guard at the hospital. There won't be any more serial killings."

"I know. That's one of the few things we have accomplished." The Devil Creek media circus had gone into high gear on two fronts at the start of this day. Another news contingent was staked out at the Town Hall after learning of Kroeger's arrest. The Reverend, a psycho serial killer. Everyone was having trouble absorbing that one, including Ben. He said, "I don't like sitting on the sidelines."

"You've got that look, Chief," said Roy. "What are you thinking?"

"I'm thinking that I could pull some rank and get on one of those search choppers, me being the Chief and all, if I pushed hard enough."

"Can't say as I'd blame you for wanting that. I'm getting right antsy myself, sitting on my thumbs down here with nothing to do but wait."

"Think I'll have a talk with one of them chopper flyboys."

"We'll find those kids, Chief. You'll see."

"I want to find them *alive,* Roy. Damn. Sure wish we could find the Curtis boy's mother and that neighbor fella, Mike Landware."

"It's kind of unusual, her not being around waiting for word with the rest of us."

"Real unusual. Stay here and keep an ear to the ground. I'm going to see a man about a helicopter."

Chapter 41

The winding, climbing road became extremely rugged as soon as it left the highway, so steep and curving, with spots of mud and clay made slick by last night's mixture of rain and snow, that it was difficult for the Jeep to build much speed. Within less than a quarter mile, they were into the pines. Time crawled for Robin, dragging slower the closer they got to where, she hoped with of all her heart, they would find Paul.

Mike gave Joe a concise briefing on Dr. Horace Bittman and the very real probability that a madman's private, unauthorized mind control experiment was being conducted upon the citizens of Devil Creek. Unlike her, Joe did not register initial disbelief or skepticism. He sat there, leaning forward, resting one arm on the back of their bucket seats, listening without comment to the recitation.

Mike concluded, "So that's why we don't know who to trust."

"That's easy," was the first thing Joe said. "Don't trust white men." He spoke without emotion, stating a simple fact of life.

"We're white," Robin pointed out.

"You're a white woman," Joe said. "That gets you the benefit of the doubt." To Mike, he said, "You, I'm not so sure about."

"That's mighty nice of you," Mike said without rancor. "Joe, let's cut the crap. Tell me what you think."

"Okay. I believe everything you just told me."

"Glad to hear it, because another thing connected to

everything else was you and me getting acquainted. Charlie Flagg's assignment was to keep tabs on what they couldn't monitor electronically, and that included you and your grandfather. Charlie 'suggested' that I visit you and Gray Wolf for a possible story for the newspaper. That was his attempt to keep tabs on the two of you. Unfortunately for Charlie, I told him you didn't exactly make me feel welcome and that was all he ever got. But anything I had told him would have been reported directly to Bittman."

"The evil which Gray Wolf saw coming," said Joe. "It was Bittman and what he's doing to your town."

"You may be an outsider," Robin said, "but it's your town too."

"No. Not my *town*. My *fight*. There's a big difference. And when the fight is over, my debt to my grandfather will have been paid in full and I'll have my ass on that Harley and be on my way the hell out of here."

She considered this. She considered Joe. The man was an enigma. A brooding, impassive man of obvious physical and inner strength. A man used to his own company, his own council; unaccustomed to helping, or asking for help. An outsider, yes. She may have been a new arrival, but Joe Youngfeather was a *true* outsider. And here he was, helping them, quite likely about to risk his life for her and her son, both total strangers. She understood that there was more to it for him. There was the "evil" they spoke of and his grandfather, Gray Wolf. This was somehow intensely *personal* for Joe even before Robin had entered the equation. She wanted to know more about this. But later, when there was time.

There was some sort of begrudging mutual respect between Joe and Mike from some previous encounters, obviously, but that was a male thing that she had little interest in at the moment. It was enough for her that they were working as a team, and that she felt she could depend on them. As for Joe, never in her life, and likely never again, had a stranger played such a key role in such a vitally immediate life and death matter to her. The thought came to her that everyone lived in a world of strangers, where people can mean nothing or everything to each other, can build or destroy, save or condemn, at unforeseeable points when the arcs of lives interconnect.

She did not want Joe to remain a stranger. As good-looking a specimen of manhood as he was, she did not have the hormonal or heart response to him that she had for Mike. These feelings for this new acquaintance weren't about that. But she hoped that a way would present itself for them to become real friends when this was over. Joe would fascinate Paul, and she sensed that Joe would understand her son, who was an outsider in his own right.

She said, "Your grandfather sounds like a wise, special man, Joe." She hoped that she didn't sound inane. Talking took some of the edge off her anxiety.

"To most people around here," said Joe, "Grandfather was the crazy old Indian who lived outside of town. They laughed at him. Hell, I don't know. Maybe sometimes I thought he was crazy too, after I'd spent too much time around white folks. I told myself that I could ride away from this after he died, him sitting out there in the hot sun in the middle of that dry creek bed, chanting away day and night. Chanting himself to death. Well, I can't ride away."

"I'm sorry I'll never get to meet him."

"If I'm right and this is the evil he saw coming, maybe you will meet him. I've seen too much over the years not to believe in Gray Wolf's magic."

"I hope his magic helps us today."

Robin had always considered herself spiritual, but she wasn't a churchgoer. Still, it was impossible *not* to acknowledge a greater power in the universe than man, a power responsible for creation. And she agreed with her New Age friends that there were most likely more planes of reality than our own. Perhaps it was a feminine "thing," but she'd had truly intuitive experiences in her life. Yes, there was more to reality than what the five senses perceived. Strange thoughts to be having as she bounced along in this Jeep on their way to hopefully—no, definitely!—find her son. But Joe's talk of his grandfather and magic brought into stark relief in her mind this collision course of mysticism, on the part of Joe and Gray Wolf, versus the powers of high tech and modern bureaucratic evil in the form of a madman named Horace Bittman.

Joe tapped Mike's shoulder, pointing to a stand of trees up ahead, alongside the road. "Pull over there, behind those rocks."

Sudden dread welled within Robin.

"How close are we?"

"Less than fifty yards from the first of the three cabins I told you about. We're on Missionary Ridge. The cabins aren't far apart. We'll go in from here on foot."

Mike parked the Jeep and they gathered in front of it. Joe drew his knife. Robin noted that Mike did not draw the pistol Joe had given him.

Joe whispered, "We have to be cautious from here on. And I might as well tell you one other thing Gray Wolf told me in my vision. He said that he would not be the last one to die fighting this evil." He stared pointedly at Mike. "Mister, you'd better be ready with that weapon."

"I'll be ready," Mike said. But still he did not draw the pistol.

Joe motioned for them to separate, but not too far apart; to stay abreast of him. They began advancing through the trees.

The world around them was alive with the chirping of birds. Here and there sunlight pierced through the branches overhead; a lush, richly-textured place, a world removed from town, from the wide-open high desert that stretched out from the base of the mountain. Robin understood why a twelve-year-old boy would find this world so intriguing. For her right now though, anxiety, a fear of the worst possible outcome, cramped her stomach into a painful knot.

Joe held up a hand for them to stop.

She and Mike drew forward to where he stood, and she then saw the cars and a RV parked in front of a rustic cabin. Smoke curling lazily from the chimney.

Mike said, "This isn't it. Paul said the cabin was unoccupied, and there's no overlook like he told us about."

"How close are we to the next cabin?" Robin asked.

"Coming up," said Joe.

They withdrew, circling away from the cabin site. Mike still hadn't drawn his pistol. Robin recalled his vow, made over the graves of his parents, never to kill again, not after what he had been through in war. With everything else unfolding so rapidly last night and this morning, she hadn't recalled that conversation with him until now. She had not thought to ask Joe for a weapon when he'd handed the pistol to Mike. She herself had never fired a weapon, had never even held a gun, and for the first time in her life she wished now that she knew something about firearms. An extraordinary set of circumstances had drawn her to this point in time and space with these men, moving stealthily through the forest on the side of a mountain, searching for her missing son, and it all boiled down in her mind to one bitter truth. She had always thought of herself, had always prided herself, on being self-reliant, independent. Yet she lacked even the most rudimentary, fundamental knowledge and means with which to defend herself and her child at this most basic level of survival.

Something, a movement seen from one corner of her eye, arrested her attention.

"Look!"

They paused, looking in the direction in which she pointed.

At the base of a tree, a gray timber wolf stood poised no more than seventy paces from them. The animal's breath formed small white clouds in the cool air, its eyes clear and piercing, observing them, not in the least intimidated by their presence in this, his domain.

Joe whispered, "Grandfather," the word heavy with awe and reverence.

Standing beside him, Robin barely heard him.

The wolf heard. With its head cocked at an angle, unhurried, the animal backstepped. Then, with one rearward look from those piercing eyes, the animal trotted gracefully away, vanishing into the depths of the forest.

"A timber wolf," said Mike. "They're common enough in the high country, Joe. You know that. Don't let it throw you."

Joe calmly looked away from where the wolf had disappeared into the trees. "Don't worry. It doesn't throw me. I expected to see Grandfather up here. It doesn't matter what you believe."

"You're right about that. All that matters right now is Paul."

"The cabin is beyond those trees."

Joe led them to the brow of a ridge that overlooked another cabin. There were no vehicles in sight. A driveway connected with a gravel road. Power lines bordered the property line. The cabin overlooked Devil Creek, a rectangular pattern of streets and buildings in the distance. Between the town and the mountain was the small landing strip used by local flying enthusiasts. A pair of men in camouflage fatigues, each armed with a rifle slung over his shoulder, stood lookout, one to either side of the cabin.

"Bingo," said Mike.

Robin tried to speak. The words wouldn't come. She cleared her throat and managed to whisper, "Paul . . . do you think he's inside?"

"Let's find out," Joe said. "Hey, Mike. You ever kill a man?"

"Some."

"Ready to kill one now? I say we split up and cut along the tree line. You take the guy in the driveway, I'll take out the one behind the cabin. Can you do that?"

Mike drew the pistol. "I'll take him out. But we don't have to kill them. We're not killers."

"They are."

"We can neutralize them without killing them."

Joe frowned. "I thought the life of this woman's child was at stake. I thought you asked me along to even up the odds, so we'd be able to save his little ass. Did I get that right or wrong?"

The harshness of the words slapped Robin across her face like an open palm. Indecision rippled through her.

"Of course Paul's life is at stake," she said, "but Mike is right. There's been so much killing. Isn't there some other way?"

"There is," Mike pressed. "A blow to the back of the head, right behind the ear. You were Special Forces, Joe.

You can do that. Do it my way."

Joe's eyes grew unreadable, alternating between them. "No. We do it my way. I'll tell you what I learned, and I learned it the hard way. When it's your life or their life, you off the bastards. There's no in-between. You want me in on this, it gets done right."

"It'll get done right," Mike said.

Robin said, "But are we sure Paul is down there? I don't want you risking your lives if we're not sure."

Joe ignored her. He glanced at his wristwatch. He spoke to Mike. "Mark time. We hit them in sixty seconds."

Mike glanced at his watch. "Mark."

"Both of you, please be careful." Now it was fear and apprehension that engulfed Robin. "And thank you from the bottom of my heart for what you're doing."

"Save that for when the job's done," Joe said. "Keep your head down."

"I will." There was nothing else she could do sensibly. Half-remembered moves from a half-baked martial arts class a few years ago would be a laughable match against armed, professional soldiers.

Mike went one way with the pistol, Joe gliding in the opposite direction, holding the knife held as if it were an extension of him. It was the biggest, meanest-looking knife Robin had ever seen. Neither man made a sound, their footfalls deadened by fallen leaves and pine needles. They faded into the forest.

Chapter 42

Beneath the bed, the dust and the semi-darkness pressed in on Paul. He slipped in and out of consciousness, as he had last night. Nausea and delirium made him lose track of time. He knew only that he could not stay hidden here forever. A complete silence enveloped the cabin. Eventually, probably because he had remained stationary for so long, the pain of his wound subsided somewhat and full consciousness returned. Were the men dressed like commandos still around? They were not inside the cabin. He was sure he was alone. What should he do? Where was his mom? Where was Mike? Were they on their way? Would they find the cabin? Would they find him? The questions swirled through his brain. He had to find out what was happening.

Using his elbows and knees, he crawled, inch by slow inch, out from under the bed. The throbbing agony returned as soon as he began moving. At last, though, somehow he was standing, supporting himself with one hand gripping the bed's headboard. He paused like that, waiting for the bedroom to stop spinning. When he thought he could manage it, he crossed the bedroom to the stairs and started down, one agonizing step at a time. The pain grew worse.

He would go down the driveway, to the road. He would walk along the road. Someone would come along and help him. That is, if his mom and Mike didn't come first. He would make it. He'd have to be extremely careful, but he could make it. He was going home.

When he was halfway down the stairs, the scab across his

wound broke open and fresh blood oozed from his side. The pain was excruciating. He reached the bottom step and started toward the front of the cabin. When he was less than five feet from the front door, the world began spinning crazily. Sunlight faded. The world became a darkening place. Almost to the door, with his arm outstretched, his hand reaching for the doorknob, Paul's knees buckled.

He pitched forward onto the floor.

Chapter 43

Taylor stood near the sun deck at the side of the cabin. The panorama of the town beyond the base of the mountain, and of the high desert beyond the town, green with scrub brush and pinion, seemed to stretch into infinity. His gaze followed the direction taken by Bittman and Mace. No sign of them yet.

What a pair, those two. A couple of psychos. But Taylor told himself that his predicament was his own damn fault. He should've learned from experience. Sign on with psychotics and it becomes a whole different ball game. He knew Mace's reputation in the merc network, of course; knew how totally amoral the guy was. But he was flat-ass broke when the offer came, so he'd signed on anyway.

Taylor was a man who, in his thirty-seven years, had done many bad things in many hells on earth. But he had never done what he'd seen Hickey do last night. He'd never killed a child—even though he had fired on the other boy, God help him. What would happen when Bittman and Mace returned from not finding the kid? And of course they wouldn't find him. How could they, when the boy was hidden under the bed upstairs in the cabin?

Taylor wished Bittman and Mace would hurry the hell up so they could withdraw to the van and get the hell away from Devil Creek. Or maybe when those two psychos got back, they'd smell something wrong because of before when he'd stupidly sounded off on them what he thought about hunting down and killing children. That had been real dumb. What if they made their own search of the cabin?

When they found the kid, both he and the boy would become dead meat real fast. Bittman was nuts and so was Mace. The unit should already have been long gone, as originally planned. There was such a thing as being too careful. Bittman was endangering everything with his phobia about tying up every loose end. Taylor wished he was back in Tucson, home with his Lisa.

He'd promised her that he wouldn't take any more merc assignments after they were married. Then he told her, when he'd signed on for this job, that it would only be a two-week deal, which is what Mace had told him. Taylor realized now, in retrospect, that there had been more than enough strain on his marriage due to their financial problems. He'd screwed up royally and had surely only made matters worse, disappearing the way he had, leaving a note telling Lisa how much he loved her and that he'd be home soon. Maybe she'd forgive him when she saw the money, but he didn't think so. He loved her precisely because she put more stock in things like honor and trust, and with this job he'd let her down big time on both counts. Since the day he left he'd felt nothing but disappointment and disgust with himself. He submerged these emotions because he was a professional. A job was a job, once you signed on. But the death of the chubby red-haired boy last night would haunt him until his dying day. And he'd be damn lucky if his darling Lisa was waiting for him whenever he did return.

He decided that he'd better check around the front of the cabin, where he'd left Hickey near the driveway. He was just rounding the corner when he saw a figure materialize from the trees behind Hickey. Hickey had no idea that a man was rushing in from behind him, raising a handgun to use as a club. Taylor started to shout a warning. Then he became aware of someone swooping down on him from behind and he knew in that instant that he was not going to make it home alive; that he would never see his Lisa again.

Before he could spin around or react in any way, a knee came to the base of his spine. A powerful arm snaked around his upper chest, pulling him off balance. And he felt the cold kiss of a razor-sharp blade slitting his throat, ending his life.

Joe stepped away. The dead man collapsed to the ground, bright red blood spurting from a severed jugular vein. Joe bent over, wiped his knife blade clean on the shirt of the man he'd killed.

Mike stepped away from having struck the other man sharply behind the ear with the butt of his pistol. His man tumbled to the ground, unmoving.

Robin left the spot from where she had witnessed everything. She ran into the clearing. She had never seen a person die before. Everything was happening so fast.

When she reached them, Mike was glaring at Joe, saying, "Damn it, why did you have to do that? I was hoping you'd change your mind. You didn't have to off him."

"When I do a job," Joe said, "I do it right."

Mike sighed, an infinitely sad, weary sound. Then he said, "Let's search the cabin."

They did not see what Robin suddenly saw. The man Mike had struck was not unconscious. He was remaining face down on the ground, but he had reached out to grab hold of his rifle. When Robin happened to see him, he was in the process of bringing the weapon around.

"Look out! He's going to shoot!"

The warning came too late.

Mike and Joe pivoted together toward the man. The rifle spat a bright orange flash and a sharp *crack!* and the bullet struck Joe in the chest with an ugly, sucking *splat!* sound.

An expression of shock made Joe's face unrecognizable. A jet of thick, red blood spewed from his back. He stumbled one, two, three lurching steps backward.

Robin heard an anguished cry and realized that it was her, her hands raised to her face.

Cursing, Mike speed-tracked his pistol at the man upon the ground. But before he could squeeze the trigger, Joe, with his final breath, raised his right arm even as he stumbled back under the impact of the bullet, coughing, hacking, gore bubbling from his mouth, and managed to throw the knife, the blade flashing like a meteor across the sun-splashed clearing, burying itself to the hilt in the prone man's throat.

The sentry let go of his rifle and reared up onto his knees, both hands clenching at the knife handle that protruded from his Adam's apple. Gurgling, eyes rolling back in his head, he pitched onto his face, trembled once and did not move.

Robin and Mike rushed to where Joe had fallen.

Joe's boots were drawn together, his arms outflung like a man crucified, his head moving slowly back and forth upon the ground.

Mike reached him first.

Joe looked straight up at him through pain-squinted eyes. "You should have taken him out." The rattle in his chest made the words almost inaudible. Joe's body convulsed once, and the life surged from him.

Mike knelt down beside Joe. "Joe . . . Joe, I'm sorry." His voice trembled. "God, man. I'm so sorry . . ." Robin had never seen such torment and anguish on anyone's face.

She touched his arm. "Mike, it's not your fault."

"Hell yes, it's my fault," he said evenly. He straightened to his feet, turned to the cabin. "Let's find Paul." It was as if a curtain had fallen over his rioting emotions, replacing them with a stoic, determined demeanor.

A voice snapped harshly from behind them.

"You will stop right where you are. Not another step. Mr. Landware, drop the gun, please."

The two men must have come up over the slope behind the cabin, wary after hearing the rifle shot, and crept through the trees.

The one who had spoken, who wore a brown corduroy jacket, western-style jeans and boots and a Sherlock Holmes-style cap could only be Dr. Horace Bittman. The pistol he held was pointed at the ground.

Beside him stood a blond-haired man, wearing commando fatigues and aiming a large revolver at Robin from a distance of no more than five feet away. The blond man ordered Mike, "Drop the gun, bud, or I'll blow this lady's head clean off. Or maybe it won't be so clean."

Chapter 44

Paul regained consciousness lying on the floor of the cabin's living room, inches from the front door. The sunshine beaming in through the windows warmed him comfortably. Then he glanced down. He saw his blood, drip-drip-dripping onto the polished wood floor. He forced himself to his feet, reached out and grasped the doorknob. *I'm going home,* he told himself. Mom. Mike. *Where are you?* His hand was slippery with his blood, making the knob difficult to turn.

He thought he heard voices from outside, from right outside this door, right in front of the cabin. He couldn't tell what they were saying. Using his other hand, he managed to turn the knob, drawing the door inward, leaning against the doorframe for support. His knees buckled. He did not allow himself to fall. He stepped through the doorway, crossed the porch, emerged into the sunshine. He thought he saw people standing there in front of the cabin.

The sky was bright blue. The world was green and smelled of pine. But things were starting to come and go for him again. His side hurt so much. It was like last night, scrunched beneath that rock when he thought he'd heard the wind carrying the voices of his mother and Mike. He was that close to delirium now. He did not know what was real. He thought he saw bodies, the bodies of dead men, three of them sprawled around the four people who stood facing each other.

The four people were so interested in each other that they were not even aware of him. He recognized two of the men from last night, the blond-haired commando and the one who had worn the white smock and given the orders. And Paul thought he saw Mike. Mike stood with both arms raised. The blond-haired man was aiming a gun. Paul shook his head to clear his vision and this brought into focus the fourth person standing there.

"*Mom!*" Paul's voice shattered the taut tableau.

Mike hadn't wanted to drop the pistol and raise his hands, but what could he do with the blond-haired hardcase aiming a .357 right between Robin's eyes? *Play for time*, he told himself. That was their only chance. God forgive him, he'd already gotten Joe killed. So he dropped the gun and raised his hands, as Bittman ordered.

At the sound of Paul's voice, everyone's eyes swiveled momentarily to the boy stumbling toward them, his arms outstretched.

"Mom!" Paul cried again.

"Oh, my God!" Robin blurted.

In that fleeting instant while Bittman and the blond man were distracted, Mike dove to the ground, lunging for the dropped pistol. They caught the movement and swung their weapons on him, but by that time he'd already hit the ground, landing on one shoulder, grasping the pistol, executing a smooth combat roll that he hadn't performed in twenty-five years. He came up on one knee, swinging up the pistol, and fired twice. The bullets smacked into the man like stiff-armed jabs to the chest, kicking him off his feet. Mike started to track the pistol on Bittman.

Before he could, Bittman fired.

Mike didn't see the flash, didn't hear the sound of the shot, it happened so quickly. He only felt the sledgehammer blow as the bullet struck him.

Robin's first instinct was maternal: to rush over to Paul, to protect her child. But something else clicked in her mind at the sight of Mike falling under the impact of the bullet.

Their lives depended not on her getting to Paul, but on her stopping a madman!

Bittman was now swinging his gun around on her.

Robin flung herself at him, seizing his arm with both of her hands, intending to pivot and use a move she'd learned in that self-defense class. She hadn't considered going up against those soldier types, but this small-boned, wiry Sherlock Holmes lookalike was different. She at least stood a chance against him and at this point, it wasn't as if she had a choice. She would use Bittman's own strength against him, unbalance him, take him down, then she would kick at his head as she'd been taught, at the same time twisting his gun wrist to wrest the revolver from him.

It didn't work out that way.

Bittman possessed a strength she would not have imagined. He wrenched his arm free from her grasp before she even had a chance to position herself. He drew back his gun arm, intending to strike her in the face with the pistol. She didn't retreat or dodge. Instead, she flung herself at him before he could strike, clutching his arm again with both hands. This time she did get into proper position to use his weight against him. She flipped him with one quick follow-through that surprised even her. Bittman fulcrumed over her bent back, landing with an audible *thud!* upon the gravel driveway. She grasped his wrist, twisting sharply. This did not cause him to release the gun the way it was supposed to. Instead, he reached out and grasped one of her ankles. With a strong yank, he tugged her off her feet.

Robin hit the ground with enough force to kick the air from her lungs.

Bittman sprang upright, the gun again in his hand, his Sherlock Holmes cap somehow remaining perfectly in place. He aimed his pistol at her, his face flushed. He peeped a strange little sound that must have been his version of a shout of triumph.

Robin became acutely aware of things on the periphery of her vision. Paul knelt next to where Mike had fallen. Mike wasn't moving. He was covered with blood, the way Joe was covered with blood. Her son looked terrible, a ghastly, ghostly pale. Paul's side was covered with blood. The boy's mouth was opening and closing spasmodically. He seemed unable to speak.

Robin refocused on Bittman. "Now what, Doctor? Please don't kill us."

"You cannot live," he said simply. "You know who I am."

Don't plead, she told herself. *Don't beg.* But she couldn't stop herself. "Why can't you just let us go? The search is still on the other side of the mountain. You have time to get away."

"I have no choice." He spoke reasonably, almost amiably. "No one must remain behind to identify me."

He was going to do it. She was going to die. They were all going to die.

She said in a voice so calm that it surprised her, "You know something, Doc? You really are one crazy son of a bitch."

"And you, madam, are correct. Unfortunately, I don't see how that is going to do you one bit of good. But I do feel merciful. I will kill you first, to save you from enduring the agony of watching your son die. The parent should die first in any event, don't you think? It is the natural order of things. Farewell, dear lady."

Robin thought, *it must be the little things you notice when you die.* The details. This had to be why the only thing she saw at that precise moment was how Bittman's thin right index finger curled as he started to squeeze the trigger.

Chapter 45

A gray timber wolf sprang out of nowhere, attacking Bittman without warning, savage jaws parted, fangs bared in a growling snarl. Robin was certain it was the same gray wolf they'd seen before.

The animal's powerful body slammed into Bittman from the side, knocking him down. The wolf landed atop him, straddling the man, ferociously going straight for his throat. Bittman raised his arms to try and fend off the snapping jaws, the flashing fangs, dropping his gun under the wolf's onslaught. The revolver landed a few feet away from the struggling beast and man.

Robin rushed over and retrieved the pistol.

As she did so, she saw Bittman reach down into his boot. While using one arm and both knees to fend off the attacking wolf, he withdrew a dagger and, in one continuous movement, plunged the blade into the animal. The wolf leaped away but did not make a sound, did not stumble or fall. Bittman sprang to his feet, gripping the dagger. The wolf crouched, poised some ten feet away. Robin saw a speck of blood on its fur. The animal had not sustained a serious wound. The leg spotted with blood was lifted, the wolf favoring it, but the three remaining paws were firmly planted. Eyes luminous. Fangs bared. Defiant. No fear. No retreat.

She had never aimed a weapon at another human being before, but she raised Bittman's revolver and aimed it at him now, grasping the gun with both hands, sighting down the length of her straightened arms, along the barrel, the way she'd seen men do in the movies.

"Stop right there, Doctor. Drop the dagger."

She was surprised at how rock steady her voice sounded. She wanted to glance sideways and see how Paul and Mike were doing, but she didn't.

Bittman did not drop the dagger.

"And if I don't?" he asked in a gentle, amiable tone that managed to be every bit as frightening as staring down the barrel of his gun had been.

"Drop it," Robin said, "or I'll shoot." She would never know how she made her voice sound so ruthless, so determined.

"I hardly think you will shoot me, dear lady." Bittman spoke in the reasonable, rational, analytical tone of a scientist. "You see, you are not the type."

From nearby, Paul shouted, "Mom, he's dangerous! Shoot him! Shoot him, or he'll kill us!"

The injured timber wolf remained stationary, observing, not withdrawing.

Bittman's lips crinkled in a travesty of a kindly doctor's bedside smile. "Don't listen to the boy. He's overwrought. You're a civilized person. You will not pull that trigger and take my life. We both know that. Now put the gun down."

She said, in her cold and ruthless voice, "I'll shoot if you don't drop that dagger. Believe it, buster."

Bittman shrugged. He dropped the dagger. It clinked upon the gravel.

"As you wish. And what would you have me do next?"

"Stay right where you are."

Robin didn't know what to do next. She did not lower the gun she held. Its grip felt slippery in her sweaty palms. Bittman advanced one step, then another. Slowly. Smiling.

"You see? What can you do? I shall walk away from here,

and the only way you can stop me is to shoot me. And you will not do that."

"Don't count on that. Stay where you are. I'm warning you."

Bittman continued advancing.

Paul bellowed in sheer panic. "Mom, he killed Jared. He hunted me down because he doesn't want anyone to know about him! Don't let him get close to you. He'll kill us."

Bittman halted, no more than six paces from her. "The boy's right, you know." With a movement so fast that she barely realized it was happening, his hand darted into a pocket of his corduroy jacket, reappearing with a small black pistol.

She'd been aiming at his head. Robin closed her eyes involuntarily and squeezed the trigger. The pistol bucked in her hands. The sound of the gunfire was deafening.

Chapter 46

Robin was surprised at the power of the recoil that lifted the gun's barrel. She opened her eyes, steadying her aim to fire again in case she'd missed. She saw Bittman sprawled on his back in the middle of the driveway, a red pool spreading beneath him. She dropped the gun. Turning away, she ran to where Paul knelt beside Mike's unmoving body.

Robin practically tossed herself down across them. An arm encircled each of them, man and boy, hugging them each with an emotion more forceful than she ever remembered feeling, embracing her son, melding herself against the blood-spattered man on the ground.

"Paul! Are you all right?"

He nodded, not pausing in his frantic shaking of Mike. "I'm okay, Mom. But what about Mike? Is he . . . is he—" He couldn't say the word.

She pressed an ear to Mike's chest, smearing herself with his blood. "He's alive. I can hear his heartbeat."

A weak voice, close to her ear, whispered, "What . . . happened?"

Mike's voice was racked with pain. She could not respond at first other than to emit one huge sigh of relief and hug him more than before. He returned the hug weakly.

Paul had no difficulty finding his voice.

"Mom shot the man who was going to kill us! Jeez, Mike, I'm so glad you're not dead!" He babbled excitedly. "Mom, you were great. You saved our lives!"

"I had help," she said.

Without releasing her hold of either of them, she looked

across the clearing. The gray timber wolf still had not moved since its withdrawal to the sidelines. With a barely noticeable limp, the wolf now warily approached Bittman's body, sniffing at the ugly gaping head wound, the animal verifying by scent what it had observed. The wolf raised its head, locking eyes with Robin. Its black nose was dotted with droplets of blood.

Maintaining eye contact, Robin said, loud enough for the animal to hear, "Thank you, Gray Wolf."

She thought she discerned the wolf return the slightest nod. The wolf turned away then and moved off, not hindered much by its slight limp, and disappeared into the dense wall of pine surrounding the clearing.

Mysticism versus technology, thought Robin, *and damn if the high tech evil hadn't been defeated with help from a reincarnated old Indian shaman!* What had happened here? Separate planes of reality? Indeed. More had occurred than met the eye. This was not her imagination. It was fact. She did not understand. *Heck,* she thought. *I don't even understand my own heart!*

She heard a peculiar, dull pounding sound, growing louder as it approached. She recognized the sound.

So did Paul.

"A helicopter!" he yipped excitedly.

And there it was, banking into view at little more than treetop level. She leaped to her feet, semaphoring her arms wildly to draw the pilot's attention.

They'd already been seen. The helicopter descended toward the parking area. As the chopper's landing rails met the ground, the backwash of the rotors generated a mini-windstorm of swirling dust. The pilot shut off the engine. The rotors slowed and the dust dissipated.

Chief Saunders stepped from the helicopter. He came

jogging over toward them, bringing with him a small metal first aid box. He seemed to take in and assimilate everything he saw at a glance, including the fact that although Paul's shirt was torn and bloodied, it was Mike stretched out flat upon his back who was most in need of immediate medical attention.

Saunders crouched beside him, snapping open the box. "Appears you folks have gotten yourselves into a world of trouble."

Robin felt dazed. "Chief, thank God you're here."

Saunders inspected Mike's wound. Then he opened the first aid box and withdrew the makings for a field dressing. He peeled off two compresses, expertly applied them to the wound, and guided Robin's hand to the compress.

"Keep the pressure on here."

Pain rippled across Mike's face, but he summoned up enough strength to speak. "Sorry we couldn't wait on you, Chief. Guess it . . ." He grimaced. ". . . guess it would have made things a lot easier."

Saunders glanced at one of the bodies. "That's Joe Youngfeather."

Robin said, "He was helping us. He led us here to rescue my son. He didn't have anything to do with the bad things that have been happening in town."

"Didn't figure he did, ma'am." Then Saunders asked Paul, "How are you doing, son?"

Robin spoke first. "We've got to get them both to a hospital!"

"Aw, Mom," said Paul. "I'll be all right. It's Mike I'm worried about. Is he going to make it?"

Mike grunted through clenched teeth. "I . . . was about to ask the same question."

Saunders said, "Looks like the bullet went clean through

just beneath the shoulder blade without hitting bone. You'll live." He looked at the boy. "Where's your friend?" he asked Paul. "Where's Jared?"

"They killed him, Chief." Paul pointed. "His body is somewhere on the mountain. And they killed Mr. Flagg."

Saunders rose to his feet. "I'll call in a medivac chopper. We'll have the lot of you over to the hospital in Cruces in no time. Sure do wish you folks had called me when you first found out whatever it was that brought you here." He glanced at the man Robin had killed. "That must be Bittman."

Robin couldn't force herself to look at the body. "It is. It was."

Mike's breathing was shallow. His face was ashen. "How much do you know, Chief?"

"We expanded the search," said Saunders. "One of the search teams found a van that was fixed up so it couldn't be seen from the air. They radioed it in and a computer check was run on the plates." He indicated the helicopter where a pilot stood waiting. "All I know is what came over the chopper radio. That's how I know Bittman's name. The plates were registered to some alias he used before he dropped out of sight, is the best I could make out of it. The Feds are all hot to trot. The FBI office in Albuquerque dispatched a team that's due in any minute now." He nudged back the brim of his hat. "And you three are right smack in the middle of it, huh? No one said anything about that."

Robin said, truthfully, "I'm sorry we didn't contact you."

"To tell you God's truth, young lady, under normal circumstances I'd be a mite peeved. But I reckon in your case I'll make an exception." And he winked at her. "Just don't let it happen again."

She watched the Chief jog back to the chopper. Paul snuggled against her.

"It's over," she said. "Thank God."

Mike was staring at the sky. "It's not over," he said. "It's my fault Joe's dead."

"Mike, no—"

Paul shook his head. "Mike, you're way wrong. A guy can only do what he thinks is right. It's that creep Mom blew away, he's the one responsible for everything that's happened."

Mike didn't seem to hear. "I should have done like Joe wanted." Each word was a struggle; poignant with remorse. "I should have killed that sentry. If I'd done it right, Joe would be alive. How can I live with his death on my conscience?"

Robin said, "We both have a lot to deal with, Michael, you and I. I'm the one who urged Joe to come with us. And I've never killed a person before. But we'll deal with these things *tomorrow.* You and I and Paul *will* get through whatever we have to get though."

Paul nodded emphatically. "We'll make it. We're a team."

Mike closed his eyes, his breathing a shallow rattle.

In the middle of the clearing, Chief Saunders replaced the microphone inside the helicopter and turned to hurry back in their direction. Robin clearly saw the compassion in his expression, a real concern for their welfare, the humane concern of neighbor for neighbor.

Never again would she embrace the conceit that a person could survive *totally* on their own, detached from others, from love, as she had come to Devil Creek believing. To accept this was to embrace a delusion as self-defeating and self-destructive as pretending that the hard times would never come knocking. When she'd come here, Devil Creek had embodied the unknown. Well, that unknown had been confronted and dealt with. Devil Creek was no longer the unknown. Devil Creek was a hard lesson learned from life. A lesson she would never forget; a truth driven home forever by Michael and Paul, and by Chief Saunders and the people of Devil Creek. And most especially by Joe Youngfeather and Gray Wolf.

No one makes it alone. Everywhere—Chicago, Timbuktu, throughout life itself—good and bad would always lie in wait, often well-camouflaged, the potential for bad things to happen always there, around every bend in life's road. But she now knew that people are defined by the hardships they endure, and by how they cope with them. In this way do people determine what they are made of.

She now possessed the sure knowledge that she was capable of *anything*—even capable of taking another's life—if it meant defending herself or someone she cared for. She had been forced to face and define and accept the stuff she was made of. She hoped that she would never again be called upon to prove this to herself or to anyone else. Once was more than enough for one lifetime, thank you.

And yes, there would be much, much healing, much soul searching, yet to come. What was their responsibility in what happened to the enigma that was Joe Youngfeather? What lasting emotional scars would remain, especially for her son?

And what would happen between her and Michael? They would be forever bonded by this experience. His error in dealing with the sentry had been to err on the side of decent, deeply-held convictions. Would they, *could* they, become lovers? They made a good team. He had risked his life, had literally taken a bullet, to help her and Paul. This man had been invaluable in piecing together what was happening in Devil Creek, and in the rescue of her son. Michael cared, and cared deeply.

She would not lose her independence with Mike. She would *gain* independence, independence from having to face and cope with and endure alone the harsh, unexpected hardships of life; those inescapable hard times. They call it *sharing*, and who in their right mind, man or woman, would want independence from that?

From the surrounding tree tops, countless birds sang their songs to the sun as it climbed higher to warm a clearing blue sky. A warming breeze carried on it the rich scents of the forest.

"I do have one thing that needs clearing up," said Mike. His eyelids fluttered, but stayed open. His breathing remained labored. His fists were clenched. His pain had to be excruciating, but he would not let it show. He was not that sort of man.

"What, Michael?" she asked. "What, darling?"

"We said we'd be a couple for the night. The night's over. Did I hear you say that you wanted to fall in love with me?"

"We are a couple," she said, "and I have fallen in love with you."

Their kiss then was not lingering, but was as tender as it was fleeting, intimate with an unspoken commitment, with promise, with love.

Paul, nestled within his mother's embrace, trembled. "Mom, is it really over?"

She squeezed her son's hand. At the same time, she leaned forward and placed a feather-light kiss upon Michael Landware's forehead.

Robin told them both, "The past is over. Our future begins right now."